WANTING MORE

"Sweetheart? Do you mean to talk to me all night?"

"If that is what it takes," Max said, but then he brushed his lips across hers. His touch was light and altogether unsatisfying. She wanted more.

"What do you"—his hand curled around her breast—"oh!"

His mouth covered hers again. She lowered her arm around his neck.

He kissed her langourously as if in no hurry at all. Her bones were melting and a building urgency made her arch into him. Then he ended the kiss as if reluctant, his lips clinging to hers. "Are you done being frightened, pet?"

BOOK YOUR PLACE ON OUR WEBSITE AND MAKE THE READING CONNECTION!

We've created a customized website just for our very special readers, where you can get the inside scoop on everything that's going on with Zebra, Pinnacle and Kensington books.

When you come online, you'll have the exciting opportunity to:

- View covers of upcoming books
- Read sample chapters
- Learn about our future publishing schedule (listed by publication month *and author*)
- Find out when your favorite authors will be visiting a city near you
- Search for and order backlist books from our online catalog
- Check out author bios and background information
- Send e-mail to your favorite authors
- Meet the Kensington staff online
- Join us in weekly chats with authors, readers and other guests
- Get writing guidelines
- AND MUCH MORE!

Visit our website at
http://www.kensingtonbooks.com

A Midnight Clear

Karen L. King

ZEBRA BOOKS
KENSINGTON PUBLISHING CORP.
http://www.kensingtonbooks.com

ZEBRA BOOKS are published by

Kensington Publishing Corp.
850 Third Avenue
New York, NY 10022

All Kensington titles, imprints, and distributed lines are available at special quantity discounts for bulk purchases for sales
promotion, premiums, fund-raising, educational, or institutional
use.

Special book excerpts or customized printings can also be
created to fit specific needs. For details, write or phone the
office of the Kensington Special Sales Manager: Attn. Special
Sales Department. Kensington Publishing Corp., 850 Third
Avenue, New York, NY 10022. Phone: 1-800-221-2647.

Zebra and the Z logo Reg. U.S. Pat. & TM Off.

ISBN 0-8217-7796-3

First Printing: October 2005
10 9 8 7 6 5 4 3 2 1

Printed in the United States of America

Prologue

Roxana Winston tied the strings of her chip-straw bonnet under her chin and gave one final look around the attic she shared with her three sisters. She would never return, and she would not miss this cramped and cold space.

Bent over like an old crone to clear the low-hanging thatched roof, she skirted around the straw ticks on the floor and made her way to the ladder that led down to the cottage's kitchen.

This tiny house had once been the grounds-keeper's residence, but was quite a come-down from Wingate Hall, where the Winston family had lived for the first twelve years of Roxana's life. Now they could look across the ungroomed lawn and see their family seat, but the hall was let to Mrs. Porter and her so-called "daughters."

Roxana's mother stood at the bottom of the ladder. Perpetual worry carved lines in Lady Winston's forehead and grooves along her mouth. "You will be all right, won't you?"

"Of course I will, Mother." Roxana was more worried about the rest of them while she was gone.

Worry was familiar to her. Worries that her father would learn that she was stealing up to Wingate Hall, worries that he would return home and make their life miserable, worries that she could not produce the next meal, and worries that they would not have enough firewood to keep warm were constant companions. She was numb to worry. Yet a herd of horses seemed to have established a racetrack in her stomach. Anticipation and—dare she think it—hope weakened her knees and made her hands shake. In a few minutes she would be free of this place.

Roxana's sister Katherine turned from where she peeled potatoes, as if she had heard the false bravado in Roxy's voice. But Katherine was bravely pretending she could manage the household and take over the chores that Roxana managed.

The four potatoes were shriveled, with black spots. Katherine was careful to peel only a narrow layer of skin away. Their food supply dwindled, while spring planting remained a long way away. A month ago a fox had broken into their chicken coop and left only bloody feathers, cracked eggs and scattered straw. These four potatoes would supply the day's meals.

Roxana had to be successful. If she failed, seventeen-year-old Katherine would be the next sacrificial lamb sent out for slaughter. Katherine would never be able to withstand the pressure. Roxana would never allow that.

"Be good to the duchess. Do not do anything to anger her; you will need her help, if you . . . if you . . . if you are to be successful." Lady Winston clung to Roxana's arm with her damaged hand. Two broken fingers had never healed correctly and usually Lady Winston kept the hand tucked out of sight.

"Yes, I know, Mama." Roxana tugged her mother's slipping shawl up around her bent shoulders. For a woman of only a certain age, Lady Winston was so beaten down she could have passed for a woman of twice her years. Thank goodness she had retained ties to friends of better times. "I am mindful of the great favor that the Duchess of Trent and her stepson are granting me. I will do nothing beyond show my gratitude."

Her mother frowned. "Your mouth has gotten the better of you at times. You cannot alienate a potential suitor with your sharp tongue. Your father . . ." Her voice trailed off.

Katherine ducked her head as if their father was present. Roxana's chin tilted up with her habitual defiance.

"I shall restrain my tendency to speak my mind. In fact, I shall just keep my intelligence safely locked in a box."

Her mother wore a vague look as if she was not quite sure if her daughter was serious or not. "A husband will expect a sweet and biddable wife." Her mother leaned close and whispered, "You must fix a man's affections quickly. You are very pretty, so if you have to . . . no one will doubt . . ." Her mother found herself unable to supply the words for the fallback plan. "It is a good thing you inherited your father's looks."

Roxana's jaw tightened. Her dark hair, blue eyes and evenly matched features had come from her father, but she would have gladly traded them for

Katherine's wispy blond curls, upturned nose and freckles. Anything to look less like the man who had forced them into this poverty.

"You remember what I told you?" asked her mother.

Roxana nodded.

Lady Winston had turned beet red as she explained the contingency plan to her oldest daughter. A party lasting a little over a fortnight was not likely to produce a proposal, yet Roxana needed to garner one. So she had been given instructions that she may get compromised, thereby forcing a proposal or a settlement. A girl of her birth could reasonably expect a proposal.

"I know what I need to do, Mama," Roxana said. Dissatisfied with her mother's vague hints and innuendos, she'd asked the more worldly Mrs. Porter for a full explanation and pointers on how to prompt a man to take such a treacherous step. Mrs. Porter's reluctantly given information had been much more illuminating.

While her mother offered it as a last resort, Roxana, with her more pragmatic nature, thought she'd do better to get compromised. A legitimate marriage proposal was unlikely and the worst thing that could happen. Roxana had other plans. They did not include marriage.

"Yes, do not set your sights on the duke, because he will do everything too correctly. My understanding is he would never . . . breach the bounds of propriety. A younger man is more likely to be swayed by his passions. You will need the duke to demand the proper recompense for you. And do not under any circumstance acknowledge our tenants."

"Yes, Mother." Lady Winston had managed to avoid calling Mrs. Porter and her girls by name for the last half-dozen years. Roxana should not even know about their sort of people. She gave her mother a perfunctory kiss on her cheek. "Goodbye, Mama."

In the parlor that at night doubled as her thirteen-year-old brother's bedroom, Roxana looked around ascertaining that every scrap of lace and usable button was packed. She no longer noticed the cracked and yellow plaster or the smoky, rattling windowpanes. Her poverty would not be evident in her wardrobe, at least. She closed the trunk in the center of the room. Her brother lifted one side and they carried it out to the waiting pony cart.

"I can ask around in town and get work," said Jonathon as he lifted the trunk and shoved it into the cart bed.

Roxana's eyes stung as she considered the idea of the future Baron of Wingate working as a common laborer. "Let me see what I can do, first."

Her brother threw himself at her, wrapping his arms around her tightly. "It is bad enough that you have had to work as a seamstress. I cannot stand the idea of you marrying just to provide for us. If I were older I could join the army."

Roxana rubbed her brother's shoulders. "I like the sewing, and do not fret about my future. This could be the best thing to ever happen to me."

A thick lump blocked her throat as she hugged each of her sisters.

As she held Katherine she whispered, "The Christmas gifts are tucked under the end of the mattress in the attic."

Katherine leaned back. "You said we would not exchange gifts this year, that we could not afford it."

"Yes, well, they are only small gifts, and I am selfish enough that I want you to think of me on Christmas Day when you open them." Roxana touched her sister's cheek and smiled even though it was painful and she had much rather cry, but Katherine needed her confidence boosted. "Besides, I am sure I will want for naught at the Trents' house party. I hardly need any gifts."

Katherine nodded.

Her heart heavy with not knowing when she would ever see them again, Roxana climbed onto the pony cart. She was to sell it and the rickety old nag in town to have the money to hire a post-chaise and outriders to reach her destination. Roxana had already determined she could ride the mail coach for less, even with paying extra to transport her ancient trunks.

The hope and fear on Katherine's face, the quivering lip that Jonathon tried to control and the tearful kisses of her two younger sisters made an ache spread under her breastbone. She could not let them down. She would find a way to keep them fed and warm.

Her sisters deserved the chance to make decent marriages and Jonathon should not have to face the prospect of becoming a laborer. Roxana was determined to succeed with her own plans. This was her golden opportunity and her last desperate chance to save her family and herself from this hopeless existence.

Chapter One

"Oh, Max, I am so glad you've arrived home. You will know the right thing to do. You always do. You have invited a few of your bachelor friends to the house party, have you not?" asked the Dowager Duchess of Trent without lifting her pen from the paper. Her smooth forehead crinkled with worry, and she puckered her lips in concentration.

"Ah, are you ready to toss out your handkerchief again, Maman?" Maximilian Adrian Xavier St. Claire, otherwise known as the Duke of Trent, smiled indulgently at his stepmother. "It is about time you remarried."

"Pish!" said the young dowager duchess. "Well, there is you, and I invited the Breedons, and they will bring their son."

Since his stepmother was not likely to count him as possible marriage material, nor did he think she would consider the Breedons' son, he did not suppose she was on the hunt for a new husband. This was just as well, because he was rather used to

Fanny running his home, first for his father and now for him.

Since she was only seven years older than Max, would she want to remarry now that her year of mourning was done? "I could send for Scully," Max said.

"Did you call me 'Maman'?" She paused in the middle of writing.

"Did I?" asked Max. She had halfheartedly tried to get him to call her that years ago. They had eventually compromised on first names. He knew that calling her "Maman" would jar her loose of her preoccupation with whatever current problem wrinkled her brow. He'd hoped for a laugh, but she had not laughed much of late.

She put her pen down and rose, her blue eyes contrite. "I am so sorry. Welcome home, Max. I trust you are in good health?"

She crossed the room and pressed her cheek to his.

"Excellent health. And your grace?"

"Stop being so formal, Max. You know I cannot abide it." She tugged the bell pull. "And do not send for Scully if he means to tag after me like a lovesick puppy. But if you can think of any other unmarried men, you should invite them, posthaste. I need eligible men for our houseguest. It is probably much too late to send her home. I am quite in a dither with this situation."

"What situation?" Max settled in for the wait. Fanny was likely to circle the issue many times before it became clear to him.

"I did not know she was coming, or I should have planned this all differently. I shall invite more young ladies of marriageable age too. You should be thinking of setting up your nursery."

"I can hardly boot my own brother and sister from the nursery, Fanny, dearest." Plus, Max had no intention of marrying and setting up his nursery.

"Well, Julia is too old to keep in the nursery and Thomas will be off to Eton next year. The timing is perfect for you to settle down. You are not getting any younger, you know."

"Do not invite any young ladies for my benefit." At thirty, Max had no reason to be discontent with his life. He would not muck it up with a marriage.

His half brother's prospects were much better if Max stayed single and kept Thomas the heir presumptive. Max would rather not lose yet another younger brother to a war on foreign soil.

"I invited the Malmsburys on your behalf."

"Oh hell and damnation, tell me they did not accept."

"Lady Malmsbury accepted." Fanny wrung her hands. "You did not want her to come? She said you would, and are you no longer . . . ?"

"Do not fret about it, Fanny. You could not have known." He was not in the habit of discussing his affairs with his stepmother, although he just realized she had always managed to include his latest paramour among the company at the house parties. His parting with Lady Malmsbury had not been quite as amicable as he would have liked, but she was a lady and he a gentleman. "I am sure we shall manage to be civil to each other."

"Well, then that is all the more reason why I should attempt to include more of the marriageable set. If I use the rooms on the west wing, we could house a dozen more guests. Are there any young ladies whom you would like me to include?"

He could only imagine Lady Malmsbury's

reaction to his paying any mind to young lady of a marriageable inclination. Her increasing possessiveness had prompted him to end their liaison. "Why are you hell-bent on matchmaking?"

A footman opened the drawing-room door.

"Please send in a tea tray. I'm sure Max is famished," she instructed the servant. "Pray tell the children their brother is here and do see if you can locate Miss Winston."

"Very good, your grace," said the footman before he bowed out the door.

"Who is Miss Winston?"

"Our houseguest." Fanny's lips flattened. "The reason I must have more younger people. I promised her mother, you see." Fanny wrung her hands. "I never intended to match make, and I am not quite sure that she is everything she should be. But I cannot send her home now, can I?"

Max pulled his stepmother to a chair. "Perhaps you had better begin at the beginning."

"You remember my friend Beth from my Bath days . . . Well, no, you probably don't—"

"Your friend"—prompted Max, knowing Fanny could wander about quite a bit before she got to the point—"from school."

"Yes, well, she married Sir Winston—or was it Lord Winston? He is a viscount or a knight or—"

"He's a baron. Baron of Wingate." Max sighed. Would he have to listen to Miss Winston's entire life story? "Do hurry, dear, before the children attack me."

"Why, Max, my children would never attack you," said Fanny with her hand at her chest.

"Yes, but if you hurry you might explain before they demand all my attention." Max wanted to know why his stepmother had invited this young lady and why she was now having regrets. "Miss Winston is the product of this union?"

"Well, yes. Her mother and I were quite good friends and we have corresponded over the years, although lately not near as much. She wrote earlier this year and asked if Miss Winston could be invited to our house party, there were so few prospects for her in Montgomeryshire, and the Winstons would not be able to present her in London. Apparently nothing can be spared to bring her out. And she has no dowry at all. There are other children and a brother who should be in school and they have been trying to get him in as a King's Scholar."

Max tapped Fanny on her hands, hoping to redirect her conversation to the problem of Miss Winston and not her entire family's concerns.

He could hear the thump of feet above him, racing for the stairs. Julia and Thomas would be upon him in a moment.

"Beth, er, Lady Winston asked if I might invite her—Miss Winston, that is—to one of my house parties, so she might have a chance of affixing a gentleman's interest."

"And now she is here." What was the problem? Was she bracket-faced? Were her manners boorish? Was she unmarriageable? "Whatever is causing your misgivings?"

"I never received an answer. I did not *know* she was coming. And, well . . ."

"Yes, well?"

"She arrived on the *mail coach*, alone. She said it was more economical than traveling in a post-chaise and—"

"Miss Winston traveled on the mail coach alone? Her parents do not attend with her?"

"She is all alone. So you see my dilemma. I certainly expected that Lady Winston would accompany her daughter. I was rather looking forward to seeing Beth again. I never thought—"

"Are her manners amiss?" Max was quite sure he did not see why Fanny was in a fret. It was a bit unconventional, but hardly unusual for an unmarried miss to stay with her parent's friend.

"No, she seems a lovely girl, but her clothes—"

"Are rags?" So Miss Winston was a charity case and poor as a church mouse to boot. While it was not well done of the Winstons to send their daughter without escort and on a public conveyance, it did not make the girl a total liability. She was, after all, wellborn.

His siblings clattered down the uncarpeted staircase from the third floor. One more flight of stairs and a carpeted passageway before they were upon him.

"No, that is just it. Her clothes are to die for—a bit too fast for a girl not out—and, well." Fanny tapped her lip with a forefinger.

Max wondered if Fanny had forgotten how revealing the current London fashions were. Nearly sheer, dampened gowns were found in all drawing rooms. The duchess's black silk gown was cut modestly, a somber tribute to her widowed state.

"I suppose she should have been presented last year. She arrived with two monstrous trunks as well as two smaller bandboxes as if she meant to stay forever. I suppose she has a great deal of clothes. But I do not understand how she could afford such fashionable and well-made things. She seems quite enamored of my lady's magazines—"

"Fanny," Max cut her off. So if Miss Winston's clothes weren't rags . . .

"I sent my dresser to help her unpack, you see."

No, Max didn't see. He heard Julia's exuberant laughter and Thomas calling out as the carpeted passageway muffled their footfalls.

"She wouldn't open one trunk at all. I hate to think what might be in there."

"Fanny."

As red stained Fanny's cheeks, her voice dropped to a strained whisper. "But my maid says that Miss Winston has undergarments made of red silk. Shifts and drawers and—"

The door burst open. Thomas and Julia flew across the room, knocking into Max. They were big enough to almost bowl him over and too old to be so rambunctious. He hugged them tight anyway.

Over their blond curls he saw what must be the owner of such scandalous undergarments made of red silk. His first thought was that even without a dowry, she should arouse enough interest to be satisfactorily settled.

She took a step into the room. Her gown caressed her slender form and the only thought he could raise was that with her dark hair and midnight blue eyes, she'd look damn good in red silk. But then again, from the way the jade green material slid against her body, he was not sure she wore any undergarments at all. In either case, he'd really like to see for himself what was under that dress.

Then he banished the thought as totally uncharacteristic. He never bothered with innocents and he had no plans to start now.

Roxana Winston entered the massive drawing room more sedately than the youngest St. Clairs. Both of them had raced past her on the stair, shouting, *"Max is home."* Julia and Thomas threw themselves at the newcomer. He enfolded them in a bear hug, lifting both the nearly grown youngsters off the floor.

The joyous greeting for the return of the head of household was a far cry from what happened in Roxana's home when her father arrived after an extended absence.

The intensity of the duke's gaze on her started flutters in her stomach. Then he ruffled Thomas's hair and grinned down at Julia. Instead of looking imperious and imposing, he looked . . . friendly, perhaps kind. "Good grief, I believe you both have grown an inch. Have I been gone so long?"

His tousled tawny brown hair appeared windblown and his skin was ruddy. As she neared him, she caught the scent of the outdoors, crisp with the cold.

Even the Duchess of Trent appeared quite excited by her stepson's presence. Her color was high as she clapped her hands together to restrain the boisterous antics of her son, jumping up and down clamoring, "Max, you have to come see me ride. I can take the paddock fence now."

Roxana glided forward and waited quietly to make her curtsy. She'd practiced, looking in her cheval glass. This was probably the only time she would ever make a curtsy to a duke in a social situation. In the future she would be shunned by the ton. Persons of trade were not welcomed in polite society.

"Roxy is designing a new gown for me," said Julia as Roxana neared the family group. "You should see it."

"Oh, dear," said the duchess.

The Duke of Trent cast a glance at his stepmother and then turned his brown eyes Roxana's way, his warm gaze roving over her gown.

Roxana supposed that was good. She wanted her dresses noticed, but she was not entirely sure that he was looking at just her creation. An edgy energy crept up her spine.

He urged the children to step back. "Allow me to meet our guest."

The Duchess of Trent performed the introductions.

Roxana pasted what she hoped was an appropriate smile on her face and dropped to her curtsy. "I am most grateful for your hospitality, your grace."

As her lowered gaze returned to his face, she noticed the way his buff unmentionables clung to the muscles of his thighs and the cut of his chestnut-brown coat emphasized the breadth of his shoulders. Her curtsy had been designed to emphasize the bias cut of her dress; instead she noticed him.

"Charmed to meet you." He cast a disparaging glance in his stepmother's direction. "I have heard so much about you, Miss Winston."

The Duchess of Trent hardly looked old enough to be a mother of the two youths, let alone as old as Roxana's mother, although they were of an age. "I cannot imagine that you have heard much. I am sure I was never much more than an afterthought in my mother's correspondence."

"I was just telling Max of your interest in fashion and how I so admire your wardrobe." The duchess rolled her eyes toward her stepson as she sat down.

The duke gestured for her to sit and Roxana complied, perching on the far end of the sofa. As soon as the Duke of Trent sat, Thomas leaned against his half brother's knee and Julia crowded the sofa next to them. How different from when

Roxana's father returned home and everyone scattered. Giving Lord Winston a wide berth, with only the kitchen, bedroom, parlor and attic to provide refuge, often proved difficult.

"Thank you, I do enjoy clothes and could spend hours discussing them, but the Duke of Trent will surely not want to be bored with such feminine diversions."

"On the contrary. Perhaps you could describe the dress being made for Lady Julia," he said.

While the question seemed innocuous enough, an undercurrent of caution threaded through the words. Had the Duchess of Trent's "Oh dear" signified an objection to Julia's new dress?

Fearing she'd broken an unwritten rule, Roxana turned toward the duchess. "Would you rather I did not help Julia construct a new gown, your grace?"

The Duchess of Trent looked left, then right, before she answered. "She is only fourteen."

"Pray tell, what color is this gown?" asked the duke.

The duchess rapped her stepson with a closed fan.

"I thought a simple day gown in white muslin, as would be appropriate for a young lady." Roxana looked down at the green dress she wore with pride. Was the neckline too low? Was her lace fichu too transparent? Was the movement from the innovative bias cut a problem? Until this minute Roxy had thought the gown, which could be worn day or evening, one of her better pieces. "I was thinking of pink ribbons in love knots. I could show you the sketch I made, your grace, to see if there is anything you would alter."

"Oh no, Mama. It is perfect."

"I apologize." Roxana ignored Julia's interruption. "I should have asked your permission first."

"How could you?" said Julia. "We were just discussing it before you came, Max. It is only a little grown up. Roxy said it would not be appropriate to dress as if I were out. You should see her dresses; she has the most splendid ball gown in red silk."

The Duke of Trent coughed, then patted Julia's knee. "I'm sure I will have the privilege during the festivities. So do you often *design* gowns, Miss Winston?"

She ran a finger over a seam. "I dabble a bit."

Roxy had not meant to be so transparent with her ambitions. She just desperately needed to know if her designs would fly in fashionable circles. She'd been told her creations were to die for, but she had never been within an ames-ace of London to really see for herself. She sucked in a deep breath and then said, "A dressmaker in my village made up my wardrobe. She wants to open her own shop in London."

It was only a small untruth, since she was the dressmaker. While here, she hoped to discover if members of the ton liked her dresses. Well, that and to follow her mother's instructions to get herself compromised, not exactly to the letter.

She stole a glance at the Duke of Trent. The very thought of what she would have to do to accomplish her mission made her go hot, then cold, as if she were struck with a bad case of ague. Until now, the man she would need to enact her plan had been a shadowy, unreal figure, not a real, flesh-and-blood man. Not that *the duke* would be the man she picked to be her pawn.

He turned toward her, as if aware of her gaze.

Doubt that she could accomplish her mission clawed icy fingers around her neck. She was not usually so false, and Roxy did not know if she could manage this deception well. But then, she had no choice. This was her only chance to be free of her father's household and keep the rest of her family from the poorhouse. As her mother had said, it was all up to her. And she would not fail them.

"So you see my dilemma, do you not?" Fanny wrung her hands and crossed the drawing room, empty except for her and Max. "She is very alluring and I cannot adequately chaperone a creature like that with all my duties as hostess."

Max paused in writing an invitation to a friend. He considered that his first thought about Miss Winston had been sinful. He found a small amount of relief that Fanny expected that sort of reaction from men, but that did present a bit of a problem. A chit like her could never be left alone with a gentleman, a prospect that was unavoidable at the house party. A less attractive young lady could be allowed a longer leash. Given that she was on the hunt for a husband, Miss Winston would be treading a thin line between respectability and temptation.

"I will watch over her," Max said.

Fanny spun and faced him. "I can hardly ask that of you. She is my responsibility."

"Worry no more. You know that you may trust me to keep her reputation safe. She is my guest too. And her family has seen fit to entrust her well-being to us."

"You have duties too. You can hardly provide escort for her every moment when I cannot."

Max put down his pen. He would have to lead

the gentlemen on afternoon shooting expeditions and arrange a fox hunt as well as daily rides. "I am sending for Scully. I will tell him if he wants to please you, he will focus his attentions on guarding Miss Winston."

Fanny frowned. "Can you think of no one else? I know I can trust you to do the proper thing, but asking Scully to help is a bit like asking a wolf to guard sheep."

"He has six sisters. He of all people knows how to keep a young lady in line." Max dismissed Fanny's distrust of his friend. Scully may be a ladies' man, but he knew which women were off limits. He never preyed on innocents, either. "Between the three of us, we can protect Miss Winston's reputation."

Max wondered what Miss Winston might have on today. Yesterday, she had worn the same green gown to dinner. She'd removed the fichu around her neck and added a crocheted lace shawl. As much as he'd studied her, he really could not name anything truly amiss with her attire. But his gaze was drawn to her form rather more than was comfortable.

Fanny wandered across the room.

He finished his letter and began one to his friend the Honorable Devlin Scullin. Having his friend back in the house again would be good. After he finished, Max folded the letters and sealed them. "I shall just take these to town. Is there anything you need?"

"I have several additional invitations too, if you will be so kind as to post them." Fanny sighed. "Have you seen our guest today?"

"No, she seems to spend an inordinate amount of time in her room. I sent a footman for her a while ago."

Max paused in his trip to the door. Fanny seemed listless. Was she upset that he meant to invite Scully again? Usually by now she would be animatedly discussing the meals and the room assignments and ordering new linens, carpets or chairs. There had been endless discussions about the number of horses needed for the hunts with his father, who had countered with his own strong convictions about all the details. She should order blue carpets, not yellow, and they could purchase another dozen horses, none of which would arrive in time to be of any use.

But his father was gone now.

"If you need to argue about whether you will serve apricot tarts or apple fritters with the first remove, I am at your service."

Fanny waved him off. "You are no fun. You will just say serve apricot tarts on Friday and the apple fritters on Saturday."

"Perhaps I could urge Miss Winston to have a strong opinion one way or another." Max watched Fanny. Did she long to indulge in a fit of redecorating? His father had been endlessly indulgent, buying his stepmother anything she wanted, be it house furnishings or extraordinary court dress. Max supposed that was the province of a beautiful younger wife with an older husband. But Max would not offer to let her redecorate, and she would not ask. A wave of guilt washed over him, even though he knew indulging her the way his father had would not be proper.

Fanny smiled a watery smile. "I do miss him."

"As do I." Responsibility weighed heavily on his shoulders at moments like this. Yet he had so much that he could not complain. "I shall be back before too long. I have to procure the services of the farrier and a few whipper-ins for the hunt."

When Max reached the stairway leading to the great hall, Miss Winston was descending the stairs. He waited until she reached the landing. Today she wore a long-sleeved navy gown with a white habit shirt filling in the neckline. The dress was slightly more sedate than yesterday's, but still not in the style of a young miss.

"Miss Winston," he acknowledged.

She paused on the landing, her hand on the banister. She looked down into the main hall, where the footmen stood ready with his overcoat and top hat. "Are you going out, your grace?"

"I have errands in town."

She bit her cherry lip and for a moment her mouth was all he could think about. That and the mistletoe that would be spread about the house when the festivities began in earnest.

"Is there a linen draper in town?"

Max snapped his attention back to more mundane subjects, such as clothing. "I believe so. Would you like to accompany me?" If Miss Winston needed to go to town, his duty required him to escort her.

"I would indeed. Will you wait while I fetch my bonnet and cloak?"

"Certainly, Miss Winston."

She had turned to go back up the stairs, and Lord forgive him, he thought he caught a glimpse of a red petticoat. Surely not. Fanny had said shifts and pantalets, not petticoats, which was quite bad enough. He stared at her skirts, trying to direct his thoughts to anything else. Conjugate Latin verbs or some such. He had never seen any woman in red undergarments, but that did not stop him from imagining the sight.

She paused, then looked down at him. "Your grace, might I ask you a question?"

"By all means." He put a boot on the lowest step, and then wondered what the hell he was doing. He was supposed to be going downstairs and out, not following her upstairs.

"Is something amiss with my dresses?"

That she was wearing them. "Er . . . no."

She folded her arms across her middle and stared him down. "Go on."

"I am done." He paused, searching for the proper response. Lord, he was a slowtop today. "Your gowns are quite lovely."

She took a step down, and for just a moment he could see the outline of her thigh under the dark material of her gown, then her skirts slid back into place.

"You have been to London. Are they fashionable?"

He hated conversations about clothing. But then again his conversations normally concerned the exorbitant costs, not if the style was au courant. Was this gown cut a little lower than the one she wore last night? Would the habit shirt disappear before dinner? "I believe you are bang up to the nines, Miss Winston. You would quite cut a dash in the city."

"Then why does the duchess look at me as if her eyes would cross?"

"Envy?" volunteered Max, deciding he should leave now. Reluctantly he lifted his foot from the stair.

Surprise flashed across Roxana's face, but then her eyes narrowed with skepticism. "You do not offer that explanation with great conviction. If it is only envy, why then did she have misgivings about my designing a dress for Lady Julia?"

He stopped and swallowed hard. "You are very direct, Miss Winston."

"Yes, I promise to make an effort to curb that disagreeable tendency when the rest of the guests are here. But I am green to society and should like to know if I am taking any missteps."

He spun around. "Being direct is not always disagreeable."

"Isn't it?" She had descended to the landing again and he regretted that he had not watched. She pursed her mouth. "I am told that gentleman prefer a more demure countenance."

"I find plain speaking refreshing." Fanny's hints and prompts could drive him crazy with her unwillingness to just spill whatever it was she wanted him to know. "My stepmother dearly loves fashion, but she has been unable to indulge since donning her weeds."

Roxana was close enough he could see how the dark blue of her dress emphasized the color of her eyes. He could not help think of dark nights and forbidden pleasures. A direct woman had no qualms about asking for what she wanted. He shook his head to clear it. He had no business thinking such thoughts about a young unmarried woman, and he, as a rule, did not.

The knowledge that Miss Winston—Roxana— wore red silk undergarments muddled his thoughts. Now that he had stepped into the role of chaperone, thinking about her undergarments was just wrong.

"Do you really believe she is envious?" She scrutinized him.

"Yes, I am sure of it." He took a step back, wanting to break the web of fascination woven around him. Perhaps he should resume his liaison with Lady Malmsbury. He had mayhap allowed too much time to pass without a mistress.

It occurred to him only then that he needed to send word that he would need the curricle and a tiger to accompany them, rather than the gig he'd asked be sent around. They could not ride alone to town without an escort. Not that he would ever allow his improper thoughts to solidify into bad behavior.

Hoping to catch the servants before they had harnessed the wrong rig, Max stepped onto the landing to lean over the rail to call down to a footman waiting in the front hall.

Roxana shifted to the side, flinching. For a second he stared at her. What had she expected him to do?

"I am delaying you," she said softly. "I can walk to town another time."

He could not allow that, not if he meant to be a proper guardian. "I would welcome your company. I would enjoy some *direct* conversation. I hope that we can become friends."

Friends sounded nice. He had not known her very long, but she intrigued him, and friendship would keep him from thinking too much about her undergarments.

Miss Winston folded her arms and cocked her head to the side as if taking his measure. He felt lacking. He had not been wholly forthright.

"Miss Winston, if Fanny has any objection to your wardrobe it is that young ladies just out dress in white muslins and muted fabrics. They leave the silks and satins and bolder colors to their married counterparts."

A faint furrow appeared between her brows. In a very small voice she said, "Oh."

He watched as emotions raced across her face. She suddenly seemed young and inexperienced and a bit crestfallen. Society would eat her up if she always wore her heart on her sleeve. "I suppose that is how being direct can be thought disagreeable."

"No, oh no." She lifted her chin. "I am quite glad you told me. Friends are honest with each other, are they not?" She gave a little laugh and a skittish wave of her hand. "I have other gowns . . . but with my coloring . . . ah, well."

Which only made him look at her lily-white skin. But if she had had all new attire made up just for this house party . . . "It is only a smallish gathering, after all. I am sure you need not abide by the most rigid of strictures. Darker colors in the evening should be fine. I am sure none of the Lady Patronesses will be among the company."

"Since I shan't be presented in London, I will never need their approval for Almack's. But I should not like to embarrass her grace. She has been very generous in offering this opportunity to me."

She clenched her fist and Max wondered at her circumstances. Then he remembered that she was here to affix a gentleman's interest. Good lord, was she here to fix his interest?

Chapter
Two

Roxana located a bolt of plain muslin in the sea of fabrics and headed toward it. The duke stood near the door and the proprietor had jumped to serve him, even though buying fabric clearly was the province of females. But the diversion gave her a chance to check the quality and estimate how much remained. She would need to make several more gowns in addition to the one she had planned for Lady Julia.

After tucking her darned gloves in her reticule, she touched a length of patterned calico. She inhaled deeply, loving the mingled scents of wool and linen, even the faint freshness of cotton.

The flattery of the linen draper droned on and Roxana stopped listening to the Duke of Trent's polite inquiries about the man's wife and daughters. Apparently he knew the townsfolk well. Completely at ease with the shop owner's ingratiation, her escort folded his arms and lounged against the wall.

"Would you like to see that spread out, Miss?" The shop owner addressed her. "Fine print it is."

"It is lovely, but alas, not what I am looking for this day." The Duke of Trent watched her. A shiver of awareness shortened her breath. "How much is this muslin, sir?"

"Four shillings a yard," said the linen draper.

Had he had inflated the price because she had arrived with the duke? She swallowed down her distaste at haggling in front of him. "That is too dear. I do need quite a bit, would you take three shillings a yard? How much do you think is left on this roll?"

"I have another bolt in the storeroom, if you need more." The man gave a slight nod, but did not counter with a higher price.

"And how much for a cone of white thread?" She unwrapped a bit of a watered silk. The whisper of the material and the drag of it across her fingers made her wish she could afford it and that unmarried misses weren't confined to insipid clothes. But enacting the first part of her plan was more important than drumming up business for a dress shop that was only a dream right now. Without money, her dream would never be realized.

"Ten shillings, Miss."

"Would you take two guineas for the muslin roll and a spool of thread? I should hate to delay the Duke of Trent with measuring it all. If I find I need more, I shall return."

The duke pushed off the wall. "We have plenty—"

Roxana shot him a quelling look.

He inclined his head slightly, with the faintest hint of a grimace. "—several errands to complete this morning."

The shopkeeper did not respond. Was he waiting for her to sweeten the pot? Roxana wandered to the spools of assorted trim and located a pink satin ribbon. "Oh, and another shilling for two yards of this."

The draper nodded. "Very well, Miss."

Roxana moved to the counter, reaching for the strings of her reticule. She hated to spend the money, money that would have fed her family for a whole month. She had scrimped and saved to pursue her dream, but if she accomplished her purpose she would be able to set up a dressmaker's shop in London. With success, her family would never go hungry or cold again.

She'd earned pennies by taking in mending and sewing the last few years. More recently she'd fashioned gowns for her father's tenants, Mrs. Porter and her so-called daughters. Perhaps she had relied too much on Mrs. Porter and her daughters' opinions about the appropriateness of her clothing.

Smelling of bay rum and the outdoors, the duke brushed up beside her. He removed his purse from his coat. "Allow me."

"Oh no, you cannot," said Roxana. Part of her mind screamed *let him pay, he can afford it*. Another part said she could not allow him to pay for her clothing in any way. She had to remain above reproach until the moment she threw her reputation to the wind. "I thank you truly, but I wish to purchase it myself."

"The material is for Julia's new dress, is it not?" asked the duke.

"Not all of it. And it is my gift for her. To allow your hospitality to extend so far as my purchases would not be seemly, your grace."

Had she given him the slightest hint of impropriety? Roxana pulled out the two gold coins and a shilling, plunking them down on the counter.

The Duke of Trent slid his purse back in his pocket. His offer to pay confused her.

The linen draper measured out the ribbon and snipped it with his shears. With a stoic face he slid the muslin off the wood core and then wrapped brown paper around the material, the ribbon and the cone of thread.

After the duke handed the tiger Roxana's purchases to stow in the boot of the curricle, he moved to hand her up into the seat. "You drive a hard bargain, do you not, Miss Winston?"

"I am sure the linen draper has still turned a profit, your grace." Roxana stared straight ahead as she climbed into the seat. Her father hated women who could think and might have gotten the better of a man in a negotiation. God forgive a girl for showing the least amount of acumen.

"Are you quite sure? How many yards were on that roll?"

Had he seen her counting the layers? "Twenty, but there may be fewer."

The duke turned her hand, reminding her he still held it. He ran his thumb over the mended palm. "A hard bargain, indeed."

Roxana snatched her hand back, mortified that he should home in on where the reins of the pony cart had worn through her outdoor gloves. He must have watched her closely enough to know exactly when she was ready to deal with the shopkeeper.

"I admire anyone who can negotiate well, for I am of the habit of paying whatever price is asked."

Her bartering did not embarrass him? A little of the rigid tension that marked her every move in the Trent household eased.

With an easy grace he swung into the curricle

beside her and gathered the reins. He flipped the reins, starting the horses. "Shall we stop by the mantuamaker's place to engage her services before we leave town, Miss Winston?"

Roxana blinked and then lowered her head. "No, I will not need her assistance for Lady Julia's dress."

"And for your gowns, Miss Winston?"

She tilted up her chin. Did he realize the extra yardage was for her? "I can manage to sew a few simple gowns."

He settled into driving. Not wanting to stare, she turned her head away. December had denuded the trees and their branches crisscrossed across the pale sky like nature's lace. She forced herself to watch the scenery. She would by far prefer to watch the man to her side.

Would he catch her out at her plans? Her heart beat a little faster. He seemed very awake on all suits, too canny for her to even think of making him the object of her deception. She sighed. Not that she could really consider using him. She would need Max to be her champion. Her plan would work only if her host filled his role in her little Machiavellian scheme.

After they had traveled a ways, Roxana stole a peek at him. A bit of a smile hovered around his mouth. She hoped his offer of friendship was sincere. She needed a friend.

He pulled the gig to a halt in front of an open building a little away from the center of town. The acrid scent of hot charcoal and molten metal told her this was the smithy. The duke hopped down. "Would you like to remain here, Miss Winston?"

That was probably the proper thing to do. Instead

Roxana reached out her hand. "I should relish the heat from the fires, if just for a brief moment."

His brows came together for just a second before he handed her down. Thinking of her darned gloves, she should have stayed in the carriage, but he made no notice of them and dropped her hand quickly, offering his arm instead.

"If you are too cold you should have said so."

"I am fine, just too curious for my own good, I suppose. I have always been curious about how things work." Anything she could learn of how a craftsman conducted business could only help.

With her fingers lightly on his arm they ducked under the low beam that supported part of a wall of the three-sided building. She stayed well back of the furnace, where stray embers darted into the air.

He greeted the blacksmith, again by name. She nodded as the smith tugged his forelock in her direction.

Ducking between sledgehammers and tongs dangling from hooks on the open ceiling beams, the duke negotiated a path through troughs and buckets of water cluttering the dirt floor.

Roxana tried to remain inconspicuous as the duke engaged the smith's services as farrier for the upcoming hunt. Startled, she looked up. There was to be a hunt? How long had it been since she'd ridden a horse? The best of her father's stable had been sold long ago. Only a couple of draft horses remained to pull the carts. She had not even thought of making a riding habit. How could she have been so remiss?

The smith wiped his hands on his leather apron and grinned. "Right good, yer grace."

"And as many of the lads as you can round up to serve as whipper-ins. We are expecting extra guests this year."

"I know six or seven that would be right happy to be of assistance."

"Seven or even eight would be good."

"Yer grace, my sister could use the work if'n you need extra maids at the house. Seeing as you have so many guests."

The duke nodded. "I'll mention it to the duchess. Have your sister come out Wednesday next, although there may only be kitchen or laundry work."

The smith could hardly contain his elation, although he was properly deferential in his thanks. Perhaps the duke was not so awake on all counts.

He did not say a word as he handed her into the curricle and then carefully tucked the carriage robe around her. Roxana was too aware of his hands brushing along her sides, although without an ounce of true impropriety. Nevertheless his tawny head bent over her lap made her thoughts stray to his kindness. He seemed a generous man, too kind for his own good, perhaps.

He slapped his top hat on his head and swung into the curricle with such athletic prowess she almost forgave him for allowing the smith to take advantage of him. For surely the smith had asked for too much; she could see the glee in his eyes. His expression was much different than the linen draper whom she had met with such a hard bargain, as the duke categorized it.

They had gone only a few yards when the duke turned to her and said, "You can quit looking so appalled, Miss Winston. He did not take advantage without my consent. If I wanted to be parsimonious, I could have sent my steward."

"Oh, was I scowling? I daresay I should not allow my opinions to be so clear." She also feared that the townsfolk were in the habit of making a cat's paw of the duke.

"You should allow for the differences in our positions. It is the right thing for me to appear generous to the townspeople and those who are dependent upon my estate. Whereas you have only to think on your interests."

That wasn't exactly true; her family depended on her success. But she couldn't disabuse him of his assumption. No one would understand how much they depended on her finding the means to support them. "*Appear* generous? Are you not?"

One side of his mouth quirked up, and he leaned forward, urging the horses to a fast trot. "I perhaps did not phrase that correctly."

"I'm sorry. I have had every example of your generosity and I have no business questioning it." Roxana felt contrite. She was being overly familiar. While she craved a friend, she could not relax her guard too much. "My only concern was that you were being grossly misused. That your kindness . . ." *allows others to take advantage of you, as happens to my father.* Although with her father it was less generosity and more gullibility. His efforts to make himself rich had bankrupted the entire family.

The Duke of Trent twisted to look at her, his brown eyes much warmer than they had been throughout the morning. He really had quite fine eyes, honest and steady. . . .

"I am afraid, Miss Winston, there are those who would say I am too parsimonious."

Roxana stared until both corners of his mouth lifted in a self-deprecating smile.

"I hardly see evidence of that."

Everything she had seen from the moment she arrived at the immense landscaped manor spoke of a casual disdain of economy. The drapery and fabrics on the sofas and chairs showed no signs of wear, the china had none of the chips of a well-used set and there seemed to be no end to the food that was served, yet the duchess had apologized for the meanness of the fair before the house party started in earnest.

"I hope it is a temporary condition," he continued.

"I am sure it must be," she managed. "You would not have offered to pay for my material else wise."

"Ah, I did not mean to offend, but I was brought to mind that I may have curbed Fanny's spending too much. I am in the habit of paying for my sister and stepmother's gowns."

"I see," said Roxana.

"Do you? For in years past, we employed more of the townsfolk in plastering, painting and papering. I have asked that the renovations cease. I fear that my decision may have hurt local commerce."

Roxana digested his unexpected admission. "Why did you stop, then?"

"I had never started. My father authorized the renovations." He straightened to that rigid stiffness she had seen last night at dinner and stared at the road. "I so dislike all that dust and banging."

Roxana had the sense that he had dropped a curtain between them. "Shall you really have a larger party this year?"

"I believe her grace has invited several more guests."

He pulled up at the inn where Roxana had arrived less than a week ago in the mail coach. He removed a dozen or more letters from his breast pocket. The official start to the house party was just days away, with the winter soltice.

"Are those additional invitations?" she asked.

"Yes. I shall just be a moment posting them, unless you should like to stay long enough to warm your hands."

She was plenty warm, and the idea of his tucking the carriage robe around her again did strange things to her insides. "Why would the duchess invite more guests now?"

He gave her a questing look.

Had the Duchess of Trent invited more single gentlemen because of her? That must be the explanation. Roxana looked down at her lap where her hands were tucked under the carriage robe. "I must seem very naive. I did not realize that I should be the cause of extra work."

"No, Miss Winston, you are just as you should be. Besides, the extra guests are not all for your diversion."

"No?"

"Some are for mine." He grimaced and turned on heel to enter the posting inn.

Was he being pressured to marry too? He did not look as if he liked the idea much.

Two days later, Roxana had been enlisted to act as secretary. Her pencil poised above the paper, she trailed after the duchess. Her grace threw open the doors of a room along the passageway containing Roxana's bedchamber. "I shall have to install the Breedons here. Sir William will expect the very best."

Roxana peeked over the Duchess of Trent's

shoulder into a cozy pale-green sitting room. Four-poster beds were visible beyond the two interior doors. Shimmery drapes extended from the floor to the high ceilings.

"Mark down the green suite for the Breedons," said the duchess with a sniff. "The carpets are new. I should hope they will consider it grand enough."

The Duchess of Trent marched out of the room, as Roxana looked down at the apple-green and yellow Aubusson carpet on the floor. The rooms were fit for royalty, but then this manse was far beyond her experience. Even her father's hall paled in comparison to the grandeur of this ducal estate. And the cottage had nothing more than a few worn straw mats over the bare wood floors. Roxana felt guilty surrounded by all this luxury while her mother, sisters and brother were undoubtedly huddled in the cottage kitchen, struggling to stay warm.

Roxana finished writing and trailed after her hostess. They stood at the doorway of a spacious room, the room that was across a servants' passageway from Roxana's room. A fireplace flanked by bookcases dominated the outside wall and two high-backed chairs faced the empty grate. The cherry poster bed stood to the right side of the door on the interior wall, just as Roxana's bed was in her room.

"Room assignments?" asked the Duke of Trent from the doorway.

The duchess stepped into the room and ran a gloved finger over the table. "Just so."

"Whom do you plan to install in the blue room beside mine?"

The Duchess of Trent turned and studied her stepson. "I should not install Lady Malmsbury"—she stole a covert look at Roxana—"in the blue room?"

"That would not do. I can remove to another room, so that you might be able to use the suite for a couple."

"No, Max, we are not so crunched as that. I am having the children move to rooms in the old part of the house, so that I might use their rooms on the nursery floor for guests. They are still young enough that they think sleeping in drafty old rooms a grand adventure."

Roxana smiled. Julia had been bouncing up and down when she told Roxy that she would sleep in the chamber where Queen Anne had once slept.

"I thought I would put all the unmarried gentlemen on the nursery floor."

"Except I shall still be here on this floor. And you cannot put a man in Julia's room. It is too pink," said Max.

Remembering the primrose chintz curtains, the flowered wallpaper and ruffled bedcurtains of Lady Julia's bedchamber, Roxana silently agreed.

"Oh dear, I had planned to put Mr. Breedon there."

"Put Lady Malmsbury in Julia's room. Put Mr. Breedon here. He will complain if he has to traverse all those stairs daily. Put Scully in the blue room."

The Duchess of Trent dropped her chin and ran a finger along the dresser, looking for dust that clearly wasn't there, judging by the smooth patina of the wood.

Roxana had the impression they were talking in a veiled code. Was the blue room part of the master suite of rooms? Who was Scully? "Would you like me to write this down, your grace?"

The Duchess of Trent nodded and stalked toward the side door.

Roxana scribbled furiously. "Lady Malmsbury in Julia's room. Mr. Breedon in—what do you call this room?"

"Just put down my former room," said the duke.

Roxana looked up to see him staring at her as if he could see through her dress. She looked down at the white muslin gown, still only basted together on the side seams.

Lord knew she was trying to appear as she should. The gown was very plain with a gathered top, tiny cap sleeves and an empire waist covered by a length of red silk, hastily stitched into a band this morning to cover the less-than-perfect seam between skirt and bodice. The neckline was not low, but she had not bothered to fill it in with a fichu.

"I copied it from a fashion plate in the duchess's latest *La Belle Assemblée*. Is it inappropriate?" she asked.

His eyes jerked up to her face, and she felt her body responding. She resisted the urge to cross her arms in front of her chest, a chest that reacted with tingling and tightening.

"Perfectly appropriate, Miss Winston." The duke leaned back against the door frame. "Might I speak plainly?"

"I should much prefer it if you do."

"Did you take my words so much to heart that you are revamping your entire wardrobe?"

"Ah, I fear you see through me, but I shall not toss aside all my clothing."

His gaze traveled down her body, and heat seared through her clothes.

"How vastly disappointing, Miss Winston," he murmured, and then left the room.

Roxana wanted to throw something. Did he think she should redo her entire wardrobe? He had seen only four of her dresses so far. Yet, she was aware of the heightened cadence of her heartbeat and the weight of her muslin gown against her skin. How odd was that?

Max pulled his horse to a halt atop a ridge near his house. The vantage point gave him a view of the better part of his estate.

Julia and Thomas crossed over the ridge and raced down the other side. Roxana pulled her horse to a stop beside him. He liked the way the crisp air brought a bloom to her cheeks and the morning sun caught indigo lights in her dark hair. Would those dark strands feel like silk, slide like satin, smell like secrets?

He shook his head. He spent far too much time watching his guest instead of seeing which of the fields were in need of attention and which should be designated to remain fallow next season. His brother had gotten away when he had intended to spend the morning ride educating him about the estate. Julia had begged to go with them and invited Miss Winston.

Roxana had initially declined, and Max had sent the children to get ready before asking her if she had brought a riding habit. She had blushed as she shook her head no. Fanny had immediately insisted on loaning one of hers.

"Thomas, come back," shouted Max.

Roxana discreetly tucked down one of the beaded pins holding the waistband. Fanny's loaned riding habit was too large for her and the style not the latest, but Roxana's gratitude had shown in her face. "You cannot know how much I shall enjoy riding," she'd said to Fanny.

Miss Winston had a streak of honesty that he admired. She had not learned or was not willing to play the polite games that he encountered in society. She had a quietness that encouraged confidences. During their trip to town he had almost divulged his financial burdens to her.

Thomas brought his horse up alongside Max's.

"Can you point out the edges of the estate?" Max asked his brother.

"I have been here with Papa," said Thomas.

"And?"

"As far as one can see to the east, the hedgerow on the north and . . ." Thomas's voice trailed off. "Oh, the creek."

Max rocked forward in his saddle. By the time he was half Thomas's age he could point out the boundaries and name the tenants on all the farms. He lifted his riding crop and pointed west. "The creek is over there, and the two farms owe us rents. The Tillsbury and Wilbur farms are just this side of the hedgerows."

Thomas slumped in his saddle.

"You need to know these things, Thomas. You are my heir."

"Papa said I should not fret about it, as I was not likely to ever become duke, and I should not covet the title. He said he would buy me a commission when I came of age."

Alarm jabbed Max's spine. His horse sidled nervously, no doubt responding to his sudden cowhandedness. "Things are different now."

Roxana looked up from her gaping waistline, which was where Max was doing everything he could to avoid looking. If the skirt slipped low enough, might he catch a glimpse of red petticoat?

He told himself that was the only reason for his excessive interest in Roxana's undergarments.

"Do you know how many different breeds of sheep we keep?" Max asked Thomas.

"I know the shepherd brings them on the lawn Tuesday and Friday and I cannot practice cricket those days. I will need to be good at cricket when I get to Eton."

"Those are two different flocks."

"Yes, may I give my horse its head now? Julia is so far ahead she will say she trounced me."

"Thomas, you need to know these things. This estate shall be yours to manage one day."

Thomas looked at the ground. "I should very much like to be in the Horse Guards. Papa said I could."

Max winced. He supposed that as far as the military went, guarding the royal residence was less dangerous than the divisions his other brothers had chosen. "Go on, catch up to Julia. Then wait for Miss Winston and me."

Max turned and realized Roxana was scrutinizing him. Heat spread outward from his center.

"Your holdings are quite vast," she said mildly, watching Thomas race his horse after his sister. She sounded so unimpressed. She had not even looked while he pointed out boundaries to Thomas. If she were angling for Max, surely she would be interested in the extent of his estate. Perhaps her preference was just for the friendship he offered.

"Yes," answered Max.

"It must take a great deal of time and effort to manage all this, and you take your seat in Parliament, do you not?"

"Yes, I take all my responsibilities seriously."

"I do not think Thomas wishes to become your man of business. In the time I have been here, it seems to me that he much prefers physical pursuits to the classroom."

"Most boys do."

"Did you?" She turned her blue eyes in his direction and a heaviness settled in his lower half.

She continued to watch him and he belatedly realized she was waiting for an answer. He tried to engage the gears in his brain box. She had asked him a question. Did he? Did he what? "Excuse me?"

"When you were Thomas's age, did you prefer being out of doors to lessons?"

A memory of his brothers racing ahead while he walked his horse alongside his father, listening to the lectures and answering the questions that tested his knowledge, sprang into his mind. Being out of doors did not offer escape from lessons for him, but being the heir to this grand estate required that he gained the knowledge necessary to manage it. "I applied myself to learning what was required, indoors and out."

She tilted her head, a small smile lingering about her delicious lips. Would she taste as sweet as she looked? He shook his head, trying to erase the immoral urges crowding out his rational thoughts. He could not think this way about her when he was chaperoning her.

He needed to survey the estate, check the cottages and outbuildings for needed repairs, note any trees that might need removing, observe anything out of place in his lands.

"So shall you buy him his promised colors in the Horse Guards?"

"Good God, no. He is my heir."

Roxana looked startled by his vehemence. Perhaps if he had been concentrating on their conversation rather than the smooth curve of her cheek, he'd have masked his reaction better. He rolled his neck. As he forced himself to stare at the sky, he acknowledged that the curve of her cheek wasn't what drew his attention, but the curves below her neck.

"Surely, he will be displaced before he is old enough . . . to be commissioned in the army." Her voice trailed off.

"No, Miss Winston."

Her brows knit and her slight smile disappeared.

Now was as good a time as any to disabuse her of any notion she might have that he was available. "I lost two brothers in combat. I intend for Thomas to remain my heir. When he understands that I shall not marry, he will be glad of it."

"Will he?" she murmured.

Bloody well right, he would. "How could he not want all this?" He waved his riding quirt in a half circle.

She studied him with an unmoved countenance.

Did she not understand how vast his holdings were? His title, his income, even his hunting lodge were coveted by a great many. How could anyone want more?

"I am sorry for your loss."

He nodded, unable to say anything as he remembered his brothers so full of life, racing their horses over this very hillock. Now they lay cold and still in their graves not far from here. They would never gallop, laughing, over these fields ever again. But he could keep Thomas from courting danger.

He would not encourage him the way he had his brothers. He could keep him home. He would keep him safe.

Their horses ambled forward. Max tried to regain his equanimity.

"Would you like to run the horses?" she asked. "I am sure I have found my seat well enough to manage a good race."

"How long has it been since you've been riding, Miss Winston?"

She shot a look at him as if unaware of how much she revealed. "Four or five years." Then she snapped her quirt and her horse leaped forward.

He held his horse close until he was sure she would keep her seat and then the race was on. She rode well, her movements fluidly in rhythm with her mount's stride. With her horse carrying the lighter burden and her head start, Max's horse nosed ahead only as they neared Thomas and Julia.

As she reined in her mount, Roxana laughed. The sound ran through him like the chime of church bells. He stared at her flushed cheeks and sparkling eyes as she circled her horse around behind Julia to fix her skirt again. God, he wished the damn thing would just fall off.

"Who is that?" asked Thomas, pointing across the stretches of field where a carriage lumbered up the drive to the house. Numerous trunks loaded down the top and no less than ten liveried outriders flanked the richly appointed coach and six.

"Looks like the Breedons."

Roxana looked up and blanched. She stole a look at Max. "The one with the son of marriageable age?"

Max's horse wheeled. No doubt the gelding was

dismayed by his jerk on the reins. "Yes, Miss Winston, Mr. Breedon is of an age to marry." She would not want Gregory Breedon, in spite of his deep pockets and eligibility, and he was not likely to want her.

Roxana focused on Julia. "Is there a way to enter the house so I might get into my room to change before I am seen?"

"Oh, of course, we may go through the French doors in the library," answered Julia.

Apparently she did not mind him seeing her in ill-fitting, borrowed clothes.

"Good. For I should not wish for my skirt to fall off in front of your guests." She looked straight at Max.

Damnation. Did she realize he'd been watching her skirt with just such an interest? "No, that wouldn't be the thing."

"Does Mr. Breedon like to ride?" Roxana asked. "I see several horses being led by grooms. Or do those belong to his parents?"

"Those are his. Mr. Breedon is quite proud of his horseflesh," Max answered.

Roxana swiveled toward him. She wore an expression of grim determination that he had not seen before. "I shall have to adjust the fit on this habit quickly, then."

Did she mean to snare Breedon? Why not? He was young, rich, not encumbered by a great deal of responsibility. Her birth was better than Gregory's.

Max closed his eyes. When he opened them, Roxana, Thomas and Julia had already started their horses to the ridge. "Shall we return to the house, then?" he asked the air.

Annoyance that she had not set her sights on him tugged at him. Max dismissed it. Miss Winston was just practical. Had he not warned her off, himself? He admired her sensible nature, didn't he? Surely only his pride was at stake in his dislike of her preference for a man she'd never met.

Chapter
Three

With Julia's help Roxana made it to her room unseen. She'd changed into one of her simple muslin gowns. She added a dark blue spencer and tied a blue ribbon around the topknot in her hair. She would not be able to create an entirely new wardrobe. When the holiday house party was in full swing, her richly colored gowns would have to suffice for the evenings.

She entered the drawing room. Stealing in unnoticed was not a possibility with the footman opening the door. At home, the servants had dwindled to nonexistent before the family had moved into the cottage. Even without renters the upkeep of the hall was too much without servants.

She nodded her thanks, swallowed hard, then glided into the room, a small smile pasted on her mouth. Now was the time for her to perform as if her very life depended upon it. Her stomach churned and her knees threatened to give out on her. So much rode on her ability to sway one of the guests into becoming her means of founding her future and the future of her family.

The Duchess of Trent introduced her to Sir William Breedon and Lady Breedon. Roxana curtsied and made polite inquiries about their health and if their travels were pleasant. She spent a few minutes chatting with Lady Breedon about the awful state of the roads, agreeing without actually making any comment. She kept her eyes wide and nodded a lot, expressing a sympathy Roxana had a hard time mustering.

Compared to the cramped journey Roxana had taken in the mail coach, Lady Breedon's experiences with musty lap robes and a foot heater that would not stay lit sounded trifling. Although the longer Lady Breedon talked, the more Roxana suspected the source of the unpleasant trip was her traveling companions, but Lady Breedon had managed to transfer those less-than-savory feelings about husband and son to inanimate objects.

The duke blocked her view of Mr. Breedon. Their conversation did not carry the length of the massive room.

Finally, Lady Breedon patted Roxana's gloved hand and told her that she was a good girl for listening to an old woman's complaints.

"You are hardly old, my lady."

"Aren't you a dear? Let me introduce you to my son, Gregory."

Ah, the moment of truth. Or really the moment of untruth, corrected Roxana in her head while taking a deep breath.

Lady Breedon led her across the wide room to her son. Mr. Breedon was short, his face a full moon with poked pale dots for eyes, a nose too small for breathing and the merest slash where a mouth should be. He closed it and stared at Roxana's chest as she was introduced.

She dropped her eyes as if bashful and fought back a sigh. She extended her hand and dropped her curtsy. "How do you do, sir? I have so been looking forward to your arrival."

Mr. Breedon looked up, mildly surprised.

Max raised his glass to his lips in a mock toast as if to say *I told you so*. She didn't dare look at him. Her sights were set and Mr. Breedon presented her the best candidate. He had a rumored ten thousand a year, but his breeding was not as nice as hers. After all, his father was only a knight, so he would not inherit a title.

Yet, she had inferred from the Duchess of Trent's comments that Breedon was not particularly looking for a wife, which suited her plans. Given that the first place he looked was her bosom pointed to the kind of interest she needed to encourage.

Roxana lifted her eyes to Mr. Breedon's moonish face and smiled. "It is so comfortable to have one near one's age to discourse with, don't you agree?"

Mr. Breedon nodded, that slash, really more of a slit, of a mouth falling open.

"Pray tell how was your trip? Your mother was telling me the roads were quite uncomfortable."

"They were indeed dreadful. I have thought the Luddites had sought to ruin them, the holes were so bad."

Max took a drink and watched her over the rim, his eyes narrowing.

Roxana blinked, not knowing how to respond to such an outrageous suggestion. Destroying textile machinery was a far different thing than destroying the roadways. She chose to ignore it. "Travel

this time of the year, when it is so chill, can be unpleasant."

Mr. Breedon shivered. "Do not remind me."

"I don't believe that the Luddites have taken to
destroying the roads," said Max.

"Well, it just seemed that it was more than nature's fury. Such jostling ought to come because
someone wished to create unease. I should much
prefer to blame the Luddites than God or nature."

Roxana laughed as if he'd spoken with brilliance.
"I quite agree. Villains are ever so much more fun
to blame."

Mr. Breedon made an attempt to pull in his
puff-guts, and Max stared at her as if she'd lost her
mind. She didn't care. Mr. Breedon was a perfect
candidate to compromise her: he was rich, a bit of
a slowtop and would think himself blessed lucky to
pay her off rather than be tricked into marriage.
Then she would have money to open her dress
shop.

Beyond that, she felt absolutely nothing but a
vague pity for Mr. Breedon, unlike for the duke,
for whom she felt things she would rather not feel
for her intended dupe.

Now she had to persuade Mr. Breedon to compromise her, and then rely on Max to insist on
compensation.

By tea time the drawing room had grown more
crowded. Scully had arrived as well as two of Max's
aunts with their families. The next three or four
days would see a steady influx of guests. Max had
been down to the entry hall, welcoming Scully and
showing him to his room, but he was more interested in seeing their first guest.

He scanned the drawing room and found Roxana standing by a window. She cast only a cursory glance in Max's direction, but her gaze had lighted on Breedon and she took a step toward him. She had been stuck to Breedon's side ever since his arrival. Max was tired of watching her fawn and flirt with the self-absorbed fool.

Weaving his way around the groups of furniture and guests, he caught Roxana's arm. He wanted to pull her aside before she homed in on the man that she had apparently singled out for attachment. She jerked back, her eyes startled.

Her stiffening under his hand surprised him. He put a hand against the small of her back, pressing ever so slightly to guide her in a different direction. He was too aware of the delicious curve of her spine and his inclination to leave his hand long after it was necessary. "Allow me to introduce you to our newest guests."

Roxana's gaze darted over the groups of people and came back to his. For a moment time stood still as he looked down at her midnight-blue eyes. He resisted the urge to pull her closer.

"I . . . I believe I've met everyone," she said.

"Then allow me to escort you in a turn about the room. There are more guests who will join us and most of them already know each other." He pulled her hand into the crook of his elbow and leaned close to whisper, "You do not wish to appear too eager to snare Breedon in a parson's mouse-trap."

She shrugged and walked beside him. He looked down on the straight part and the very simple loose knot of her hair. She seemed determined not to look at him as he steered her toward the far reaches of the room and the alcove that flanked the far side of the massive fireplace. Just a little nook where they could be private, without actually leaving the room.

When he had her far out of earshot of the other guests, he asked her, "What are you about, Miss Winston? You cannot be enamored of Mr. Breedon."

Her delicately arching brows flattened, and she backed away from him, folding her arms across her breasts. "Why ever not?"

Her arms drew his attention to her neckline. Was it perhaps just a little low? In any case he would not complain, since his eyes feasted on the gentle swell of flesh. "Well, I daresay you would not be the first young lady to be enamored of his flush pockets, but it will not fly with him."

She dropped her arms, lowered her head and stepped farther back into the corner. He wanted to keep their tones low, so he followed her into the recess.

"Pray, what concern is it of yours?" she asked.

Max searched for adequate answer. In truth, she was his concern, but she would not appreciate knowing that he was watching over her. "I had thought you might be glad of the guidance of a friend. You said you wished to know if you made any missteps."

She gave him a startled look and pressed her lips together.

"If you appear too eager, he will think you are just another fortune hunter," he continued.

"My family . . ." She broke off and looked at the floor. "I have to be practical and I do not have much time."

"You have not even met all the men who have been invited for your perusal. I mean, if you are looking for a rich husband I would have thought you would settle on me, and I invited other gentlemen who are comfortable enough they would not balk at your lack of dowry."

"But you do not intend to marry, and I should not like to be so poor a guest that I lay out traps for my host." She fought a smile. "Besides, I thought I would not face much competition for Mr. Breedon's affection."

Max couldn't argue with that, but his affection wasn't why young ladies sought out Breedon. Most were after his wealth and Roxana apparently was too. Even if the idea of her fixing her affection on Breedon both annoyed Max and filled him with concern, he kept thinking she must have a reason that would make sense to him. Did she want nothing more than beautiful gowns and jewels? Or had her family instructed her to marry a man of good fortune? "What traps do you mean to lay?"

Her eyes flitted up and then away. An expression of alarm crossed her face. She flattened against the wall and darted to the side.

Good grief, he must have made her feel cornered. He turned and leaned against the wall and made sure his gaze did not stray below her neck. "I assure you, Miss Winston, you are perfectly safe. We are in a room full of people."

She caught her elbows in her hands and the gesture made her neckline gape for just a second, and his promise to himself to look no lower than her chin was broken. He mentally chastised himself and then decided he had done no harm in looking.

As he raised his gaze he noticed the simple cross she wore on an old chain. Most of the young ladies in the room had strands of pearls and earbobs made of gold and precious jewels.

"I doubt you can bring any gentleman up to scratch in the few weeks of the house party."

She looked up at him. "I have to try." She turned as if she would rejoin the company.

He reached out and touched her arm. A flash of heat traveled up his hand and snaked down to his gut. Damn his abstinence, which was making him react with too much heat. "Why?"

"Because this is my only chance to secure a decent future for my family."

Not for herself? How bad was her situation? She was not the first girl who would be sacrificed on the altar of family finances yet unease crept through him. How could he protect her from the travails of self-sacrifice?

He looked at the determination in her jaw, the strength of will that radiated off of her, and smiled. "I highly doubt that, Miss Winston. You strike me as the sort that would manage to avail yourself of another opportunity and another until you achieved success."

She looked at his hand on her arm, and he resisted the urge to stroke up her sleeve, across her shoulder. Putting his hand around her nape and drawing her to him would be simple. He could feel her still, like a skittish horse, prepared to bolt, yet not quite of a mind to, yet. "Come, you like plain speaking, Miss Winston. Are you thinking of what you shall have to bear if you marry Mr. Breedon?"

Did she understand she would have to bear Gregory's complaints and fancies of persecution as well as his children? The idea of that lout touching her curdled Max's spleen.

She looked at him directly. "I have only this opportunity, and I have no intention of wasting it by being undecided."

"Miss Winston, you are beautiful enough to attract a great many admirers. Surely you do not mean to settle on a suitor so quickly."

She stared at him, a hint of uncertainty around her eyes. Was she unused to compliments? His mistresses had often complained that he was ungenerous with them.

"And Mr. Breedon was not one of the gentlemen invited because he is in want of a bride. He is invited only because Fanny is fast friends with his mother. He has slipped the noose on many occasions before."

Roxana's head dipped, and he stared at the white part in her dark hair. Damn, he wanted to pull her to him and whisper dozens of compliments in her ears. But he had not pulled her to a corner to seduce her. His thoughts swam. He had pulled her aside to warn her that Breedon had made it clear he wanted a woman who brought as much wealth to a union as he did. Nor would it be the first time a penniless young woman had dangled herself in front of him only to look foolish when Breedon failed to take the bait. Or worse yet, nibbled at the bait, but threw the hook back.

"See here, Mr. Breedon has said time and time again that he will marry only a woman of equal wealth. He may be flattered by your attentions, but he is not likely to marry you." Although, Roxana's fresh-faced beauty might be enough persuasion for even Breedon to throw over his long-held plans to further gild his pockets.

Scully peered around the corner. "A turn about the room or a tryst in a corner?"

Max pulled his hand back from Roxana's arm and looked at his friend's quirked eyebrow. Scully had managed that unpardonable trick of raising one brow and he tended to make use of it whenever he found opportunity. He took an exaggerated long step, sliding his tall lanky body around the corner and pushing back a shock of straight dark hair that defied all but the most liberal of bear-grease applications.

Apparently Scully had forgone the application of pomade and was suffering for it, but then the idiot had arrived a full two days before his traveling carriage and valet. His clothes must have been stuffed in a valise tied to his saddle, given their sad, wrinkled state. Max introduced Roxana and Scully.

"Miss Winston," Scully acknowledged, raising his glass to his lips as if he was offering her a toast.

"Is that tea?" asked Max, amused but wishing his friend to perdition. No wonder Scully drove Fanny to distraction.

"Of course not. Found your brandy in the library. Haven't been here in a coon's age, but I haven't forgotten where things are. Malmsy is looking for you."

Scully looked at Roxana and sidled up beside her, crooking out his arm. "Trust me, all will go better if you hang on me."

Roxana looked at him as if he was half-crazed. But then, Scully had that effect on people.

"He has a good heart," said Max, suppressing a smile. "And it is your own fault that you haven't been allowed in the house forever. My father banned you."

"Oh, good, I thought it was Fanny."

"She said you could not come if you meant to make a fool of yourself."

"But that is what I do best." Scully turned toward Roxana, who was leaning away from him, although she delicately placed her fingers on his raised arm. "Ah, but then I am directed to make a fool of myself over you, Miss Winston."

Pain flickered in Roxana's expression. "Really?" she asked.

Scully's white teeth flashed in his face as brilliant as a stroke of lightning. His smile was one of his best assets. Max watched Roxana to see how Scully affected her. An answering smile tugged at her lips. Max felt a wash of relief. He could always tell from their reaction the women that would fall under Scully's charm. Roxana was amused, but not buoyed.

Scully patted her hand on his arm. "And here when I expected a dreadful task, I find a most delightful charge. I cannot think of a better way to spend my holiday than to tag after a fetching morsel like you."

Max kicked him.

Scully looked at him, startled. Hell, Max'd startled himself. He couldn't remember the last time he'd kicked anyone, perhaps when he was twelve in a cricket match. Probably Scully then too. He'd never thought to request Scully keep mum about the task given him.

Scully took another drink and reached over to set his glass on the mantelpiece. "Here she comes. I must say I am surprised to see her here."

"Fanny did not know."

"Ah yes, well . . ."

"What are you talking about?" asked Roxana.

"Ah, sweetness, it is time for us to take a turn about the floor," Scully said to Roxana. "I shall be the envy of every gentleman in the room, and of course the ladies will be coveting your gown. Shall we stir the pot a bit, my most pretty Miss Winston?"

"Do not let his flattery turn your head, Roxy. His heart has long been given," Max warned her.

She glared at Max. "All these ineligible eligible men at my disposal, whatever will I do?"

Scully laughed. "How droll. Is she always so droll, Max?"

"You would not want Scully anyway. He is poor as a church mouse and without expectations," Max told her.

"Max, there you are!" Lady Malmsbury flew forward into his arms. "I have been looking all over for you, darling."

Red curls tickled his nose and cloying perfume made him want to sneeze. What had he seen in her? She pressed her full breasts up against him as she kissed his cheek. Ah, he remembered. But her figure suddenly felt too fulsome.

"Ah, Lady Malmsbury, have you met our houseguest, Miss Roxana Winston?" He put his hands on Eliza's shoulders and pushed her back, heaving in a deep gulp of breathable air.

Eliza's reddened mouth rounded into an *oh*. She swiveled. Her pale-green skirts dragged over Max's legs. Fondling her necklace—his parting gift of emeralds—she batted her darkened eyelashes at him. More than one of his shirts had been sacrificed to her penchant for artifice.

Finally, she acknowledged the introduction. Lady Malmsbury slowly looked Roxana up and down. Max winced.

Scully pulled Roxana closer to him. "Isn't she a pretty thing, my lady?" Scully flashed his smile at Max's ex-mistress.

But his comment reminded Max of what Roxana had said earlier. "By the by, I am only two years older than Breedon."

"You have got it bad, son." Scully shook his head as if Max were a lost cause.

Max bit his tongue to keep from disputing Scully's right to call him "son." Even if Scully managed to convince Fanny to marry him—and marriage had never been a sure thing when it came to Scully—they would have to have a long heart-to-heart about whether marrying Max's stepmother would confer the title of stepfather upon Scully or rather would not.

And what did he mean, Max had it bad?

Lady Malmsbury leaned in close and said, "You will hate the room I am in. It is all pink ruffles and lace."

"That is my sister's room."

"Oh, dear. Well, I suppose it is more private."

"I thought you looked good in pink," muttered Max, but no woman could look better than Roxana. His gaze followed Roxana walking away on Scully's arm. They headed straight for Breedon. Christ, he couldn't trust Scully with anything.

Eliza had said something about green, and Max had no idea what she'd said, but her eyes were narrowing as she looked across the room to where Scully led Miss Winston around. And just what traps was Roxana planning to lay?

Roxana pulled her crochet hook through her lace and looked around the room. She sat beside Lady Angela DuMass, a young woman near Roxana's age. Other women were engaged in various activities; Lady Malmsbury preened before one of the gilt-encrusted mirrors, the duke's two elderly aunts sat across the room, playing cards, several women sat gossiping in one corner, but most of the gentlemen were absent. Max had led the men off on a masculine pursuit after nuncheon.

"That is lovely lace," commented Lady Angela, pointing her long sharp nose at Roxana's lap. "You do that very fast."

"Thank you," said Roxana.

Lady Malmsbury wandered over, glancing at Roxana's handiwork and sniffing. "I confess I much prefer Brussels lace."

Roxana resisted the urge to grit her teeth. "Of course, there is none prettier." Nor more expensive. "I prefer it too." The impulse to touch the chemisette that filled in the neckline of her green dress guided her hand to her neck. She wanted to point out that it was trimmed with expensive Mechlin lace. She lowered her hand. "I'm fond of Battenburg lace too."

"Oh, but one uses that only for table linens," said Lady Malmsbury.

The duchess entered the room with a couple followed by a petite young woman whose fawnlike eyes dominated her face. Fanny led the newcomers around, reacquainting everyone. They eventually made their way to where Roxana sat.

She stood and made her curtsy to Lord and Lady Lambert and their daughter. After a polite exchange Miss Lambert greeted Lady Angela with a hug. They began an excited chat, catching up on things that had happened since the close of the London season. Fanny patted Roxana's arm before moving away.

As the older Lamberts drifted to other acquaintances, taking Lady Malmsbury with them, Roxana's status as an outsider was painfully obvious. She moved to the side of the sofa so the two girls could continue their animated exchange. But she could not help but overhear their conversation.

"Mama said we must come posthaste, for if the Trents were inviting us, the duke must be considering marriage. Before, when they invited my parents, my older sisters were not invited," said Lady Angela.

Miss Lambert appeared startled by the notion, her brown eyes growing larger. "Do you think he picked us to come?"

"The duchess invited you," said Roxana and then wished she could bite off her tongue. She didn't know what prompted that tiny irrational surge of jealousy to make her want to burst their bubble.

Two pairs of eyes, one of pale blue and the other of velvety brown, turned in her direction.

"After the duke came home, they decided to invite more of the younger set," Roxana said, trying to undo the damage. Who was she to interfere with their hopes and aspirations?

"Who?" asked Lady Angela.

"Yes, who else is invited?" echoed Miss Lambert.

Roxana knew the names only from the place cards she'd written out and the room assignments. The names meant nothing to her. She searched in her mind's eye for the last minute additions, who had not arrived yet. "The Misses Ferris, Lord Hampton and a Mr. Allensworth. Mind you I do not know if they will come."

"Oh, no one would turn down an invitation to this Christmas party unless they were on their deathbed," said Lady Angela.

"Yes, everyone fights for invitations. I have heard their hunts are the best and the food is to die for, and then the gifts they give . . ." said Miss Lambert. "We were so afraid they would not continue the house parties after the old duke passed."

"Gifts?" said Roxana weakly.

"And the other sons," said Lady Angela. "The duke has had a great deal of tragedy in recent years."

"But he bears it so well," said Miss Lambert.

The girls both sighed in unison. Roxana wondered if Lady Julia was more mature.

"Did you ask about the gifts?" asked Miss Lambert politely. "Last time all the ladies received beautiful carved ivory fans. And the men ebony walking sticks. One year it was cloisonné snuff boxes for the men and gold lockets for the women."

"I just have handkerchiefs for everyone," said Lady Angela. "Mama said one can never have too many handkerchiefs."

"My parents said a young lady cannot give personal gifts or she'll be thought fast." Miss Lambert grimaced. "So me too."

"What are you giving, Miss Winston?"

"Ah, you'll just have to wait and see," she said. Oh stars, she would have to come up with gifts for everyone. "Perhaps, I'll give Lady Malmsbury my lace."

"Oh, do not waste it on her," said Lady Angela. "For I would dearly love it."

"She's bamming us," said Miss Lambert. "She probably has handkerchiefs too."

"No, I assure you I do not." Roxana didn't have sufficient lawn to make handkerchiefs. Store bought would be too dear. Red silk wouldn't suffice.

The gentlemen began entering the room, bringing in the scent of the outdoors, and the duchess rang for tea. The duke entered, his cheeks reddened from the winter cold. He looked in her direction and their eyes met. Heat snaked up through her body and she lost count of her stitches.

"He looked our way," said Miss Lambert with a titter.

Lady Angela looked at Roxana. "He looked her way."

"I'm sure he is just observing that you have arrived." Roxana nodded toward Miss Lambert.

As the duke broke free and started in their direction, Roxana hastily scanned for Mr. Breedon. He stood near his mother.

Roxana gathered her crocheting and stood, hoping to get to his side, before the duke waylaid her. She heard his gracious welcome of Miss Lambert as she had nearly reached Mr. Breedon.

"I am off to that walk now, Mama. Do you still wish to go?"

Lady Breedon sent her son off with a wave. "Bundle up, it looks cold out there."

"Do you want tea, Miss Winston?" asked the duke behind her. His voice ran down her spine like quicksilver.

No, she wanted to catch Mr. Breedon, but as he slipped out the door she knew she'd have to snare him after his walk. Lord Lambert approached and Max greeted him and politely engaged him in conversation.

Roxana managed to move away and avoid Max until Fanny suggested it was time to change for dinner, dispersing the crowd in the drawing room. Steering clear of Max when nearly all of his guests wanted to engage him in conversation was easy. He played the gracious host to the hilt, politely conversing with each and every one who approached him.

Roxana was determined not to let him distract her, and considered how best she could encourage Mr. Breedon.

"Fanny is avoiding me as if I carried the plague." Scully aimed his cue stick.

Max crossed both his hands over the top of his stick and leaned on it, waiting for Scully to take his shot. "Mmmm."

They were in that odd part of the early evening after tea when the ladies all disappeared to dress in all their finery for the evening, but the gentlemen were at loose ends, not needing hours to don their breeches and evening coats.

Scully pulled up and looked at Max. "Your mind is on the evening ahead?"

Actually Max's mind was on Roxana. What pressures bore on her?

"How about loaning me clothes for this evening? I had only one change of evening clothes and I wore them last night."

"My clothes will hang on you like a scarecrow. What did you do? Race here as soon as you got my invitation?"

Scully rolled his eyes. "Of course. I do hope the stable hands can save my horse. I rode him near to death."

"I am sure if you survived, your horse will." What would Roxana wear tonight? No doubt it would be remarkable.

"I am not at all sure that I do myself any favors by keeping close my hand. Can you ask Fanny where her heart is?"

"For God's sake, Scully, you're not a schoolboy. Ask her yourself."

"Ah, well, I have not succeeded in getting her alone, and there is all the squiring about of Miss Winston."

"You have hardly been doing that."

"Of course I have, when Breedon isn't doing it for me. Does Fanny not ride any longer? I asked her to ride out with me and she refused."

"Of course she rides, Dev, but not while there are guests in the house." If Roxana wasn't hanging on Breedon's arm, Scully was ready to step up and engage her in conversation. Scully was almost taking his duties too seriously. Max should have been relieved that he did not need to keep Roxana under his thumb every minute. "Have you ever met Lord Winston?"

Scully finally took his shot. The clack of balls against each other hardly penetrated Max's brain.

"Met him at the races at Newmarket one year. He plays rather deep. Drinks deep too."

"Does he take his seat in Parliament, for I do not remember him there?"

"Doubt it." Scully rubbed chalk on the leather tip of his stick. "I gather he's a bit of a Sunday man."

Which would explain Roxana's desperation to marry a rich man. Had her father landed himself so deeply in debt that he dodged prison? A man could not be arrested for debt on the Lord's day.

"I swear Fanny went around by the servant stairs so she would not pass near the mistletoe when I was near it," Scully said.

Max avoided being near the stuff too. A sprig would be strung up just outside the dining room for those persistent young women who might loiter about waiting for the gentlemen to finish their port. One sprig hung in the corner of the ballroom, for those bold enough to seek out its location in the midst of company. Then another hung in a niche just to the right of the staircase leading to the bedchambers. That was the dangerous one.

"Your turn," said Scully.

Max took aim.

"Look, it is Breedon returning from his afternoon constitutional," said Scully just as Max took his shot.

Used to his friend's attempts to distract him, Max nailed the shot, the balls clicking neatly together as he'd intended. "Is he? I need to speak with him."

"Sending him packing?" inquired Scully with an arched eyebrow.

"Don't be absurd." Max leaned his cue stick against the wall. "I want to sound out Breedon about his intentions toward Roxana." Breedon should know that Max took his duty as her stand-in guardian seriously. "Do excuse me while I catch him, unless of course you really did not see him."

"How is it you manage to turn every disadvantage to your advantage?" asked Scully.

"I have no disadvantages, just friends who would offer useless distractions."

Scully followed Max out of the billiard room, toward the entry hall and the stairs to the ground floor.

A form darted toward the niche where the servants had removed the ornate table and Grecian urn that normally resided there.

Scully started, "Is that—"

"Roxana." Max recognized the green dress that clung to her figure like a glove, or a scarf—or a wet sheet. Was she dampening her gowns? Every time he saw the way that the material clung to her perfect form, his breath caught and desire stabbed low in him.

Scully grabbed Max's shoulder, stopping his forward progress.

Max wanted to shake free of Scully's hold. Was Roxana planning for Breedon to catch her under the mistletoe?

Scully tugged him back. "She must have been watching for him to return," he whispered.

In the dim twilight of the evening, before the wall sconces had been lit, Max felt himself sink into a blackness that he didn't understand. "We should stop her."

"You know Breedon won't take advantage in an open passageway. It's just a harmless kiss under the mistletoe."

Scully wrapped his arm in Max's and yanked him back. Max could have broken free, but he knew Roxana wanted Breedon to offer for her. Max stood his ground as Breedon reached the top of the stairs and rounded the newel post.

Roxana stepped out.

Max could not see her expression, but he could see Breedon's round-faced surprise.

After greeting her with a short nod, Breedon walked past without stopping to kiss her.

Roxana's shoulders dropped, and she folded her hands across her front.

"If Breedon doesn't mean to honor the traditions of Christmas, I shall do the honors." Scully started forward.

Max grabbed him by the scruff of his neck. "No!"

"Stop. You're destroying my oriental."

"If that's an oriental I'll eat my hat. You cannot tie more than one knot, Dev."

"Never made it my life's ambition to stand in front of my looking glass, perfecting my cravat."

"A gentleman of my standing cannot neglect such a detail." Max whispered as Roxana turned and trailed after Breedon, her head down. "Go fix your cravat."

He gave Scully a good tug backwards just to be sure he would make himself scarce.

Roxana noticed their presence and stood still as a deer.

Max did not even realize what he intended to do as he strode forward, caught Roxana by the elbows, then backed her into the niche. Her blue eyes glistened with moisture as she looked up at him.

"Breedon is an idiot," he said as he lowered his lips to hers.

He hadn't meant more than a small kiss, but her disappointment incensed him. She should not have been so casually cast aside. Yet, as his mouth touched her petal-soft lips, rational thought escaped him. Her mouth had fallen open as he pushed her back and that was too much temptation for him to resist.

Chapter
Four

A squeak of alarm left Roxana's mouth just before the duke touched his lips to hers. His warm fingers slid around her nape, his thumb stroked along her jawline and his mouth pressed against hers. She had been prepared to submit to a kiss . . . just not with Max.

His hold was gentle, but left her in no doubt that he was in charge. Her pulse leapt as his lips moved against hers, making this kiss different than any she had ever experienced before. His tongue prodded at the seam of her lips, and he stepped closer, his firm body brushing against hers. Tingles danced along her spine. His masculine scent filled her with a heady intoxication.

Her thoughts and emotions swirled in senseless patterns until the only thing she could think about was the rough burr of his tongue against hers and how very odd she felt, all melting and weak. He pressed her further into the niche. She relished the solid pressure of his chest, as if she could draw from his strength. Prickles danced along her skin, her breasts tightened and grew heavy.

He deepened the kiss. She opened to him, allowing him access. His taste filled her. She had never realized that she could feel so undone, as if she were unraveling, but at the same time, feel completed and yet hungry for more of him.

His fingers stroked along her skin behind her ear as if he would pet her into compliance. Then her back met the wall and Max continued to push into her.

She welcomed the solid warmth of him. The growing response of her body compelled her to continue to explore this physical union of their mouths. Her knees weakened and her will to resist was only a tiny cry in the overwhelming fervor of her response.

She raised her hands to his chest, feeling his broad solid strength and his quickened breathing. A low growl left his throat. With the three walls around her and Max in front of her, she was trapped. Fear cut through her fog of fascination. Roxana shoved against his chest.

He abruptly ended their kiss. Lifting his head, he looked down at her, his brown eyes dark and bottomless. For a second it was as if he looked inside her. She shut her eyes, unable to bear the idea that if he looked too deeply, he would not like what he saw.

Air filled her lungs in quick pants and her heart raced. She shoved harder. He backed away, although she was still cornered in the small space. With her body no longer molded against his, her thoughts cleared. What was she doing?

Max reached above her head and plucked a berry from the sprig of mistletoe. He held it out to her. "Your luck should be in good stead this coming year, Miss Winston."

His roughened voice stole through her, touching parts deep inside of her. The intimacy of their kiss had opened her to him in ways she hadn't meant or expected. This was different from friendship.

She stared at the small white fruit in his fingers.

Surely this was not the kind of kiss she should have permitted or encouraged. Her lips tingled. She pressed the back of her hand against her mouth, trying to regain normal feeling. But on a deep level she had changed, and she did not ever think she could go back.

Max stepped back, his manner returning to that rigid correctness that she now suspected was his way of shutting out others.

She squirmed out of the niche—there were too many places in this house where a man could trap a woman. Only her disordered thoughts reminded her that she had laid this trap, but caught the wrong man. Mr. Breedon had either not noticed the mistletoe or had not wanted to kiss her.

Why had Max? He had forced her back under the kissing bough when she was several feet away from the corner.

"Was that a gesture of friendship?" she asked, dropping her hand down to her side.

"No. I . . . ." Max raised his free hand and pushed it through his wavy brown hair.

"Was it to teach me a lesson?" She suffered a moment's regret that she had not taken the opportunity to touch his hair, but things had happened so fast, she had not thought of what she could do. She should not play with fire.

Max still stumbled with his words. "I . . . Miss Winston, I . . ."

His inability to find what he wanted to say suggested he had been shaken in the same way that she had. What had they done?

"I apologize. That was most unhandsome of me."

Hurt stabbed and cut her insides. Her emotions had turned into delicate crystal easily shattered. "Are you apologizing for kissing me?" Her voice crested up unnaturally.

"Not for kissing you, per se. You were under the mistletoe."

"Not when you seized me and marched me back here." She pointed to the niche. Her heart refused to slow its mad race. "There."

He stared at her. Did he regret kissing her? He had spoken before he kissed her, but she had been so surprised by his handling that his words hadn't registered.

She folded her arms across her middle.

He pushed his fingers against his forehead. "I apologize for breaching the bounds of propriety."

"Oh." She looked at the little cubbyhole set up for the purpose of stealing kisses. Their exchange had been too heated. "Perhaps I should have offered more resistance. I did not know. I have never been—"

"You did nothing wrong." He reached out and caught her shoulders.

She froze as his gaze dipped to her mouth and then back up. Would he kiss her again? She could feel that welling response, the weakening of her limbs as if she was about to turn mindless. She sucked in a heavy breath.

He dropped his hands and took a step back. "Should you not be dressing for dinner?"

"Yes, yes, of course." Roxana swirled, thinking

she could not make it to her room soon enough if she flew.

"Miss Winston," Max called behind her.

She did not stop. She had not known how being held in his arms could approach wonderful heights. Yet, she could not fully appreciate the experience. Not knowing would have been better, because experiencing such kisses in her life was unlikely. And, oh God, she was such a ninny to fall for the high-and-mighty duke who would not marry any woman, let alone a needy, poor woman like her. Nor would she marry any man, let alone a man who could control her with a touch, turn her mindless with a kiss, make her forget her imperative plans with a caress.

Yet worst of all was his reaction, that he had drawn up stiff with regret. Pain swirled in her stomach. He had not meant to kiss her so freely. That had been apparent in his dismayed expression. She could not let it lay, but had challenged him. Would she never learn to curb her tongue?

Max stared at Roxana's retreating back and wondered what fever had invaded his brain. He'd never treated an unmarried lady to such an unbridled kiss, let alone treated any woman to such a kiss without a gentle seduction of hand kissing, touches, indications of his intent. He had been close to allowing his hands to roam lower, to capture and caress her curves in a way that conveyed an intention to bed her.

Had she sensed his slipping control when she pushed him away?

Scully approached him with a smirk on his face. "Shall we finish our game?"

"I forfeit."

"The game?" asked Scully with that infuriating lift of a single eyebrow.

"What else?"

Scully grinned, but did not reply, which was probably wise of him.

"Did Breedon . . . ?" Max gestured toward the kissing bower.

"Walked him to his room, warned him that you were taking your duties toward your guest seriously and expect him to be above board in all *his* treatment of her. He is oblivious to your waylaying Miss Winston."

Max did not know if that relieved him or not.

Scully studied him. "That is what you meant to say to him, isn't it? Far too soon to demand to know his intentions."

Max did not think he could bear the scrutiny at the moment. He did not understand why he failed to toe the line. Perhaps it was because the minute he touched Roxana he had thought of her most improper undergarments. Or that he had not slept with a woman in months, or just that she was under his protection . . . but not under his protection in the way that gave him the right to take indecent liberties. What was wrong with him? He never violated the rules of proper behavior.

He could not think of that, and he should not have seen her so revealed and unaware.

Max raked a hand through his hair. "We should get ready for this evening."

"Or have a drink," suggested Scully.

That sounded like a splendid idea. A drink might cool the heat in his blood. Max strode toward the stairs.

Roxana was just a lovely girl, young woman, young lady. Max could not even think straight. So fresh and sweet, the imprint of her body flooded his mind.

"You are a better catch than Breedon," offered Scully slyly.

"Do not finish that thought," warned Max in a tone that he knew Scully would not contest. "I could not afford a wife even if I wanted one."

Max would keep his distance this evening through dinner. "You keep an eye on her the rest of the day, and for God's sake do not let her be alone with me."

Roxana smoothed her hands down her dress and wondered if she had made a mistake. Lady Malmsbury's dismissal of Battenburg lace had probably influenced her decision on a dress to wear for dinner. That and she hadn't really been thinking straight after that kiss from Max. Or she needed to wear a dress that made her feel powerful.

She had made the dress from table linens and sewn it in a harlequin pattern, mostly because she had to work around the stains and had not had enough of either tablecloth to do a complete dress. A thin strip of gold piping ran down the seams between the alternating diamonds of bright white and butterscotch. Instead of gathers she had sewn gores into the waist of the skirt. While it had a high bodice, the dress fit more closely than the loose empire gowns most of the other women wore.

The normally circumspect footman hesitated before opening the drawing room door. She felt like running, but the footman was hardly frowning.

He opened the door and she turned to look at him inquiringly before he shut the door after her small train cleared the entry.

She had sewn on it for days, and she wondered as she looked around if it was too innovative, too different, too admired by Mrs. Porter and her girls. What on earth had possessed her to rely on the advice of a pack of Paphians?

The duke turned from across the room, glanced her way and then looked again. She saw him swallow, his cravat shifting with the motion. His eyes moved down her from her slashed sleeves to her midsection and seemed to linger on her hips. Roxana looked for a place to sit, steeling herself against the idea of running away. She would be under a table most of the rest of the evening and she wished she was there now.

Lady Angela approached and Roxana nearly sagged with relief.

"You continue to amaze us," said Scully, tugging her elbow and pulling her away from the door. "You look stunning, Miss Winston."

Miss Lambert hung behind Lady Angela and peeped over her shoulder.

"Bit of revenge?" whispered Scully near her ear.

Relieved her limbs worked and she had not frozen in place, Roxana heard the murmurs around her. She cast Scully a skeptical glance as if she didn't know he was referring to Max.

She had not even thought of Mr. Breedon. She turned looking for him; instead she encountered Fanny's frown. The duchess wore a modest evening gown in black silk with an overskirt of gray net. They were dressed as different from one another as night and day.

"You look famous," said Lady Angela. "Where did you have your gown made?"

"Yes, did it come from France?" echoed Miss Lambert.

Roxana sighed with relief. Improvising as she went along, she said, "My mantuamaker is from France."

"Is she in London? Oh, my mama would never allow me to wear a dress like that," wailed Lady Angela.

"She plans to open a shop in London, soon," answered Roxana.

"It should help to have a figure like that," whispered Miss Lambert.

"Oh, no, it is the way the diamonds are positioned." She knew that she wasn't really meant to hear Miss Lambert's comment. Roxana started to show how the points came together toward her waist and the white diamonds were cut narrower, which made her midsection appear slimmest.

Scully cocked an eyebrow at her.

"Miss Lambert, you are near to my size, perhaps you would like to try it on. If you two want to come to my room, I could show you . . . things." She could show them how to show off their best assets and minimize their worst features.

Miss Lambert shook her head. "I would never be allowed to wear dresses like yours."

Remembering what Max said about unmarried misses sticking to white muslins, Roxana queried, "Not even after you're married?"

"What is your modiste's name?" asked Lady Angela.

Roxana went blank. She had not even thought of a name. At that minute the drawing-room door opened and Lady Malmsbury entered wearing a gold gown cut so low that it was a wonder her nipples did not show. Nearly every inch of fabric sported a bead or a spangle. With her red hair in long dangling curls and diamonds flashing from her throat she paused in the doorway, flipped her hair and waited for a response from the company.

Roxana, much to her chagrin, looked to see Max's response. He barely looked at Lady Malmsbury and then looked back in her direction.

Roxana was appalled by how much her freezing at the doorway imitated Lady Malmsbury's bid for attention. She hoped that no one thought she was making "an entrance."

Then she realized she had to give Lady Angela an answer, but when she turned the two girls had drifted away. Roxana stared at their girlish dresses with ruffles and ribbons, one in light yellow and the other in a pale peach.

And Max was approaching.

Scully held out a hand to stop him. "Go away, she's mine."

"I'm taking her down to dinner," said Max imperiously.

Just then Roxana caught Mr. Breedon's eye. He looked stunned.

"I promised Mr. Breedon," Roxana muttered. That was the only good thing that had come of her waylaying him near the mistletoe.

Scully arched his brow and silent communication passed between him and the duke. "I'll go get Fanny."

"Yes, go speak to her grace."

Max held out his arm and Roxana reluctantly took it. A flush crept up her neck and heated her face. She remembered the kiss under the mistletoe. She wished she could forget it. Mr. Breedon cast a questioning look in her direction and Roxana shrugged.

A circle seemed to have opened up around them. Max looked down at her with a warm smile. "Remarkable dress, Roxana," he said in a low voice. "Try not to blush."

"At least it is mostly white," she tried. "I'll stick to the muslins from now on."

"No, you won't."

Fanny approached, with Scully following, his hands clasped behind his back.

"You amaze me, Roxana. I wish I could wear such beautiful things."

"You cou—"

Max placed his hand over hers, tapping the back of her hand like a schoolmaster might gently redirect a daydreaming student.

"You are just the dernier cri, but I suppose that is what one must expect from a girl who has spent time in Europe. You have acquired such a continental flare," said Fanny.

Scully cocked an eyebrow.

The duke and duchess flanked her until the butler announced dinner. Lady Angela and Miss Lambert cast hopeful glances in the direction of their parents.

As the company filtered out of the drawing room toward the stairs, Roxana hung back.

"I have been to Europe?"

Max shrugged. "Apparently. You did not have a season, so you must have been somewhere."

"So if you and the duchess put a stamp of approval on my apparel then everyone will accept it?"

"Exactly so." Max tilted his head back ever so

slightly and gave an infinitesimal shake of his head in a regal sort of gesture.

In his gesture was something domineering and imperious. Then he looked down at her, his brown eyes warming as he assessed her dress.

"You look beautiful." His voice was low and spread through her like melting butter cream.

"I never intended to look . . . fast."

Max swallowed hard again.

Mr. Breedon cast an uncertain look in her direction before he left the room.

"Coming, you two?" asked Scully from the doorway.

Max held up one finger and swung around in front of her. "Nothing is improper in your gown. You just have a flare for drawing attention. As a friend, I advise you to continue wearing the clothes you wear or the gossips will assume that we have browbeaten you in private."

She nodded.

Max's eyelids dropped and he leaned closer. Did he mean to kiss her again? Mistletoe wasn't above her head this time. Her heart pounded madly, but the duke was not her prey. And Mr. Breedon was getting away.

Roxana took a step back and said, "Who'd have thought wearing table linens would create such a stir?"

Max coughed, and she skirted around him, then scurried to catch Mr. Breedon, wondering how he felt about her clothing.

Max tapped on the connecting door to the blue room, with a spare dressing gown over his arm and the brandy decanter and two glasses in his hands. He could not sleep, and Scully was always good for a shared drink.

Scully jerked open the door, then stared at Max. His blue eyes narrowed. "You are not whom I wanted to see." He shook his head, the dark shock of hair flopping across his forehead. Scully shoved it back and muttered, "I knew something was wrong when I realized I was in Fanny's former room."

"Please, avail yourself of my valet until yours arrives." Max held out the dressing gown, then realized what Scully had said. "How do you know this room was once Fanny's?"

Scully shook his head. "Come have a nightcap with me." Max lifted the decanter.

"I drink too much as it is," said Scully, but he shed his coat and waistcoat, then grabbed the dressing gown. He jerked the knots of his cravat free. The clothing went sailing back into the blue room, landing on the floor.

Max had removed his outer evening clothes long ago and switched to long unmentionables rather than his evening breeches. He scrutinized his friend. "Were you planning to go out? It is well after midnight."

"I haven't the slightest idea of which door to tap on now. Putting me here was cruel of Fanny. I suffered grandiose notions of easy seduction, only to find I am sharing a suite with you."

"Sorry to disappoint, old boy." But it was that kind of night.

"Never mind. My course has never been easy."

"Fanny did not put you here, I did. I preferred your company to Lady Malmsbury's." Max pointed. "Fanny's room is two doors down. Mind you, not the next door, for that is Fanny's dressing room and her maid is sleeping in there. You will scare the dickens out of her if you tap on that door."

"God love you, son."

"You call me son one more time, I shall throw you out on your ear so Fanny won't have to. If you knock on her door, I expect you will offer marriage. Otherwise, don't knock."

Scully paused in his flaying attempts to get the dressing gown on over his shirt. "You're testy."

"Me? Never." Max turned back into his room and set the glasses down on the table between the two easy chairs facing the fire and poured brandy into them. He just needed a drink. And he needed to know that Scully would do the right thing.

"It is Miss Winston, is it not? Hell, just marry her—you do not need a woman to bring a dowry to the estate."

"I'm not marrying. I want Thomas as my heir."

"I'm not sure Thomas wants to be your heir."

"Want to or not, he is." Max did not know why everyone was so resistant to the facts of the matter. Once Thomas fully appreciated all that he would have, he would want the title and all that came with it.

"Besides, I've scarcely known her a week." Max stared into the liquid in his glass, then tossed it back in one gulp. "Should I ever marry, I'd need a heiress."

"Bad form, Max. Brandy should be warmed before you gulp it."

"I know how to drink, Dev. Just because Miss Winston's presence has affected me, does not mean I should marry her."

"Ah, her presence or her enthusiasm?" asked

Scully with a knowing tone in his voice. "For she seemed quite as engaged in that kiss as you were."

"Do not speak ill of Miss Winston. She did offer resistance." Thank the Lord, she had finally come to her senses, because Max wasn't entirely sure that he would have. He didn't even want to think about his near repeat in the drawing room. He slammed back another drink. In all his years, he had never come so close to losing control.

"That was hardly speaking ill. Quite a beautiful chit. She makes best use of her charms, does she not?"

"Scully!"

"Ah, do you mean to call me out? Defend her honor? She has caught you in her web, and I do not even think she was trying to snare you. You really should marry her. She would stand up to your superiority."

Max ground his teeth and ignored Scully's irreverence. They had known each other too long to be truly offended, but Max was skating closer to the edge of the precipice. "No, I should not."

"Yes, you should. You are enamored of her. Happens quick like that at times, happened that way for me."

"You were fifteen, and I am not enamored of her." Max did not need to pretend with Scully. What Max felt for Roxana Winston was pure and simple lust, while his friend had been enamored of his stepmother since Eton days.

"And I have been steadfast in my affections ever since," returned Scully, rolling his brandy glass between his hands.

"Hardly so."

Scully made an odd noise and threw himself

into one of the high-backed chairs. Max looked at him. Scully seemed as fretful as Max felt. Was he having second thoughts now that Fanny was free? Unrequited love for a married woman was one thing, unrequited love for a widow was an entirely different matter. In a way, Scully's professed love for Fanny had kept his heart free during his numerous entanglements over the years.

Trouble was, Max cared about both of them. He poured out a third glass of brandy and tried not to allow the memory of that kiss to crowd his mind. Of course, realizing that he had managed about ten seconds' respite from the memory of Roxana's perfect form pressed against his body made heat rise in his blood.

He shifted in his chair.

He had barely managed any other thought as he played the gracious host throughout the remainder of the evening.

"You shall to have to marry one of these days. You have responsibilities," said Scully. "I, as a younger son, bear no such need. I do not need to reproduce. My property is too modest to split among heirs."

Max closed his eyes. "I won't have Thomas going into the military. If Fanny or my mother had brought lands to marriage as dower property I could give them to him, but neither did."

His father should have considered what would happen to his heirs before he married women that brought small portions to the marriage and then allowed them to spend so recklessly. For it was not all Fanny's spending that brought about the current state of affairs. Many of the loans predated her marriage. His two brothers left debts to discharge too.

The weight of Scully's stare bore on him.

"My father's debts are monstrous. Everything is entailed, you know. I cannot sell any property to settle his loans, nor can I split off any lands to provide for Thomas."

"So you can marry only a woman who brings considerable dower property to the table?" Scully balanced his glass on his forehead and stared at it cross-eyed. "You are the only one who knows of my affection for Fanny, you know."

Max looked at Scully. "Why is that?"

"I did not want you offended if I was successful in my pursuit of your father's wife."

"Were you ever successful?" asked Max.

Scully twisted his head, catching the glass as it fell off his forehead with nary a spill. "I may have been a lark to her, an indulgence for her vanity. She has made no secret of her preference for maturity and stability. Has she asked about me once, since your father's death?"

Max looked into his glass. No, Fanny had not asked after Scully, but he had always thought she reacted when he spoke Scully's name. He knew she was lonely and vulnerable, but did she truly mean to avoid Scully? Would she be happy only with a husband who encouraged reckless spending? "It has been only a little while."

"It has been eighteen months," said Scully.

The door clicked open and both men swiveled in their chairs to see Lady Malmsbury draw up short in the doorway.

"Oh dear, I seem to have lost my way," she said as she glared at Scully.

Chapter
Five

Fanny spooned buttered eggs onto her breakfast plate. She initially lifted two scones with the serving fork and then put one back. She glanced at Roxana's plate. Her guest had moderate servings of everything. No wonder she was so slender. Although truth be told, Roxana was no twig, she just had the figure of a young woman and dresses that showed it to her best advantage. Her figure was much like the one Fanny had enjoyed nearly twenty years ago . . . before children.

Fanny sighed as she sat down at the morning-room table and pulled the cloth napkin across her lap. She hadn't grown monstrously large, but her hips had widened with each of her two children, and well, her figure was fuller and gravity was working against her.

Roxana was the full-grown daughter of one of her best friends from school days, a friend she had not seen in nearly twenty years. Fanny's own daughter would be presented to society in four short years, and Thomas would be away to school in just a few months.

Fanny felt old and yet too young to be alone for the rest of her life. Julia and Thomas tromped into the breakfast room and shoved to be first at the sideboard.

"Thomas, do let your sister go first." Fanny's words had little effect.

"I'm hungry," complained Thomas.

"I was here first," said Julia.

Across the room, Max lowered his newspaper. "If you two must behave like little children, you will have porridge in the nursery. We have guests."

The shoving stopped. A frisson of resentment surprised Fanny. She should feel nothing but gratitude toward Max, who allowed her to stay on in his household, although he could have suggested she move to the dower house. Max had done wonders stepping into his father's role without hesitation. Of course, he had been raised to do so from his infancy.

But his decreeing that his friend Devlin Scullin sleep in a room just two doors down from hers when she did not even want the man in the house bothered her. When Max had spoken to her of ending the improvements to the house and grounds and suggested economy in spending habits, as was his right, Fanny had felt chastised and humiliated.

In the near nineteen years of Fanny's marriage, her husband had never once indicated that she spent too much or that paying the bills created problems. Max stopped short of saying she should live on her jointure and apologized handsomely, blaming recent crop failures and that he wished to be sure Thomas and Julia would be adequately provided for. Fanny knew that he avoided saying her reckless spending had created debts. The former duke had indulged her and encouraged her spending to no end.

But she was not able to voice to her stepson her protest that she had not known that she was too extravagant. She should have known. She had long ago discovered that the pretty things held little appeal once bought, but by then her spending was more habit than not. Max was the head of this household now, which made him guardian of her children as well.

Although on the face of it, Fanny could not fault Max. She knew he would not have asked her to cut back if there was no need. Resenting Max's long absences and his mandates about Thomas's education was silly. Nothing had changed in the way Max handled himself, except he took his duties to Parliament much more seriously than his father had.

She was just lonely, and Max was not at fault, nor was her husband to blame. No more than it was Roxana's fault for being young and wearing beautiful clothes. Roxana would no doubt receive a great deal of attention from the men at the house party. Fanny would receive the deference due a hostess.

"Thomas, do sit here beside me and tell what you will do today," said Roxana. "Do you have studies?"

"Not today, for it is the week's end and Max gave our tutor leave to visit his family for Saturday and the Lord's day," said Julia as she took the seat on the other side of Roxana. "Seeing as how his home is a county away."

"He's my tutor, not yours. You only get to borrow him while he's here to teach me," said Thomas.

"I know more than you do," retorted Julia.

Max folded the newspaper and gave Julia, then Thomas, a look.

Roxana gave the tiniest shake of her head. "Would you not expect to have learned more? You are older, after all."

"I don't see why I have to share my tutor with her. Girls aren't supposed to know Greek and Latin and mathematics," Thomas said sullenly.

"Why ever not?" asked Roxana. "Does it harm you that Julia is fluent in the ancients?"

Thomas shook his head.

"Do you know such?" Julia asked.

As Roxana shook her head, Max cleared his throat. Both the children ducked their heads.

"But I should have liked the opportunity to learn," Roxana said.

"Then you should come up and study with us, Roxy," said Thomas with a sly look at his sister.

Max stood and folded the paper. "Thomas, have you been given leave to be so informal?"

Roxana looked at him. "I do not mind, your grace. Lord Thomas is only a little younger than my own brother, and I have three sisters. I should much prefer if Lady Julia and he call me by my given name. It reminds me of being home."

Max stood very still for a moment before nodding slowly. Miss Winston set down her fork. They seemed very ill at ease with each other this morning, when before it seemed they had gotten on well. But Miss Winston had all but attached herself to the richest eligible houseguest, Mr. Breedon. If she was not with him, then Scully was at her side.

And she had worn that striking gown that had everyone looking at her and her perfect figure.

Roxana lifted her fork, but only stirred her eggs. She now stared at her plate.

"I've read this paper already." Max slapped the paper together and tossed it down.

"Well, it does take a few days for them to reach us from London," said Fanny. The same paper had probably been delivered to him before he left town. Max was behaving oddly. He watched Miss Winston. Good grief, was he attracted to her? Had his decision to help chaperone Roxana thrust them too much in each other's company? Would that be a bad thing?

Would Max consider offering for her? While Roxana's birth was acceptable, Max could certainly find a young lady of better birth and a superior dowry. Fanny had the sudden realization that if Max took a wife, her position would be even more fragile.

"Thomas, after breakfast I should like you to accompany me to the office." Max gave a pointed look in Roxana's direction. "Unless you have need of him, Fanny."

That meant she would need to chaperone Miss Winston for the next few hours. She often had Roxana tagging after her in the mornings as she went about her preparations for the party. "I plan to spend the morning decorating the ballroom."

"I should be glad to help if you need me," said Roxana.

"I want to help too," piped Julia.

Well, that would take care of that little problem. Fanny had learned when having Roxana assist her with hanging the mistletoe that the girl had a knack for decoration. Roxana had taken a look at the kissing bower Fanny had set up in the ballroom corner and had stepped in and draped it with twisted gold ribbon, making the corner look extraordinary. Would she be so eager to help if she thought Mr. Breedon would join them soon? Was she at all curious to learn the whereabouts of Dev this morning?

But there was no need for an answer as that gentleman, wearing clothes that fit him ill and were in the brown tones Max favored, strolled into the room. Scully flashed his smile and said, "Good morning, Fanny, Max, Miss Winston, Julie, Tommy. How is everyone this fine morning?"

Fanny felt the familiar flip-flop of her stomach and a stab of jealousy. She had been half afraid that Scully would find her too old and careworn to want a flirtation with her. He would surely be drawn to the bevy of young ladies she had invited to the party. That he had spent a great deal of time with Miss Winston last night after dinner only confirmed Fanny's suspicion that he no longer thought about her. Besides, she had never had any reason to believe he had ever wanted more than to be her cicisbeo.

She rose from her chair. "If you will excuse me, I have a great deal to get done."

She told herself that she was just angry that Scully used his position as Max's longtime friend to be overly familiar, but she knew that every time he said her name she wanted to melt into a puddle of adoration at his feet. That would undoubtedly be the most humiliating experience of her entire life. A duchess should be above behaving like a ninny over a coldhearted rake.

* * *

Max looked up from his desk and noticed Thomas staring out the window instead of going over the accounts Max had assigned him.

Max put down his pencil. "Is everything correct?"

Thomas slumped in his seat. "Why should I bother adding up all the numbers when you shall do it again anyhow?"

"Because you need to know how to manage the estate. Not all of it is riding around checking the fields and livestock." Thomas took those instructions marginally better than when they were closeted in Max's office with the ledgers and correspondence. "Once I've seen that you know how to do it all, I shan't have to double-check you."

Making the youngster feel his efforts were valued was tougher than Max realized.

"I have lessons all week. It is not fair that I have to do more of the same all day Saturday with you."

Max wondered if he had ever said the things Thomas said. He remembered feeling that way, but he could not remember disputing with his father about the necessity of learning how to manage the duchy. But then, for Thomas, dealing with an older brother had to be different from Max's learning from his father. "You need to know. You are my heir."

"Yes, well, I shall hire a steward if it comes to that," said Thomas.

"I have a land steward, a secretary and a man of business. But if I do not know what is about, they could make mistakes or rob the estate." His money was stretched too thin to risk losing any through a failure to manage it properly. His income was large, but so were the estate's expenses. Paying his father's death taxes had forced Max to liquidate more than a few assets. And the debts he had inherited were more than Max had ever expected.

"You don't trust your hirelings?" Thomas gawked at his older brother.

"Of course I trust them. I would not keep them on if I had any reason to doubt their loyalty." Max sighed. Why was this so difficult to explain? "The lord has to oversee everything."

Thomas folded his arms. "It is not fair. Julia is helping decorate the ballroom, and Roxy said she would show me how to cut paper decorations if I joined them."

"Very well." Max pointed to the door. If Max showed Thomas the total amount of the outstanding loans of well over a hundred thousand pounds, would he understand the need to account for every penny? But Max feared his brother might tell Fanny or become angry with their father. "Go on, then."

Thomas was out of the office before the words were finished. He nearly crashed into the butler holding a silver salver.

"Correspondence, your grace."

"Thank you." Max nodded as he retrieved the stack of letters and bills from the tray. Three letters were for guests, addressed to his care, so that the recipients would not have had to pay the postage. One was for Roxana.

Too late to call Thomas back to have him deliver Roxana's letter. Max rubbed his forehead, knowing that he had to dig the estate out from the quagmire of debts, yet fearing he would never be successful.

He pushed back from his desk. He might as well inspect the ballroom while handing Roxy's letter to her. Ignoring the rise of anticipation in his gut,

Max closed up the business affairs that had seemed so pressing a moment earlier.

In the midst of uncovering holiday decorations, Roxana spied a heap of wine-colored velvet in the corner of the attic. "What is that?" she asked Fanny.

"Just some damaged bed coverings. I should throw them out."

Roxana bit her lip, wondering if she could salvage the material.

"One of the maids scorched it with a warming pan. I've told them not to let them sit," Fanny explained. "It is a wonder she did not burn down the house."

Roxana opened her mouth to ask if she could have it, when a footman entered the room.

"Your grace, a traveling coach is on the drive."

Reaching to straighten her lacy cap, Fanny stood and then swiped at her skirts as if she felt unkempt. Every time a new guest arrived, the duchess stopped whatever she was doing and went to greet the new arrivals and escort them to their rooms and make sure their needs were seen to. The servants always knew where to find her, and one must be assigned to watch the drive at all times.

"We can finish the ballroom, your grace," Roxana told Fanny, noticing the harried look on the duchess's face.

Roxana opened a carton that contained wire wreaths with a bit of dried leaves stuck in the joints, while Julia unearthed a box of silver stars. She took one out and rubbed it with a polishing cloth.

Fanny nodded. "Thank you. Julia, can you tell Miss Winston where everything is? The fresh holly is—"

"We have the list." Julia waved her mother's hand-written note.

Roxana stole a glance at the list. *Hang stars from chandeliers. Drape columns with tinsel. Wrap holly around wire frames . . .*

"Truly, your grace, decorating is a treat for me," said Roxana. "If I don't understand anything, I'll be sure to find you and ask."

"Oh, do just call me Fanny. You are nearly family, after all."

Roxana ducked her head, uncertain how to respond to that. Was it because she had befriended Julia and Thomas, who seemed largely abandoned while their mother flitted around seeing to her hostess duties? Or did she know what had happened with Max under the mistletoe?

"Do not, fret, Mama. We shall make it look wonderful."

Fanny nodded, and with a backward glance over her shoulder, she followed her servant downstairs.

Thomas entered the attic storeroom, looking over his shoulder. "It's not fair. He hardly ever comes home and then he expects me to slave over the accounts with him."

Roxana gently urged Thomas to assist with the decorations while he vented his spleen about his brother's expectations. Roxana forbore answering. After a while Thomas settled into decorating.

They steadily moved back and forth between the attic storeroom and the ballroom. A couple of footmen magically appeared with ladders to assist in the hanging. Roxana dismissed them as she set Thomas to cutting paper snowflakes. She returned to the storeroom to wind the holly around the wire wreaths.

Julia had stood and watched. "You make those

look so wonderful. Mama just throws on the stuff, then insists they are horrid."

"I am sure that hers look wonderful, far better than mine." Roxana took one last look at the pile of material in the corner. With a sigh she lifted the wreath, while Julia lifted another.

"No, Mama hates the holly because of the sharp points. It is about like how I hate to play the piano, but Mama says I must, and my teacher says I do not practice enough."

"Would you like me to sit with you when you practice?" It had been almost a decade since Roxana had played the piano. She remembered her mother had taken great pleasure in playing before her fingers were broken and she could not play any longer. Then they moved to the cottage, which was not large enough to hold even a harpsichord.

"You would hear how very horrid I am."

"I assure you, I am probably worse." Roxana's piano lessons had ceased the day her mother's hand had been injured.

Julia looked at her skeptically.

Roxana laughed. "If I promise to show you my lack of skill, will you play for me?"

Julia nodded.

Holding the large holly wreath, Roxana entered the ballroom. A frisson of anticipation passed through her, as if the room had garnered fairy magic in her brief absence to retrieve the last of the decorations from the attic storeroom.

Thomas leapt to his feet and called out that he was done as he raced out of the room.

Shiny silver stars hung from the ceiling, interspersed with dozens of snowflakes cut from white paper. Traditional evergreen boughs covered the two mantelpieces and lent their crisp fragrance to the air.

The room resembled a holiday paradise, thought Roxana. Swags of forest-green velvet framed every tall window, and she and Julia had just finished replacing all the tiebacks with thick gold ribbons. Fat candles sat on the sills waiting to light the windows in the holiday spirit.

The room was so much more formal than the ballroom at Wingate Hall. Besides that, the last time Roxana had seen that ballroom it had been draped in red silk to resemble a harem's tents. Mrs. Porter had ordered yards and yards of what she called sari silk from India. The silk had been draped all over the ballroom to create little semi-private tent rooms for her party. Mrs. Porter filled the bowers with every cushion that could be found and a few more that Roxana was commissioned to make. Roxana guessed there was not much dancing at Mrs. Porter's party.

That none of the girls commissioned new ball gowns disappointed Roxana. Although, she did have a high demand for peignoirs and undergarments. Apparently a regiment of soldiers, temporarily stationed nearby, had needed entertainment.

The silk became Roxana's after the party. Mrs. Porter had said to throw it away; the stuff was too transparent to be of any practical use. Roxana had doubled it, sewed it into dresses and then cut undergarments of the same cloth.

"Oh, Max, isn't it lovely?" said Julia. She carried a holly wreath too.

Roxana drew up short, and Julia plowed into her from behind. The sharp holly leaves pricked through the simple muslin gown.

Max stepped out from behind one of the silver-tinsel-wrapped columns. He walked toward them. "Quite."

She had been looking so much at their newly finished decorations that she had not noticed the figure at the far end of the room, standing behind one of the columns. But she had sensed him, hadn't she? Was he the reason she felt magic when she entered the room this time?

"Roxy and I made all the snowflakes."

Roxana mentally nudged her frozen limbs toward one of the fireplaces, lifting her wreath to place over the mantel.

"She's very good with scissors," said Julia. "She taught me how to cut the patterns just so. Every one is different."

"Indeed," answered Max.

Her heart thumped erratically as she strained to catch the wreath on the hook.

He moved behind her. "Allow me, Miss Winston."

"I have it," she said mulishly and bounced on her toes and missed the nail again.

He reached around her and guided it to the wall. Since she hadn't relinquished the task to him and stepped aside, the brush of his body against hers was inevitable. Heat flashed and spiraled into her stomach. With every ounce of willpower she possessed she restrained the urge to lean back, to feel that broad strength with the length of her body, and she did not want to think of the antics Mrs. Porter encouraged in a ballroom.

The holly wreath in place, he stepped back and leaned a hand against the carved mantelpiece. "All is well with you?" he asked.

She nodded.

"I'll go get the last wreath," said Julia, and like that, they were alone.

The ballroom was vast. She could put yards between them by just walking to another place in the room. Her feet refused to move.

He looked down at her, mesmerizing her. Looking upon his countenance was so much more pleasant than looking at Mr. Breedon. Roxana gave herself a mental shaking. Pleasant looks weren't everything.

He reached out and touched a stray tendril of hair that had escaped her topknot. "You look beautiful this morning."

His voice reverberated down her spine, leaving trails of soothing warmth. How did he do that? She brushed her bare hands over the apron she had donned to protect her dress. She was thoroughly coated in dust and pieces of holly. "I look a mess."

"You do not like compliments, Miss Winston?" he asked as he rubbed the strand of hair between his fingers.

"Why, of course I—" She gave up the pretense. Why was Max comfortable enough to treat her with an intimate gesture, but she had not managed to make Mr. Breedon so much as touch her hand? "No, I do not like insincere flattery, but thank you just the same."

Max smiled, and she could hardly tear her eyes away from his mouth. The change from a stoic expression was slow and measured, not a lightning flash of teeth such as Scully treated her with. But it tugged at her just the same, as if her insides were turning to mush. Everything would be so much easier if she wanted to be married.

He pulled his hand back, and she felt bereft.

"I have a letter for you," he said.

"A letter?" she echoed stupidly. What had her father done now? Heaviness pulled at her heart.

Max reached into his breast pocket and drew out the sealed missive.

She took it, feeling the warmth of Max's body on the paper. She clutched it at her breast, fearing that whatever it contained, the news would not be good.

Max's smile disappeared. He gestured toward one of the chairs that lined the walls of the ballroom. "Would you read it now?"

"Yes. No. I shall read it in my room." Dread tightened her spine.

"Roxy, if you fear it contains bad tidings read it here. I will assist you in whatever way I can."

"I . . . no . . . I just am surprised to get a letter. I did not expect one so soon." She tried to laugh, but the sound that left her mouth was more of a nervous titter.

What was she doing with Max? She needed to be with Mr. Breedon. She needed to spend her time pursuing her goal. She had to encourage Breedon to behave recklessly. How could she persuade him to her room if he had shown little interest in seducing her?

She had long ago accepted that she would not take her place in the world as part of the privileged and pampered upper ten thousand, but that she would slip into the working world of the middle class. But she was unsure she could pull off the first part of her plan.

If she could not get money to start her business . . . her future as well as her sisters' and brother's future yawned before her as a dark black hole, their grasp on dignity pried loose by the wicked hands of a fate they did not deserve.

She could feel Max watching her, waiting for her to speak. Max held out his hand. Roxana put her hand in his, aware of the pounding of her heart.

His hold steadied her. "Roxy, read me the letter."

She could not. Her mother would write of the urgency of their situation. She would plead for Roxana to save the family by marriage to a man of means. Or there may be worse. Anxiety clawed at her insides.

She pulled her hand back and walked away, concerned Max would penetrate her fragile hold on her emotions. She did not want him to notice her trembling.

She wanted to confess to him, to tell him the only reason she was here was because she needed money to start her business. Her sisters and her brothers were living no better than crofters. She had to save them, but she had never accepted her mother's plan to marry as the only course. Marriage certainly hadn't saved her mother. Marriage had broken her mother.

Max lived in opulence and comfort. He would never understand the horror of not knowing if food would be on the table, or if the knock on the door was the sheriff to escort them to the workhouse. Or that the idea of turning over her trust to a man who should protect her struck terror in her heart.

Max's hand closed around her upper arm. Memories of her father jerking her around doused her in panic. She wrenched free and spun away from his grip.

"Roxana?" He folded his arms in front of him. "Tell me your situation so I might help you."

She wanted to confide in him. She wanted to believe he could help her, but everyone she had confided in had scoffed at her plans.

She had tried to get a loan through the local bankers, through applications to a group of investors and finally from Mrs. Porter, who knew how well Roxana made clothes, but all had refused. She was a young woman who should get married and have babies, not become a mantuamaker. Besides that, she was underage and could not be held to a loan without a guarantor. Everyone had thought her scheme bacon-brained. But she knew she could make it work. She had to.

"Unless you wish to loan me money, I do not see how you could offer more help."

"There you are, love," said Devlin Scullin. He'd seen Fanny head down the stairs for the great hall and followed her. "Where have you been hiding this morning?"

"I was preparing the ballroom for the festivities a week hence, but guests are arriving," said Fanny.

She sidestepped away from him and cast herself into the mid-morning sun shining through the window. Her hair caught the light and reflected off the honey-colored curls peeping out under the edges of her lacy cap. Devlin leaned back against the newel post of the great staircase and crossed one booted foot over the other. "Do you intend to avoid me the whole time I'm here?"

She twisted her hands together in front of her. "I'm sure I don't know what you mean."

She knew what he meant.

"Is all hope lost for me, then? Do you trample my hopes and crush my dreams?" he asked with an exaggerated clutching at his breast.

"Do not," she whispered.

He eased out of his relaxed pose, catching her around the waist. "You look like an angel with the sunlight dancing in your hair."

She twisted away from him, out of his grasp. "Do not trifle with me, Scully. You are kinder than that."

She reached to tuck stray curls under her cap. Years ago, when her hair had streamed across her pillow, it had been lighter, more the color of bright sunshine. Perhaps he'd said something like that. Yes, he had made a remark about her hair resembling sunshine then. But then he had remarked on everything from her dainty toes to her Cupid's bow mouth.

"You have no husband who could be wounded now," he said.

Fanny turned her startled blue eyes in his direction, eyes he had seen fill with tears of remorse. The happiest night of his life, and she had regretted it, wished it away, wished him away.

"Do not think I shall be easy pickings because I am alone now." Her chin lifted, but he could see her hand shake. "Other women are available for you to amuse yourself. I want no part of your . . ." She looked about as if she would find the words she wanted stuffed in a corner. Perhaps she would discover them in the gilt around the mirror, or the bowl holding wax fruit, or the Chippendale chair in the corner.

"My what?" Devlin crossed the marble floor, narrowing the gap between them. Why wouldn't she look at him?

"Your stable of discarded loves."

"You are hardly discarded, my pretty Fanny. You sent me away, remember?"

"Do you like Miss Winston?" asked Fanny.

"Well enough. She is an interesting girl."

"You might amuse yourself with Lady Angela DuMass or Miss Lambert. The Misses Ferris are joining us too."

Devlin studied Fanny. Since she was no longer married, did she want him attached to preserve her distance? Had that night meant anything to her? Or was it just a moment's indiscretion, a bad choice instantly regretted? "But I am already pledged to dance attendance on Miss Winston. Max said that would best please you."

"Yes, that pleases me." Fanny's blue eyes narrowed in such a way as to make him think she did not like his escorting Miss Winston around. "Do not break her heart."

"I do not believe Miss Winston's heart is at stake, Fanny."

"No, well, you break many hearts, Dev," Fanny paced away from him again. "I have seen you collect them like so many pearls to a string."

He had made sure she had seen him and his conquests. What a foolish notion that had been. "Fanny, none of them ever meant anything to me."

"Yes, I know, Dev," she said in a soft tone riddled with weariness.

He clenched his fist. "You are the—"

"If I hold a special allure merely by virtue of refusing you, do give over. It is nonsense that shall pass."

The butler crossed the hallway and opened the front door and the Ferris family entered, two unmarried misses and their parents. Footmen followed with baggage and the hall transformed into a hive of activity with servants pouring out of the woodwork to take outer coats, hats and muffs.

Fanny stepped forward and greeted her newest guests with smiles and hugs. She had not given him so generous a welcome when he had ridden overnight to reach her at the first possible moment.

Had he waited too long? Should he have pushed his advantage when she fell into his arms but begged him to leave? He had waited years, and now she no longer wanted him? Anguish clawed at his throat as he stepped forward and greeted the two Misses Ferris with his usual bland flattery and teasing about his fluttering heart. Only it was not all teasing. Fanny did make his heart skip and race . . . and bleed.

Chapter Six

Max stared at Roxana's door, his mind on her plight. Her face had gone pale when he handed her the letter. Her request for a loan had left him flat-footed. When he did not answer her right away, she had fled the room.

He wanted to help her. It was his duty. How to assist her was the question. The last thing he expected her to ask for was a loan. He was cash starved himself. He could not take on more debt. Besides, what means would she ever have of repaying a loan?

He wanted to be sure she was all right when she emerged from her room. He'd escort her to the drawing room and see if he could not persuade her to divulge the contents of her letter. Besides, it was his turn to play chaperone since Fanny and Scully were otherwise occupied.

Lady Malmsbury strolled toward him. Too late he turned to walk away. Had she realized he was loitering about waiting for Roxana to exit her room?

"Max, darling, you are neglecting me dreadfully. Won't you show me about your home?" Lady Malmsbury threaded her arm through his.

Her cloying scent flooded his nostrils, and his instinct was to recoil, but the right thing to do was to be unfailingly polite. "Of course, my lady."

She tugged him toward his bedroom as if she hoped for a midday tryst. Instead, he aimed her toward the next flight of stairs and the ballroom. As they strolled down the gallery, he made the required comments about the portraits.

Lady Malmsbury cooed and claimed she saw resemblances to his ancestors.

"Would you like to see the ballroom, my lady? It is decorated for the winter solstice ball."

Lady Malmsbury leaned close, pressing her breast against the back of his arm. "You are so formal, Max. Come, we know each other better than this. I have missed you so. Surely you have missed me a little."

Max felt unease slide down his spine. Malmsy acted as if she planned on cavorting on the ballroom floor. "I have been busy."

Malmsy stuck her lower lip out. But then she spied the kissing bower and headed straight for it, dragging him along with her.

Repugnance skittered down Max's spine. The last thing he wanted to do was taint his memory of kissing Roxana under the mistletoe, by being forced to go through the same motion with Eliza.

Roxana was shaking like a leaf by the time she sat down near the window of her room. She had seen from Max's stiffening that he was offended by her mention of a loan. He would not help her in the way she wanted. He had told her he would not marry, and that of course would be the only way he would see as a way to help her. She knew from Thomas's complaints earlier that Max was quite serious about keeping his half brother as his heir.

She popped the seal on the letter, dreading what she would find. Her mother's tiny script crisscrossed the page.

Dread snaked down her spine as she leaned so the natural light would shine on the paper.

Her mother's letter started with the news that all the girls were well. With a hacking cough from the cold, Jonathon had hunted unsuccessfully for deer three days. He had finally returned with a rabbit just in time to feed their father.

Roxana hated the idea that the slender amount of meat would be wasted on Lord Winston. Remembering the chill of the cottage in winter, Roxana drew her shawl tighter around her shoulders.

As near as Roxana could figure through her mother's disjointed comments, their tenants' risqué party had angered the baron, and he'd evicted them. Roxana suppressed a sigh of impatience. What did he expect when he rented their home to a semi-retired abbess and her girls?

She tossed the letter onto the writing desk and sat on her trunk that contained many of the scraps of dresses and peignoirs that she had sewn for the women renting the main house. She had used their leftover cuttings to trim her own dresses. The ladies' fondness for lace had been a blessing in disguise, giving Roxana the expensive touches to her gowns without costing her a penny.

Roxana castigated herself for being distracted by Max's attentions.

She needed to be more active in pursuing her plan; time was running out. The only thing she knew to do to calm her overset nerves was to create. She crept out the side door of her room, the door that led to the narrow servant passageway and the back stairs. Across from her room was Mr. Breedon's bedchamber. He was so close, yet so far away.

Stealing up the back stair, she headed for the attic storeroom to see if she could use the discarded bedcovers. The habit she had from Fanny was pretty, but its cut and color were better suited to an older matron. Roxana fretted as she moved stealthily. She thought she could use one of the Duchess of Trent's lists. Flirt with the richest gentleman present—Mr. Breedon. Seduce him, but let him think it his idea.

With that income from the rent gone, what would her family do? The estate had been so neglected and crops so poor in recent years that little income could be had from the land. Her mother had gone on to say that her father had consulted a solicitor about breaking the entail and selling the estate. Cold hard doom stabbed at Roxana's spine.

She could not allow the other guests at the house party to guess her circumstances. Only Max knew a bit of her troubles and she had probably erred in sharing hints of her family's plight with him.

With the Porters no longer paying their lease and suing, the family's main source of income was gone. Their creditors were hounding them, the green grocer refused to deliver any more food without payment . . . and then there was the mortgage her father had taken on the property. If her father succeeded in breaking the entail and selling the heavily mortgaged estate, it would just be a matter of time before nothing was left.

A sense of fatalism bore down upon Roxana's shoulders. Even if she wanted to go home, her main source of income—sewing clothes for Mrs. Porter and her "daughters"—was gone. Her mother had closed with pleas for a successful conclusion to her daughter's mission. She must urge a man of means to marriage, by any available method, before her family was thrown into the workhouse.

A teardrop obscured the writing near the bottom of the page. For a minute Roxana was not sure it had not come from her. She had touched her fingertip to the stain on the letter and found it dry.

She opened a door to the long gallery that ran outside the ballroom. Relieved to find the room empty, she ran toward the storeroom. She found the bedspread and gathered it up.

A large scorch mark on the satin lining showed the damage. Roxana shook out the material and sneezed as a cloud of dust rose in the air. The dust surprised her, because the army of servants kept the household so neat. Still, there was plenty of material if she cut judiciously. If she started on it this afternoon and worked through the night, she might be able to finish it in time for the hunt. Perhaps that would help impress Mr. Breedon. Or should she concentrate on the Duke of Trent?

Her heart stumbled to a trot. No, her involuntary response to the duke made keeping her head unlikely, even if he did mean to offer more than a flirtation.

Roxana could not see that marriage even to a wealthy man would be anything more than a stopgap. Her father's gambling went unabated. A new source of income would just provide him with license to continue his reckless course. That he had the right to destroy her entire family with his behavior went beyond unjust. But a man had total control over his family's resources, and no one could say him nay.

She had to get the money for her dress shop, and soon. Even then she was not sure it would be enough to save her family from complete and utter ruin. She heard sounds from the ballroom. Curious who could be in there, Roxana leaned her head into the room.

Max was in the kissing bower with the red-haired Lady Malmsbury, and their embrace was more than familiar. Lady Malmsbury had her fingers threaded in Max's hair and she stood on her tiptoes, her back arched as she pressed her bosom into him. A stab of pain shot through Roxana's chest. Her breath whooshed out as if she had been dealt a doubler blow. Did the duke go around kissing every woman at the house party?

Hearing a noise behind him, Max swiveled. A figure in a white muslin dress moved away from the open doorway. Who else would be up here besides Roxana? Alarm skittered down his spine. What had she seen?

"Max," Eliza protested. "Kiss me." She pushed her hips against him, swaying in a provocative rhythm.

He grabbed her arms and ripped them away from his neck. "Excuse me."

He strode after Roxana.

"Max!"

He turned and bowed at the door. "My lady."

Eliza glared at him and planted her hands on her hips. "What? Are you afraid that our relationship will disturb your pursuit of Miss Winston?"

"I am not pursuing Miss Winston," said Max.

However, since he was itching to follow her, his words rang hollow. He clasped his hands behind his back.

Lady Malmsbury sashayed toward him, her green eyes narrowing. "No?"

She moved close enough to put a finger on his chest and traced it over his lapel. Her voice dropped to a purr. "She is just an inexperienced girl. I know she cannot offer you the pleasures that I can."

His skin began to crawl.

"Really, Max. It is clear she means to snare Breedon."

"You should not have come to this party, Eliza."

She pouted. "I was invited, darling."

"Not by me."

"Have I hampered your seduction of Miss Winston? I promise you she has no need to know of any night games we play."

"I am not seducing her." Max winced.

"She is seducing you, then," snapped Eliza.

"She is a perfectly modest young woman. No one is seducing anyone." Max closed his eyes in an attempt to modulate his rising anger and lower his voice. "I will not have you speak ill of her."

"Then I want what I came here for," Eliza demanded.

"I assure you the entertainment will be exemplary," he said, banking on the idea that Lady Malmsbury would not be bold enough to state her desire so baldly again. "Now, if you will excuse me, I have duties I must attend."

Was it too late to catch Roxana? He hurried toward the stairs, abandoning Eliza to find her own way. What could he do to help Roxy anyway? If she needed money he could not help her in that way.

But then she had settled on Breedon, and he could help her with capturing him.

Lady Malmsbury's accusations of seduction swirled in his brain. Lord help him, the idea of seducing Roxana excited him far more than it should. That was one thing he could not do.

The right thing to do was assist her in landing a rich husband. He just wished his duties lay anywhere else.

After dinner, Roxana listlessly wandered around the drawing room while waiting until the gentlemen joined the ladies. She did not know what to make of Max. Were they friends or something more? He had called her Roxy this afternoon, but then he'd had a tryst with Lady Malmsbury.

The drawing-room door opened and the gentlemen filed in. Before Roxana could even react, the voluptuous redhead, Lady Malmsbury, latched on to Max's arm. Who was Lady Malmsbury to Max?

Obviously her conduct was too warm for them to be just casual acquaintances. A sinking sensation settled in the pit of Roxy's stomach as she thought about the way Lady Malmsbury had plastered her body against his. She was always following Max around the room with her eyes when not attached to his side. Roxana was at a disadvantage with not knowing so many of the people present and their unspoken connections.

Max met her eyes across the room and Roxana deliberately turned her gaze away. She should not waste time ogling her host. That he knew too much about her situation undoubtedly made her breath catch in her throat. It could not be the broad breadth of his shoulders or the masculine shape of his mouth that made her feel lightheaded around him. She would stay well away from the sprigs of mistletoe around him. Clearly he was indiscriminate about taking advantage of the license to behave with more freedom.

Mr. Scullin had glanced in Fanny's direction, then headed toward Roxana. She was glad to see him in better-fitting clothes, a blue evening coat over a gray waistcoat. The colors suited him better than the brown he had worn this morning. Not that anyone else cared about clothing as much as she did. Following Max's advice to continue wearing her outlandish clothing, Roxana wore her best evening gown, sewn from the red silk.

Mr. Breedon headed directly toward the tea tray.

"Would you like some tea, Mr. Scullin?" asked Roxana as he took his place at her side and offered his arm. She didn't particularly want tea, but Mr. Breedon was filling a plate.

"Call me Scully. Everyone does. And yes, I could use a spot of tea." With her hand in his elbow he tugged her toward the tea tray.

"I have to tell you her grace's cook prepares the most delicious scones. I always think they will melt in my mouth."

"That good, mmm?" said Mr. Scullin. He looked to the tea tray containing the silver service. "I shall have to have some, then."

He pulled her up to where the tea tray had been placed on the low table in front of the sofa. A tea cart laden with platters of sandwiches and sweetmeats stood in the center of the floor between them and where the duchess poured tea into fine china cups and handed them to her guests.

Roxana noted the flush to Fanny's cheeks and her animated conversation. Scully greeted those around them, although he turned away before speaking to the Duchess of Trent. "Got enough there, Breedon?"

Gregory Breedon turned his moon face their direction. Roxana glanced at his plate, which contained four of the thin sandwiches and so many scones, tarts and biscuits that she could see nothing of the ivy leaf pattern around the rim. His little eyes opened wide and the few scraggly hairs that passed for eyebrows lifted high up on his forehead.

"Ah, the food here is too die for, is it not, Mr. Breedon?" Roxana pasted an indulgent smile on her mouth.

"It is adequate," he answered, but he looked slightly relieved.

His moon face settled into a frown. "Would you like a plate?"

"Please, sir." Truth was, Roxana had eaten enough at dinner to last her until breakfast. She took the plate he shoved her direction. "You are too kind."

"And would you prefer coffee or tea?" asked Scully, reminding her that he still had her hand trapped under his hand, on his arm.

She could only hold the empty plate with her one hand, not dish anything upon it.

"Oh, I could not hold a cup and saucer, but do get whatever you wish." Perhaps he would let her loose. Although she wanted to know why he had been charged with watching over her. Since the guests had started arriving, if Max was not at her side, Mr. Scullin was. Since the kiss it was more often Scully. Although Max seemed to watch her constantly.

Scully looked straight at Mr. Breedon and said, "I do believe Miss Winston expressed an interest in the scones."

Mr. Breedon gave a short snort and set his plate down so he could dump four scones on her plate, more than she could eat under the best of circumstances. She smiled and thanked him as if he had just slayed a dragon for her. Scully rolled his eyes. She slid her hand out from under his, and he took her elbow. "Right this way, Miss Winston, I believe there is room on this sofa for us."

"Mr. Breedon, would you join us?" asked Roxana.

The three of them headed for the open sofa. Roxana sat in the middle with the gentlemen flanking her.

"I shall fetch us tea, then," said Scully, leaping up almost before he had finished sitting down. Roxana watched her appointed guardian move across the room. She noticed he walked with a loose-limbed stride. Scully had a contained energy that unsettled her, although it was Max who tended to make her jump.

She knew most men were unlike her father. Most men did not lash out with violence when displeased, but that was the only explanation she had for the strange way the air felt charged when she was close to Max. As if a storm were about to break.

Yet, as she looked up, she saw him moving toward her, Lady Malmsbury plastered against his side. Roxana's throat caught. Although, Max looked mildly displeased, the same way he looked when his brother and sister fussed at each other. On the other hand, he looked quite ducal as he greeted his guests, stopping often to exchange pleasantries.

She forced herself to turn to the man beside her.

"How are you settling in, Mr. Breedon? Is your room comfortable?"

"A bit smaller than what I'm used to," Mr. Breedon said around a mouth of food.

Roxana suppressed her shudder of distaste. His assigned bedchamber was twice as large as hers. "I'm sorry to hear that, but you know, these ... older houses are just not built with modern comfort in mind."

"Oh, it is well enough for a guest, I suppose. Although my house is much newer. I have put many of the public rooms on the ground floor. No reason to be traipsing up and down the stairs all day long. It is not as in the olden days when one had to build a house to withstand attack."

"How very clever of you."

Mr. Breedon's sparse eyebrows shot up. She imagined he was not often told he was intelligent.

"My father broke his leg once; I assure you, it was quite difficult for the servants to take him up and down the stairs." Actually it had been mostly Roxana and her mother who had to convey him up and down the stairs, until she'd finally told him to make his bed on the sofa. His fury was restrained until his leg was healed well enough to bear his weight.

Roxana did not know that she would have continued to cater to his whims, knowing the outcome of that protracted stay of her father. Really, that moment convinced her of the need to succeed, convinced her of many things, the least of which was the certainty that she would never willingly place herself under the control of any man.

"Your parents are not here, Miss Winston?" asked Mr. Breedon. Crumbs decorated his cheek.

"Mama cannot get away with the younger children and Papa is still tied up with his affairs in London. The Duchess of Trent has been gracious enough to invite me to stay. She and my mother are fast friends." Exchanging a letter once a year hardly made them bosom bows, but Roxana was taking a lot of liberties with the truth these days.

She steeled herself for the uncomfortable questions that were sure to follow.

"You did not have a season, Miss Winston?"

She smiled brightly. "Not yet."

He frowned.

She wondered if she could wipe off the food without belittling Mr. Breedon, or if she should just let him wander around with crumbs on his cheeks.

Out of the corner of her eye she saw Lady Malmsbury using her handkerchief to wipe away a reddish spot on Max's cheek. It was where Lady Malmsbury had kissed him, and it also meant Lady Malmsbury used vermilion on her lips. Mrs. Porter and her daughters used pots and pots of the stuff.

Since Roxana did not have a napkin, she reached for her handkerchief and turned toward Mr. Breedon. "You have a bit of food on your cheek, sir. I could get it if you would like me to."

Mr. Breedon stared at her blankly. Roxana leaned toward him and was well aware of when Mr. Breedon's gaze dropped to her cleavage. Well, she had learned a few tricks from Mrs. Porter and her daughters. She gently brushed the crumbs away. His cheek was soft and smooth like a baby's.

"See there, all better." Roxana straightened,

knowing that her neckline reverted to its proper position. She thought she had managed the whole maneuver without being obvious, but as she turned back around and lifted a scone from her plate, Scully's raised eyebrow and Max's scowl greeted her. She looked down, certain that they could not have had the same view Mr. Breedon had.

Scully leaned forward, extending a saucer with a steaming cup on it. "Your tea, Miss Winston."

Lady Malmsbury bumped Scully from behind, then grabbed his arm to steady herself, and the tea went sailing. The shock of scalding liquid against Roxana's bare chest jolted her out of her seat. The now-empty cup fell to the floor, although she made an ineffective grab for it.

"Oh, I say!" exclaimed Mr. Breedon, lurching to his feet. "What a clumsy oaf you are."

Scully looked blankly at the empty saucer in his hand.

Roxana wasn't quite sure if Mr. Breedon was talking to her or Scully, but her chest burned.

Max jerked out of his coat, tossed it around her shoulders, and grabbed it closed just below her chin. She hunched over and tried to pull the steaming material of her bodice from her skin.

Max tugged and she had no choice but to follow. Curious stares followed her out as they crossed the immense room and Roxana was aware of the sting of humiliation. Worse than that, as she tried to point to the Limoges china teacup on the carpet, Mr. Breedon, the unmentionable region of his unmentionables coated in clotted cream, stepped on the cup, shattering it into a thousand pieces.

And where on earth was Max dragging her as if she were a pest a cat deposited into the middle of the company? As soon as the drawing-room door closed behind them, he barked orders to the servants. "The door, James."

A footman sprang forward to open the door of another room. "Fetch cool water and towels. Send for Miss Winston's maid and tell her to bring a dressing gown for Miss Winston. Do not allow anyone other than the duchess or the maid in here."

He pulled her around in front of him and looked her in the eye. "Are you burned?"

He loosened his grip and Roxana swiveled away, leaving the coat in his grasp. A large table with red balls on a recessed baize top blocked her path. Roxana realized this was a billiard room. Nearly every occupation possible owned its own separate space in this house.

Her efforts to peel away the soaked bodice made her neckline gape, and she tugged it up. She was a little scalded, but nothing that wouldn't heal. "I'm fine."

She looked down at the reddish cast to her skin. "If I could just go and change."

"Your maid is coming. I'll get Fanny."

"Vinegar eases the sting of a burn," said Scully from the doorway.

"For God's sake, get out. Miss Winston . . ."

"Pretty sure we are the only ones who saw," continued Scully. "Breedon is making a fuss. I am so sorry, Miss Winston. Fanny is on her way."

"Tell her not to bother. I am all right. I shall just go to my room and change." Roxana wondered if Mr. Breedon would associate his own humiliation with her. Would everyone at the house party think of her as the victim of Lady Malmsbury's clumsiness?

"I'll tell her," said Scully.

"Wait—"

The door clicked shut.

Max's "wait" trailed off. "Damnation," Max said.

Roxana looked at her chest. The redness wasn't going away, although the material of her bodice had cooled. She dabbed at her front with her handkerchief, which came away pink. If she rinsed the gown right away the tea might not stain it.

"My apologies, Miss Winston."

She wasn't sure if he was apologizing for his language or the whole incident. "I would just like to go to my room now."

"You cannot. You must wait for your maid to bring you a dressing gown. I . . . am sorry for your discomfort."

"There is just one problem," she said. "Well, two problems, really." She turned around, wadding the stained handkerchief in her hand. The silk was too cheaply dyed, but that was problem number three.

His eyes darkened and he seemed to struggle to breathe. "Miss Winston?"

"I do not own a dressing gown and I do not have a maid," she said.

For a long second the rasp of Max's breathing was the only sound. The air charged with raw energy and she felt edgy.

"You cannot go through the house like *that*."

Roxana realized Max's gaze was trained below her chin. "My skin is red, but it does not hurt." Although as she spoke, a tingling spread across her chest.

His gaze threatened to burn through her, warming the skin that had started to chill with the dampness. What on earth had him so transfixed?

She looked down and realized the thin layers of saturated red silk were transparent. Worse than that, the material was molded against her breasts, revealing *everything*.

"That is the most striking of your gowns thus far, Miss Winston," he said with a low burr to his voice that reached right down to her toes.

"Oh, God!" she whispered, folding her arms across her chest and spinning around to present her back to him.

His hands settled on her shoulders and Roxana wanted to melt to the floor. Yet the feeling wasn't all mortification. His touch affected her like the flash of hot water followed by cold. Her heart thumped erratically and her skin tingled and tightened, and the paper-thin layers of silk felt like heavy fur pelts, startling her with every shift across her skin.

Chapter
Seven

After retiring last night, Roxana had heard lots of doors, and now she sat impatiently in her room, waiting for the sound of Mr. Breedon's door. The midmorning sun peeked in her window. He must be a very late riser.

She had done a fair amount of sewing this morning, but now she was at a place where she needed to try things on. She feared that the minute she removed her morning gown to try on the riding-habit skirt, Mr. Breedon would leave his room.

Fanny had appeared sporadically throughout last evening to check on Roxana. The duchess had been dismayed to find her guest using the cold water and towels to blot the tea from her gown rather than attending to her reddened skin. Fanny's maid had shown up and whisked away the gown after that. Then a lot of fussing and dabbing with vinegar left Roxana fearing she smelled more like a pickle than the lavender soap she'd washed with afterwards.

A door snicked and Roxana crept to her door

and gently opened it an inch. Ah, finally, Mr. Breedon was up and about. Even though his back was toward her, mistaking his robust form was impossible. She quickly followed him out into the passageway. "Good morning, Mr. Breedon."

He stopped and looked back at her impatiently.

Roxana hurried forward. "Oh, I do hope I have not missed breakfast. I am famished. Have you eaten yet, sir?"

"Not yet, Miss Winston. But we shall not have missed breakfast. We are early."

"All's well, then." She moved past him as if she did not notice his extended arm. As Max said, she would gain nothing by appearing too eager. Mr. Breedon did seem put out with her.

"Are you the type of gentleman who dislikes chatter in the morning? For my father does not like us to speak before he has eaten his fill. I assure you I am quite adept at holding my tongue," she said.

"You may talk."

How absolutely gracious of him, thought Roxana. She kept her disgust out of her expression. "I do hope you suffered no ill effect from Lady Malmsbury and Mr. Scullin's collision after dinner."

Mr. Breedon closed his eyes as if the memory was painful. Perhaps Roxana should not have brought it up.

"I vow I have never been so *mortified* in all my life. I was quite afraid that everyone present would think that *I* had caused the mishap," she said in a confiding tone.

"I doubt anyone would think that, Miss Winston."

"As long as *you* do not think that, sir." Talking in a breathless, brainless manner was making her feel lightheaded. "I had, after all, told Mr. Scullin I did not want tea."

"Yes, why yes, you did," said Mr. Breedon, brightening.

"I should have fetched it myself. Women should wait on men. One is only asking for disaster by reversing the natural order of things."

Mr. Breedon nodded as if he was in complete agreement with that bit of blarney. So when they reached the breakfast room, she insisted on dishing his plate for him and setting the heaping mound of his selections in front of him. "Would you like the paper to read?"

"No, I am set," he answered.

She frowned. "Are you sure? Because I am quite sure the plate does not hold enough food. I can get you more if you wish."

"They are smallish plates, are they not?" said Mr. Breedon.

"Quite small." His plate held enough food to feed her entire family breakfast. *Just a few days,* Roxana recited in her head. She could keep up this false front for two weeks.

Mr. Scullin entered the breakfast room. He paused, seeing the two of them sitting at the table. "Good morning, my adorable Miss Winston, Breedon." He bowed slightly.

Mr. Breedon continued to shovel food into that slit of a mouth. He grunted a response, while Roxana returned Scully's pleasantry.

Mr. Scullin moved forward to hunch down by Roxana's chair. His blue eyes searched her face. "Are you all right, Miss Winston? Any ill effects from my clumsiness last night?"

"I am fine, thank you." Roxana looked over at Mr.

Breedon, who had not even inquired about her well-being. She'd have to find a way to make him think she appreciated his lack of consideration.

"Max says you have a very good seat. Would you join me in a ride before breakfast tomorrow? I will assemble an adequate party if riding would please you."

Roxana would so much prefer to ride in the early morning briskness than to sit twiddling her thumbs in her bedroom, waiting for Mr. Breedon to join the living. She looked at Mr. Breedon, who did not stop shoveling food. "I . . . I . . ."

"Breedon, you'll join us, won't you? Your horses will need exercise before the hunt."

Mr. Breedon wiped his mouth with his napkin. "My grooms will see to my mounts' readiness, I am sure. Besides, I have brought enough horses that I can change them out during the hunt. My horse-flesh is too valuable to risk damaging by too much hard riding."

"Very well, I should love to ride tomorrow morning," said Roxana, deciding that she could be back before Mr. Breedon stumbled out of his room. It would give her a few minutes every morning to enjoy before she settled into her pretense. And she did not want Mr. Breedon to feel as if he suffered unpleasant scenes any time she was around him. "If her grace approves, of course."

"Leave persuading the duchess to me," said Scully with a wink. He patted her on the shoulder as he stood, and she noticed he looked at her chest as if to verify with his own eyes that she was uninjured. Not that he could see the worst of the redness that was in the crease between her breasts, and her white muslin morning gown was cut considerably higher than the gown of last night.

Heat rose in Roxana's face. How much had Scully seen of the way the thin silk clung to her breasts, revealing everything? Mrs. Porter had told her that men would *always* look at a woman's bosoms if offered a chance. Roxana did not know that she believed that until Max had stared at her almost as if he could not look away. She had known the silk was thin, but had not realized how thin until that moment she looked down to see where the duke's gaze was focused.

Inexplicably her flush spread to other places on her body, lower, across her belly and lower still. She stared at her plate, seeking composure.

"Miss Winston?"

She looked up at Mr. Breedon's moon face.

Uncertainty hung in his expression. "Are you all right? You do not have to ride if you do not wish."

She smiled and glanced back to where Scully had moved to the tray of pastries and was selecting his breakfast. "No. You will think me terribly vain, but I have a huge desire to wear my riding habit in company."

"Your clothes are very pretty." Mr. Breedon's cheeks pinked. "And you are too."

Roxana was unprepared for the compliments she kept getting on her looks. By far the worst offender was Scully, but the most sincere seemed to be Mr. Breedon with his simplistic comment. "I am not used to being told so, but thank you. Are you sure you would not join us riding?"

"I might consider it, if I wake early."

"I hope you do," said Roxana brightly, and it was not quite as much of a strain as her earlier forced cheer.

Other guests drifted into the room and made their way to the sideboard. Scully talked to one of the gentlemen in the far corner. A few of the women asked Roxana if she had suffered a very grave injury. She reassured them she had not.

Mr. Breedon leaned closer to her and said, "I was afraid to ask if you suffered any injury last night, because I did not want to be crude. Because of where . . . where . . ." His pink drifted closer to purple.

He did not want to mention her chest for fear of seeming indelicate? "I suffered only a very slight burn. I assure you the Duchess of Trent's servants plied me with more poultices and cold towels than were warranted."

"I did not know what to do when Trent whisked you out of the room," whispered Mr. Breedon.

"I think he is just very used to controlling any situation." Roxana shrugged. Would the duke be part of the riding party that Scully made up? And her anger at being yanked around had melted when she realized her gown was transparent. Max had an odd unsettling effect on her that was not quite fear, but close enough to it; she'd do better to avoid him.

She put her fingers on Mr. Breedon's sleeve. "In truth, I should much rather not speak of it, and I appreciated your forbearance in not speaking of the incident earlier. Although I understand you would have felt remiss not inquiring, since others have brought up the subject."

"Just so," said Mr. Breedon, who had followed her every word with a sincere nod of his head.

One of the other ladies of the party sat her plate down at the morning table. Mr. Breedon pushed back his half-full plate.

Had Roxana given him too much food? As she watched Mr. Breedon, Lady Malmsbury brushed by Roxana's chair, catching her hip on the back. Roxana turned to see two white globes of poached eggs sliding across Lady Malmsbury's plate.

Roxana envisioned yellow yolk dripping down her front, just as Mr. Breedon reached up and tipped the plate so the eggs slid onto the table-cloth instead of her front.

"Careful," Mr. Breedon said.

"You moved your chair," said Lady Malmsbury.

Roxana stared at the yellow and white mess on the pale green tablecloth. Had she? "I'm terribly sorry."

"I say, Lady Malmsbury, you are extraordinarily clumsy around Miss Winston." Scully moved across the room. With an edge of warning, he said, "Perhaps you should keep clear of her."

What had she ever done to incur the wrath of Lady Malmsbury? She stared at the lovely red-haired woman and noticed that in the morning light, the woman's hair had the brassy hint of a henna wash.

"Oh dear, you are not hurt are you, Miss Winston? I am so dreadfully appalled. Of course you did not realize I was behind you when you moved your chair back. I shall have to pay better attention."

The occupants of the room looked between the two of them, almost as if unsure which woman was at fault for the accidents.

"Well, get a servant, do." Mr. Breedon tossed his napkin over the mess on the table.

Roxana decided that was a task she could man-age, and she fled for the door. In the passageway a hand at her shoulder stopped her. Roxana turned, expecting Scully, half hoping for Max, and found Mr. Breedon pulling back his hand. "You shan't cry, shall you?"

Roxana folded her arms across her middle. She was used to being attacked with little or no provocation. Lady Malmsbury's tricks were hardly of consequence. Roxana was good at dodging unwarranted attacks. She'd keep at arm's length from Lady Malmsbury in the future. "Thank you, no."

Mr. Breedon pulled his hands behind his back and rocked up on his toes, and then cleared his throat. "Well, because if you were of a mind to, I thought you might want to make use of my shoulder."

Roxana stared at him.

"Of course, I understand if you do not want to. And I just meant it as a friendly sort of offer. I . . ." He took a step back.

Roxana swallowed her fear of getting too close physically to any man and stepped forward, leaning her head against his broad shoulder. Very slowly, as if he were aware of her past, he put his arm about her shoulder and patted her arm.

She reached up and placed her hand against his shoulder and found him more solid than she had expected. Solid and comforting like an old quilt. And she did not want to like him, because tricking him would be so much more difficult if she liked him.

Fanny jerked as her bedroom door opened. She turned, expecting Julia or Thomas; instead Scully stood looking around her new bedchamber.

"Ah, a pretty little room for a pretty little woman."

She was faded, not pretty, and "little" was not a word she'd use to describe herself. "Dev, what are you doing here?"

"It is so hard to catch you alone," he said, drifting to the far side of the room and picking up a Dresden china figurine sitting on her nightstand. "Do you like your little chamber?"

She folded her arms across her chest. "You should not be in here."

"Yes, well, I am on an errand for Miss Winston." He set the expensive figurine down and touched the gold filigree box sitting next to her bed. Her heart beat harder knowing her wedding ring was in that box.

Fanny glanced at the closed door. Devlin was alone with her in her bedroom, but he made no move to take advantage of the situation. He had put the bed between them, and while her room was not as large as the one he stayed in, it was by no means small.

Shaking like a leaf she turned around and returned to her task. "I suppose it will do no good for me to insist you leave my room."

"Well, you should have to put more verve into it than that."

"What is it you want or Miss Winston wants?" Fanny sighed. Everyone was on a mission for Miss Winston, it seemed. Julia had practiced the piano for her, Thomas had finally learned a difficult passage in French so he could recite it for her and Max had put Fanny on her own task.

"Miss Winston asks if she might ride with me in the mornings," said Dev casually. "I assured her that I would persuade you to approve."

Such a spike of jealousy stabbed at her heart, Fanny wished she'd never invited the girl into her home. She closed her eyes, wondering if Max's attention to the girl, her children's attention or Dev's attention bothered her the most. Silly question. "I am not at all sure that is a good idea, Dev."

"Do you not trust me, love?"

"I of all people know you are not to be trusted." Fanny's voice trembled.

"You need not have any concerns. I have no interest in Miss Winston. Besides, she has already invited Mr. Breedon to accompany us and we will of course have a groom as escort."

Fanny winced, hearing the clink of the porcelain box.

"Fanny?"

She turned slowly. He held her ring up between his thumb and forefinger.

"Why did you take off your wedding ring?"

She stared at him, searching for the right response. The foolish hope of a middle-aged woman. She finally shrugged. "I am no longer married, am I?"

His grin flashed across his face, and she spun away. How much had she revealed? Her heart pounded. "Fine, then, take Miss Winston riding. Go on, then."

She heard her ring clink and the sound of his movement across the room. His hands landed on her shoulders.

"Go, please," she whispered. "I am not married."

"Fanny—"

She spun out of his grasp, concerned that she could not resist him if he applied the least amount of pressure. But she could not risk pregnancy without a husband to provide cover for her sin.

"Please, I beg of you, leave me be."

Max stared as Miss Winston leaned against Mr. Breedon. His shoulders tightened and a dull ache spread to the base of his skull. She was making fast work of enticing Mr. Breedon, except the embrace the two shared spoke more of friendship than a stolen cuddle.

"Joining us for church this morning, Breedon?"

The two sprang apart as if guilty of an illicit encounter. Miss Winston was again unchaperoned. Max sighed. He would have to watch over her more closely.

"Certainly, certainly," said Breedon.

If he couldn't keep an eye on Roxana, the next best thing was to keep Breedon occupied.

"How about the pheasant hunting tomorrow afternoon?"

"Uh, no," said Breedon. "I, uh, don't like killing things much." He backed away.

Max should not have interfered unless the pair risked passion overtaking their senses. Not terribly likely in Breedon's case. And surely Roxana could not find Gregory overwhelmingly persuasive.

Roxana shifted. Shaking his head, Breedon walked away.

If she could fix Breedon's attentions and be happy married to him, who was Max to interfere?

"Do not allow him to treat you with too much familiarity," Max cautioned.

"He offered comfort, no more." Roxana turned in the direction Breedon departed.

"So all appears to be going well in your laying of traps."

"No," said Roxana.

He stopped and looked at her. Hope bubbled through his struggle to do the right thing and assist her in securing a decent marriage. "No?"

Her blue eyes narrowed as she studied him and Max again felt that absurd rise of heat. Such delightfully deep a blue, like a clear moonlit sky at midnight. Did she know how striking she was?

"If I might have a word with you, Miss Winston."

"Certainly, your grace." She swiveled around and her blue eyes hurtled glacial daggers in his direction. "Shall we use the billiard room?"

Max choked. He closed his eyes, warding off the images of Roxana in her plastered-on dress. Her breasts had been perfection, full and cherry tipped. No good. His body flooded with heat. His hand itched to caress her surprisingly lush curves. His mouth watered as he thought of touching his lips to those sweet berry nipples. He could not be alone with her in his hardening condition. "If you would accompany me upstairs."

"Is there a problem?"

He took a step toward her, and Roxana took a quick step backward.

The moment grew heavy with tension. Was she aware of his arousal? She had just been in Breedon's arms, yet Max wanted to grab her to him and let her know just how she made his blood run hot. As if he could mark her as his. Which was about as ridiculous a thought as he could entertain.

He should be relieved her pursuit of Gregory appeared to be going well. Max had no place in his life for Roxana, and her problems would only compound his.

Max gestured toward the stairs.

"Lady Malmsbury does not like me, you know." Roxana paused for a second at the base of the stairs.

"I am sure that last night's incident was just an accident."

"The eggs too?"

"What eggs?"

"Lady Malmsbury's eggs that Mr. Breedon saved me from wearing." Roxana waved a hand as if it was of no import.

But it was of great import if Mr. Breedon had gained Roxana's gratitude by rescuing her from Eliza's bad behavior. And was Max's attraction to Miss Winston the cause of Eliza's spite?

"Fanny's maid said your skin was only a little reddened." Max swallowed hard as he thought about the expanse of flesh to which he referred. "Are you in any discomfort?"

"I am fine."

He put his hand to the small of her back to guide her toward Fanny's room, but he knew as soon as he touched Roxana that it was a mistake. He was the one in discomfort as he resisted the impulse to rub his fingers in coaxing circles.

He tapped on Fanny's sitting-room door.

"My lady went to greet arriving guests, your grace," said Fanny's maid. "She said to give you this. It is everything you requested." She handed Max a pouch of sorts. "I put your dress back in your room, Miss."

The maid curtsied and then shut the door, leaving them alone in the empty passageway. He slid the pouch into his coat pocket and the pocket bulged out.

Max hesitated, then he guided Roxana down the passageway. He had meant to discuss things with her in private with Fanny present, but he could not take her into a room alone. At the far end a slender table stood flanked by two unlit girandoles. Hopefully none of the other guests would intrude on their conversation.

"Where are we going?" she asked.

"The end of the hall. We shall just be a moment."

His touch at the base of her spine made Roxana shudder. She stepped a little faster so he would remove his hand and pulled her shawl closer around her shoulders. Was it proper to be alone with him?

He turned at the far end of the passageway and leaned against the little table. "I spoke with Fanny this morning about assigning one of the maids to act as your abigail."

"That's not necessary," said Roxana. "I am used to making do without one."

The mirror above the table reflected the back of his broad shoulders at her, while she could not help but notice his form from the front. She wanted to look her fill. Was that how he felt last night as he looked at her transparent dress? Seeing both sides of him overwhelmed her. Her breath felt short and her knees wobbled as if no longer capable of supporting her.

"Miss Winston, the official festivities will begin the day after tomorrow with the hunt, followed by the choosing of the Lord of Misrule at the ball, and shall be nonstop. You will need to change your gown three or four times a day. Then there is fixing your hair and everything else."

Roxana's hand shot to her simple topknot as if by its own volition. His brown eyes followed her hand, and she withdrew it self-consciously. Roxana bit down the resentment that she needed assistance.

A more rational part of her brain noted that she should just accept his offer. Other women of her station had lady's maids. Just because she had resigned herself to a working-class future did not require that she should not live as expected now.

"My sister will need an abigail in a year or two; you will be helping us by trying one of the maids to see if she can handle the increased responsibilities."

"Ah, you would turn it into a favor I do for you." Roxana turned away. His attention made her feel odd, as if he was touching her, although he stood more than an arm's length from her.

"If that would help you swallow the idea, Miss Winston."

"Very well." She was not in a position to refuse. Why was Max telling her this? He was not like the duchess, who accepted her polite demurs when asked if she needed anything. "I shall be ever indebted to you."

"Miss Winston, if I might speak plainly?" he said gently.

Bracing herself, she turned back around and nodded.

Max pushed away from the table and pulled the pouch from his pocket. The bundle was a chamois cloth tied with a ribbon.

"It occurs to me that if you mean to land a rich husband, you should not look as if you need one."

Mortification flowed through her, making her joints lock.

"I asked Fanny to go through the family jewels and select a few items appropriate for a young woman to wear. She agreed it was a good idea." He untied the ribbon and set the tie on the table, then peeled back the edges of the cloth. Gold glinted out among other shiny baubles.

Roxana swiveled away and ducked her head.

She had thought she had done a credible job of fitting in. But he had seen her mended gloves, knew she had arrived without a maid or a riding habit, and had guessed that she was the architect of her gowns. "Am I so obviously destitute, then?"

"Yes," he moved around in front of her. His brown eyes radiated concern. "I only mean to assist you, Miss Winston. Julia was dancing around me this morning quite proud of her new gown."

So was he helping her because she made Julia happy? His nearness made breathing hard.

He turned her back to him and then slid a single strand of pearls around her neck and fastened it at her nape. Shivers poured through her as she touched the gems, just above her neckline. But it might have been a strand of knotted hemp, because it was the brush of his warm fingers along her collarbone that made her skin heat and tingle and her stomach tighten.

All of the jewelry Mrs. Porter proudly displayed, along with the tales of the protector who had bestowed it upon her, raced through Roxana's head. "I cannot accept them."

"It is only a loan, Miss Winston. It is not as if Fanny will need them while you are here. The family has a great deal of jewelry that is currently not being used by anyone. If I had more than one sister, it might be a different story."

Or if he had a wife. These jewels would eventually become the province of his wife. If he married. How could she have even thought for one second that he was offering her carte blanche?

His hand against her shoulder did strange things to her insides. That was why. Gently he pushed her toward the table and the decorative looking glass on the wall. She saw her eyes, wide and dark, and tried to ease the fear from her expression. His face moved above her shoulder, and he held a teardrop pearl earring up to her ear. His thumb grazed against her earlobe and a shudder rippled through her.

Their eyes met and held in the glass. She could turn her head and her lips would brush his cheek, he stood so close. Or if he turned too . . .

Roxana wanted to close her eyes and lean back into him. As if aware he stood too close, he stiffened and stepped back.

"You are too kind, but I cannot wear these."

Every time she touched them she would think of him. Stars above, she could not forget why she was here and what she needed to do.

"Why has your father not provided better for you than to cast you among strangers?"

Roxana's hand curled around the pearls. Mentioning her father was as good a reminder as any. She closed her eyes. Pictures swam before them. Falling to her knees in the drive, her hands scraping against the rough gravel. The thought that she needed to protect her hands from injury had sustained her as the stinging whacks fell across her back.

"Roxy, are you all right? You've gone quite pale."

Roxana strode away, her gloved fingers unable to undo the necklace's catch. "I do not think this is a good idea."

"Hold steady." Max followed her down the passageway until he caught her shoulders and then undid the pearls. He put them in the chamois cloth. "It is not a good idea for us to be alone together overlong. But do take the jewelry, Roxy."

"I cannot think this is proper," she said.

"I did not expect you to object. No one ever

questions the propriety of my actions. I assure you, no one will recognize them as Trent pieces." He looked down into the pouch. "I can see a few of these were my mother's pieces. They haven't been worn since her death."

Surely he would not use his mother's jewelry to foster a seduction. Perhaps her own folly led her to misinterpret his gesture. "I do not understand why you are helping me, when you do not approve of my goals."

"Do not allow false pride to stand in the way of your ambitions." Max retrieved the ribbon from the table and returned to where she stood in the middle of the passage. He reached out for her hand, pulling it up and setting the chamois cloth in it. "Would wearing them not help you achieve your ends? It costs me nothing."

From the weight of it, she could tell the contents were more than the pearls. Max reached for her other hand that hung stupidly at her side and brought it up to hold the makeshift bag. His hands were big enough to hold the bundle in one hand, but her hands were not. He wrapped the bit of ribbon around the cloth and tied a bow. She studied his fingers as they deftly handled the narrow strip.

"I want you to use them. All beautiful women should have proper adornment." His hands closed around hers and the gentle warmth of them burned through the back of her gloved hands. "I do not know why the mention of your father upsets you, nor why you feel your course is so urgent." He smiled encouragingly. "I would hope that you could help me understand your plight."

Roxana wanted to tug her hands back, but she hesitated because she could not pull back without looking as if she was snatching the jewelry to her.

If he understood her plight, would it become a bargaining chip to persuade her with, or was his inquiry only kindness?

"Is your family's situation so dire that you must sacrifice your own happiness to marry a wealthy man?"

Roxana stared at him, unwilling to lie to him, and yet knowing she could not tell him the truth. Yes, her family situation was dire, but nothing upon nothing would convince her to marry. She'd rather be a man's mistress first. She never wanted to allow a man so much control, so many rights, not even when he made her heart pound, and her knees weak, and was too, too kind to her when he hated what she was doing.

But clearly Max was a man who wanted his own way. He cajoled and flattered and reasoned until the path he thought best was followed. Would he ever resort to the measures her father used to demand his family's compliance? Roxana suspected Max had never been so challenged. A duke was toadied to in a way that a baron could only dream about.

"I am sure Fanny could be persuaded to sponsor you in a season," Max said. "You do not need to settle so quickly."

"Yes, I am sure you could convince her to chaperone me through a London season, but I should not like to be so demanding a guest, and I do not think her heart would be in it." Besides, marriage was not Roxana's goal, and a season would not offer the opportunities to be compromised that a house party offered. "I will not protest any longer, because I can see it shall be useless. Thank you."

She pulled her hands away and moved toward her bedchamber door, the bundle clutched in her hands. And if Max had looked a little taken aback, then it served him right for making her think he was offering to set her up as his mistress. Then Roxana had to acknowledge that perhaps her own desires had warped her understanding.

Chapter
Eight

Max's horse nickered and resisted the standstill after running so long. Looking around at the gathering guests, Max saw that many of their horses were flagging, their heads down, blowing hard out of their nostrils and their hides wet with sweat. The grooms would have a difficult evening, caring for all the horses. A chill breeze blew out of the north, ruddying the cheeks of the already rosy cheeks of the riders.

The hounds bayed as the kennel master and whipper-ins yanked them back on newly attached leads, the kill left for the equestrian pursuers. Mud and decaying leaves clung to many of the riders, the result of a recent run through a creek.

As Max dismounted, he mentally counted the riders, wondering if any had dropped out or been hurt in the last hour of hard riding. His boots squished against the spongy ground near the boggy stretch of reeds where the fox cowered, the red of his brush clear through the thin stalks. Max disliked this part.

The fox had given a good run, but now it trembled, beaten, its sides heaving with fatigue. Max would have preferred to let the fox live another day; the beast had provided a good hunt. He'd kept the chase alive for three days, leading them over hill and dale. Mostly their quarry had kept to Trent lands and hadn't dragged the riders through forest until the end, when nearing exhaustion.

"There you are, fellow," Max cooed softly. "Almost done now."

Scully and Thomas as well as a few of the other hunters closed from either side, the servants taking positions on an outer ring to cut off any avenue of escape. Not that the fox had the energy left to run any longer. Besides, dusk crept through the trees, the shadows long and low.

Max reached for the fox with his gloved left hand. The animal wasn't done yet, as he snapped at Max, but it was too late. Max caught the brush of his tail, yanked him up and slit his throat almost before Scully could assist him in the kill.

Max held high the limp animal to the triumphant cheers of the hunters and the near hysterical baying of the hounds. Max gave the order to one of the servants to run back to the house and let Fanny know that the hunt party would be back within the hour. They were far enough away that he was not sure she would hear the horns.

Thomas skipped forward to receive the smears of fox blood on his cheeks.

The Misses Ferris urged their horses in to receive their mark, more because Max was bestowing it than because it was truly their first hunt. Max scanned for Roxana.

"Miss Winston." He lifted the bloody carcass. "Your first participation in the kill?"

She stared at him, her eyes glassy and accusatory. The brilliant red flush of her winter-chilled cheeks drained before his eyes. She shook her head and wheeled her mount around. For such a pragmatic woman, she had surprisingly soft sides.

Max continued forward, offering the blood to the eager clamoring of the other hunters. Many of the women who had fallen back near the end now joined the circle around him.

"Go after her, Dev," he whispered to Scully.

Scully backed away and out of the crowd, but he returned a few seconds later. "Breedon has got her."

Max thrust the fox's body in Thomas's direction, and the boy struggled to hold the animal aloft to the cheers around him.

Max peeled off his bloody gloves, tossing them in the direction of a groom.

"Has she never hunted before?" asked Scully. "Did she not know what to expect?"

Max had killed animals dozens of times. Killing the fox was expected and more humane than letting the dogs rip the poor beast to shreds. He'd never questioned the necessity of it. The cold stung his bare hands as he mounted his horse again.

Roxana's wary expression and the way that she shied away from him made him feel just a bit savage.

No doubt Breedon, with his aversion for hunting—aversion for anything physical—and his slothful movements, made her feel that he would never so much as hurt a fly.

Roxana wasn't sure why the killing of the fox had bothered her so. Perhaps because Max had gone about it with an ease and a matter-of-factness that reminded her of the way her father's hand would fly across her mother's cheek if his dinner was late or his slippers did not appear as promptly as he wished. As if the recipient of the cruelty deserved the treatment.

When they lived in Winston Hall it had been easier to avoid her father, but after they moved to the cottage, they were too on top of each other and the rages were harder to sidestep.

The poor fox had done nothing more than lead them on merry chase over hill and dale. It hardly seemed fair to slaughter the poor animal when he could run no more.

"Miss Winston, ho, wait for me," called Mr. Breedon behind her.

She pulled her ambling horse to a halt and waited for him to catch her.

Mr. Breedon pulled alongside her and bent forward to stroke the neck of his horse, cooing to his steed. The horse tossed its head.

Roxana brushed below her eyes and turned. "My, it is turning cold, is it not?"

Mr. Breedon noticed her gesture. "The end is hard to watch."

"I suppose I am quite silly, but I wanted the poor fox to get away."

Mr. Breedon smiled. "Why, Miss Winston, you have such a tender heart."

No, she did not, but such brusque violence by Max unaccountably affected her. She shuddered. Had she thought that Max could be only kind, that he was incapable of the violence that those of his sex relished?

She was being a ninny. The all-night sewing stints must have made her overtired. First had been her mad rush to construct her fashionable new riding habit. Then she cut apart her new pelisse to make scarves for the men. She started sewing drawstring reticules for all the women. Hopefully, by Christmas she would have respectable gifts for everyone.

The evenings had been quiet, games of charades or cap verses and cards. Evenings were the best time to make up to Mr. Breedon. But the hunt kept her in his presence, even if it did not allow for a tête-à-tête. So she had participated, even though riding a horse for so many hours when she was unused to it had made her sore and tired.

Mr. Breedon's horse sidled toward her and pinned Roxana's legs between the two horses. He reached across the distance and plucked a bit of dead leaf from her shoulder. She felt as much as the leaf. If Max had done that she would have experienced his touch deep in her womb—which was insane. But she tried to substitute in her head the reaction she had with Max.

"You have quite a good seat," said Mr. Breedon.

"I enjoy riding. I have been admiring your mounts all day long. You keep quite impressive horseflesh, Mr. Breedon."

Mr. Breedon looked down. "I like to ride too. I just prefer riding at home where I know all the paths."

"And walking when away from home?"

"Just so. Riding occasionally bothers my knee. It has seized up on me. I find it mortifying to be laid up in bed when visiting."

"Yes, one would hate to miss the festivities."

Mr. Breedon, for all his girth, actually exercised quite a bit. She knew things about him that she suspected he had not shared with others. In fact, she was starting to feel quite bad about her plans to trick him, but then she needed to prod him along the path. He did not act as though he even wanted to compromise her.

"Miss Winston, might I ask you a question of a delicate nature?"

Mr. Breedon's horse still brushed her leg. She slowed her mount so her legs might brush Mr. Breedon. "Certainly."

"Is there an arrangement between you and the duke?"

Arrangement? Roxana's horse neighed and backed away, so the planned gentle touch of their extremities became a bone-jarring crash. So much for her use of subtle physical enticements. "No, why would you think that?"

"The others are speculating, and Lady Malmsbury . . ." Breedon cleared his throat. "Just did not want to be poaching."

Were the others gossiping about her and Max? Surely they did not think her his mistress. "What kind of arrangement?"

"Well, since his father's passing, there are those that say he is looking for a bride."

Roxana sucked in a calming drink of cold winter air. "No, I have it on good authority he is *not* looking for marriage."

Mr. Breedon looked down at his hands. "Oh."

Panic rose in Roxana's throat. She had allowed her natural sharpness to show through her sweet-as-sugar pretense. "Not that I care about that."

Mr. Breedon looked off across the field. "No, of course not." He urged his horse forward.

Stars above, he probably thought she had cast out lures for Max and failed before she began angling after Mr. Breedon.

"Gregory—I beg your pardon—Mr. Breedon, I find the Duke of Trent too sure of himself."

Mr. Breedon looked back at her as if wanting to be reassured. Would he comment on her accidental use of his first name?

"I do not think whomever he chooses as a wife shall be very comfortable. He is a very forceful man, is he not?"

"I had not thought him forceful."

"I do not wish to be critical of our host," said Roxana. Had she set her cause back too far? Panic clutched at her throat. She was much better at her role when her emotions were not running high. "I am sure there are those that would think his strength of character one of his best assets, but I find him intolerant of dissenting opinions."

"No. He is quite tolerant of diverse opinions. He entertains all of the gentlemen after dinner by making sure all different ideas are honored."

Roxana bit down on her tongue. She could not argue with Mr. Breedon, and certainly not about Max. "I am sure you must know him better than I do. I have, after all, only just met him. I only know that I feel much more comfortable in your presence than in his."

"Yes, well, he watches you a lot," said Mr. Breedon.

Heat curled under her skin, but Roxana tried to dismiss it. "I am sure it is that he takes his temporary guardianship of me quite seriously."

Did Max watch her? Their eyes seemed to meet often across the room, as if he always was aware of where she was. When he watched over her did he feel that same odd fluttering as she did?

* * *

"There, love, the fox is killed and it is too bad we cannot eat him," said Scully as Fanny went around the massive dining-room table, checking that the place settings were in proper precedence.

"We have plenty to eat without resorting to eating vermin," answered Fanny, while switching two place cards.

Scully went behind her and switched Miss Winston's card to the place beside his seat and away from Breedon, who was farther down the table. He wandered around looking over the china and silver and made sure that Malmsy was on the opposite side of the table and far enough away that she'd have to launch a gravy boat to decorate Roxana with food.

"Thomas enjoyed his first hunt," Scully said, knowing Fanny would be worried about her son but would not ask directly about Thomas's well-being.

Fanny stopped for a second and then resumed her chore.

"I rode with him and let him regale me with all the tales of the fences he took."

Fanny turned her blue eyes toward him and then closed them. She gripped the back of a chair. "I should not have let him go."

"Never fear, Max or I had him within our sights every day." They had traded off between keeping an eye on Thomas and keeping an eye on Miss Winston. "I never would have let him take a fence that he could not clear."

Scully moved to her side.

"You should be upstairs in the drawing room," said Fanny. "I'm sure that more of the younger set are gathered up there."

"I would rather be here with you."

"Yes, well, you are making a nuisance of yourself."

"Shall I go play with the children in the nursery?" asked Scully. "For you seem determined to treat me like a little boy."

"Perhaps you should not. My children talk of nothing but you or Miss Winston." Fanny strode away.

Scully paused, wondering if he had erred in ingratiating himself with Julia and Thomas. Not that he was overplaying his role, but just treating them as a friendly uncle would. And did he hear an edge to Fanny's voice when she mentioned Miss Winston's name?

Fanny came to a complete stop when she saw the two place cards he had switched. Her gaze rose to meet his, and he did not mistake the hurt in them.

"I'm not a boy or an unformed youth who does not know my mind." As Devlin said the words he wrestled with the idea that he was not sure of what he wanted. He had ridden here fast, thinking he knew, but Max had raised the stakes and Fanny shied away from him at every turn.

A servant entered the room to light the tapers on the silver candelabrum gracing the table every five feet. Fanny exited the room without saying another word. What had happened to the woman who had delighted in his company, smiled at his cajoling and laughed at his compliments?

Was she just a distant memory he had idolized in his youth, or was the Fanny he knew and loved still hiding under her stiff widow's reserve?

He looked down the long polished rosewood table. The largest table in his home could seat no more than two dozen, but this table was set for more than twice that number. Did Fanny hate the idea of losing all this splendor? Was that the reason for her animosity toward Roxana and her resistance to him?

Roxana curtsied to her partner and then joined the polite titter of applause. A small orchestra played on a raised dais and local gentry had been invited to fill out the company in the ballroom.

Too many times she had looked across the floor and encountered Max's gaze.

"Ah, there you are, Miss Winston," said Scully as she returned to the Duchess of Trent's side. "You are looking heavenly."

Whenever Fanny's hostess duties kept her busy, Scully seemed to have taken it upon himself to make sure Roxana never stood alone.

"Heavenly? More like devilishly wicked," said Lady Malmsbury nearby.

Roxana looked up, but the words were not addressed to her; Lady Malmsbury was speaking to Lady Breedon.

"Have you ever seen such clothing on a woman of quality? Miss Winston dresses like a Cyprian."

My stars, she did not need Mr. Breedon's mama thinking she was beyond the pale. Lady Breedon's color rose, and she refused to meet Roxana's gaze. Lady Malmsbury had no such qualms. Her green eyes shot venom in Roxana's direction.

"Hell has no fury, eh, Malmsy?" called Scully.

Lady Malmsbury turned her back to them, her long red curls bouncing with the vehemence of her cut direct.

Roxana tugged Scully along. Much as she would like to confront Lady Malmsbury, nothing would be gained and much could be lost. She could not repay the Trents' hospitality by creating an unpleasant scene.

Roxana looked down at the gathered swags of red silk across her chest and shoulders. The whole dress consisted of layer after layer of swooping skirts, each layer shorter and shorter, until the top layer hung just below her hips. Or perhaps it was the matching long gloves, the gathers on the forearms mirroring the drape of her dress. Every other woman in the ballroom wore long white gloves.

"Do not pay her any mind. She is just jealous and in a bad mood," Scully said. "Your gown is simply stunning, and you are beyond compare in it."

"Don't. I do not quite fit in, do I?" whispered Roxana.

"If you don't fit in because you stand above the others, there is no fault to you in that."

"You are too kind," said Roxana.

Scully had taken over their direction and Roxana stopped walking as she realized he was leading them to the group where Max stood surrounded by a bevy of young women.

Roxana tugged at one of her gloves.

Max backed away from the group and headed toward them. "Miss Winston, Dev."

"Malmsy is on the warpath," warned Scully in a low undertone. "Fanny is precious close to where I want her."

Max nodded and extended his arm to Roxana. "Might I have this dance, Miss Winston?"

Fanny watched Scully approach with a determined stride. She looked around for an escape, but the only clear path was toward the mistletoe hanging in the corner of the room, a corner that had been conspicuously avoided thus far.

"Might I have this dance, your grace?" Scully stepped so close her skirts brushed against his legs.

She took a step back. "I have to see to things."

"No, you don't. Everything is running smoothly, as usual."

Fanny wasn't sure if she enjoyed these house parties anymore. She had at first enjoyed the increased stature she gained by hosting one of the most exclusive of holiday parties, but in recent years she found her concerns about her guests' pleasure trumping her own enjoyment. A disaster always took place, but by dint of her ability to contain it, rarely did all her guests catch wind of whatever catastrophe befell each party.

One year a certain unmarried lady, not known to be with child, had nearly given birth on the ballroom floor. Another year, three gentlemen and one lady had a horrid accident during the hunt, which resulted in two broken limbs, a broken crown and a lost front tooth. Another year, Scully had been the disaster that had haunted her ever since. Fanny was beginning to jump at her own shadow, waiting for whatever would go wrong this year.

Of course there had been the spilling of hot tea on Roxana, but with the wisdom of her years, Fanny knew that did not rise to the level of her annual disaster. More than anything she feared a repeat with Scully.

Fanny sought out her guest in the crowd and saw Roxana taking her place in a set forming with Max. She also saw the daggers-drawn glare of Lady Malmsbury. An older woman needed to learn to step aside when a man started the hunt for a bride.

Although Max had denied his need to take a wife, she knew her words had not fallen on deaf ears. Max always did the right thing. She just hoped he was not deciding so soon after realizing he needed to marry. He did not seem to single out Roxana for special attention, he just looked at her differently. Truth was, Fanny far preferred Max with Miss Winston than Scully with her.

While Fanny glanced over the company and fretted, Scully stepped closer. She tried even harder to concentrate on her stepson and his settling down. Of course that put her in an untenable position.

Scully was so close she could feel the heat off of his body. For one second she felt herself leaning toward him. She took another step back.

"Forget about me?" Scully asked with a quirked eyebrow and another step closer.

"For goodness sake, how could I forget about you? You—"

"My thoughts exactly."

"—are nearly standing on my toes." Fanny stepped back again.

"I have never trod on your toes, dearest."

"Shhh!" She put out a hand to stop him from moving closer.

His lightning grin flashed, and Fanny felt that momentary blindness that always hit her when Scully smiled at her. Of all of Max's friends for her to fall for, Scully had to be the worst. Yet he never failed to make her heart flutter. He pressed his chest against her palm and she took another step backwards. "Scully."

His blue eyes were amused, laughing at her, laughing at a too-old woman he could toy with and fluster. God, she was too old to be rattled by a rake like him. But the feel of his chest against her palm passed a current of energy through her.

"Another step, Fanny. Did I tell you that you are looking radiant? Remarkably beautiful. Ravishing, actually."

"Stop," she whispered, dropping her head and trying to put space between them, before the whole room was looking at them, before he could see her eager interest. But even if he wanted to resume their dalliance from long ago, Fanny could foresee no good outcome and many horrid ones.

"Yes, we can stop now, love," he said.

His loose use of endearments tore at her.

He pushed her hand up to his shoulder. "Look up, Fanny. There is much magic in the mistletoe this year."

Fanny frantically looked to her right and left, realizing Scully had backed her into the kissing corner. She tried to dart around him, but she could hardly do it without looking like a ninny, not a duchess of twenty years. "You—"

"Yes, me," said Scully as he gathered her to him.

Max took one look at Roxana and caught his breath. She was stunning in her scarlet gossamer silk gown. The very sheerness promised sin. Yet try as he might he could see nothing, but he could fill in details from the memory burned in his mind.

He had kept his distance, not trusting the weakness of his control around Roxana. When had he ever had trouble staying within the bounds of propriety? Max could not remember finding doing the right thing so difficult. And Scully would not let him forget it.

Roxana's light placement of her fingertips on

his sleeve made a shudder pass down his spine. Where was Breedon when he needed him?

"How are you tonight, Miss Winston?" he asked as they assumed their position in the set forming for the next dance.

"I am quite well, thank you."

"Are you enjoying the ball?" he asked politely.

Roxana looked around the room as if the thought of enjoyment had never crossed her mind. "Everyone is dressed so beautifully. I have never seen so many remarkable ballgowns all together. I *am* enjoying myself," she said, almost as if surprised to realize it.

The sparkle in her eyes indicated that she told the truth. Why was she always surprised to find pleasure? With a house party designed around indulgences, she should have expected to enjoy herself. But then, Roxana had come with a mission.

"Ah, then you would enjoy the opera."

"The opera?" she said. "Do you think so? For music is not my forte. My sister Katherine loves music. I think she would enjoy the opera so much more than I."

"Ah, well, not everyone attends the opera for the performance. It is the place to display all one's best finery."

Roxana smiled. "Then I would enjoy it."

"Then you must allow me to extend an invitation to my box, next season."

Her expression fell. Then she masked her disappointment with a soft smile. "I do not believe I will have the opportunity to accept your most generous offer, but thank you just the same."

She looked across the room, where Breedon stood with his mother, and Roxana's eyes narrowed. "Do you not expect to be in London next season?" whispered Max. "Mr. Breedon will be there, you know. My offer would of course include him."

Roxana's blue eyes clouded. A furrow pinched her brows together. "Well, I hope to be in London, then."

The pattern of the dance took them apart and Max asked himself what he was doing. Setting up a smooth path to seduction later, after she was married?

And why was Roxana no longer confiding in him? Their steps brought them back together again and her manner was so much more serious than before.

"You have outdone yourself tonight," he said. "You are beyond a doubt the most beautiful woman in the room."

"I should have worn white gloves." Roxana glanced down at her scarlet gown and then looked over to where Lady Angela and the Misses Ferris stood in their pale pastel gowns. They were like faded flowers and Roxana, a rose in bloom.

Now he knew he had lost his mind.

Perhaps the inappropriate maturity of her dress made him want to overstep the lines of propriety. Her appearance gave more than a hint of sinful pleasure. Yet she bore herself so regally. At the same time she was kind and responsive to his sister and brother. She would make a husband immensely proud.

His thoughts swirled as he and Roxana came together in the dance again and he took her hand. Heat flashed up his arm and pooled low in his gut. She was beautiful, and when he was with her he felt less alone, less cognizant of the loss of his family.

With her pragmatic nature, she was used to employing economy through her sewing. Her alluring new riding habit looked suspiciously like his old bedspread. Perhaps she would even make a good wife to a man drowning in inherited debt. How mired in dun territory was her father?

"You are very quiet this evening, your grace," she said.

"I need to speak to you in private," he said. A sensation somewhere between relief and desperation rolled through him. "When do you plan to return home?"

She frowned at him as if faintly puzzled. Then she looked around furtively, as if trapped. "When everyone else does, I suppose. After the twelfth night?"

"I will escort you there after all the other guests have left."

Roxana's blue eyes rounded in alarm. "I assure you that will not be necessary."

Max could not leap into a courtship after all his protestations. And what about Thomas, he asked himself? "I want to meet your parents," he said firmly.

Roxana shook her head. "Shall we just see what comes of things?"

Was she hoping that Breedon would come up to scratch before then? Could she actually prefer that puppy? The idea of being second best rankled. Yet, holding her, dancing with her, contemplating asking Roxana to marry him, felt deliciously right.

Chapter Nine

Max heard the gate to the cemetery clanging and the north wind blowing steadily. He crossed the yard and entered the small family plot, latching the wrought iron gate behind him. He removed his hat as he walked among the gravestones.

He needed a respite from the company. The Ferris girls wanted his opinion on everything. Lady Angela constantly made sheep eyes at him and Lady Malmsbury had continued to mistake his room for hers the last three nights. After escorting her back to her bedroom without staying, Max would have thought she would have gotten the message.

Mostly, his change of heart last night when holding Roxana's hand in the dance alarmed him. She did not fit into his plans and he did not know that he was overreacting to a strong desire to bed her.

Slapping his hat against his thigh, Max walked toward the newer graves. His ears stung with the cold. Pausing at his mother's grave, he whispered a prayer. He barely remembered her. His father's grave came next. Then his two brothers lay side-by-side in the cold ground. Imagining them so still and robbed of life after too short of lives made his throat ache.

The gate clanged behind him and he turned. Roxana wove her way among the tombstones, her head down. She read the markers and touched her gloved hand to the tombstone of his father's sister who had died in infancy.

She rounded the corner and drew up short. She looked at the recent row of graves and then up at him. "Am I intruding?"

"No. The gate was unlatched; I came to shut it." He did not come to the graves often. He found it still too difficult. If he did not look upon the markers he could think of the long silence as merely the gap between letters that happened when his brothers adventured around the world.

Max had never left England; his duties to the estate prevented lengthy trips abroad. How he had looked forward to those letters describing places he would never see.

"I saw you without a hat. I thought you could use this gift early." She reached under her cloak and drew out a muffler the color of burnished ivory. She drew up as she realized his hat was in his hand.

"My hat does not keep my neck warm. If you would, please." He held out his hat for her to hold.

She took it, while handing him the folded rectangle of fabric.

He wound the long ribbed silk scarf around his neck, pulling the edges up to cover his stinging ears. The scarf was thicker and much warmer than he expected. The lengthwise stitches gave it enough substance to stand high. "Thank you, Miss Winston."

Roxana read the markers as the first flakes of snow hurtled down. "Your brothers?"

"This was Samuel. He died in Aboukir. And this is Alexander. He died at Copenhagen." Words seemed so inadequate.

"Would you tell me about them?" she said softly.

He looked at the graves. "They both fell in battle. Samuel lingered a while, but we did not know soon enough to get to him." Max had been preparing to go the continent when the news arrived that Samuel had expired. Then their sealed coffins had arrived, dashing any hopes he had of mistake.

He could feel her watching him and he wanted to say so much more, yet his throat felt closed.

Roxana sidled closer to him as if seeking his warmth or offering hers. Yet he kept thinking how cold his brothers must be, lying in their wooden boxes in the frozen ground.

"It must be extraordinarily difficult to have lost brothers," she said. "I have been incredibly lucky to have all my sisters and brother hale and hearty."

"They were both . . ." his voice trailed off. She offered sympathy, not a suggestion that his brothers were not healthy. Good health was little impediment to a bullet. "They were both so full of life. It is hard to believe they're gone. I'm sorry you did not meet them."

Roxana glanced up at him. "You are afraid Thomas will suffer the same fate?"

Max's first inclination was to deny any fear, but he was deathly afraid of just that. When each of his brothers died it was as if a piece of him had withered and blackened too. His own role in their choices haunted him and bore down on him with the weight of a medieval press. "Yes."

"Have you explained your fears to Thomas?"

"Miss Winston, you do not understand."

"Oh, I think I do. As the oldest it is ever my feeling that I must shelter my siblings from every ill wind that blows. Accepting that I cannot protect them from every true thing in the world has been difficult for me."

Again Max wondered about her family life. She said so little about it. Yet he knew she had not offered advice that led to death. Alexander, at least, had considered taking a living their father had open, but had really wanted a chance to serve under his hero Nelson. Unable to imagine his wild younger brother as a clergyman, Max had urged him to that course. The living could be held until Alexander decided if he wanted it after experiencing the world.

"I know you want to protect Thomas, even though he has charged me with dissuading you from being so adamant with his learning the estate. Honestly, my sympathies lie more with your position."

Max clasped his hands behind his back. The wind riffled his hair, but to hold it down was futile. Snowflakes fell against his skin and hair, then quickly melted. "Do you think I am being too harsh with him?"

"I think you are teaching him as you were taught. You are not impatient, nor are you unreasonable. You have high expectations of him, but not impossible expectations. I believe that Thomas feels the rules have changed without notice."

Max gestured toward the graves. The rules had changed. Death had changed all their lives. "When did Thomas tell you this?"

"When we were decorating the ballroom." Miss Winston turned her head back toward the graves, her bonnet hiding her expression from him. Her voice was evenly modulated, not shrill or accusatory.

"I hope I am not too forward, but I promised Thomas I would speak with you."

Had she watched Max for a moment to catch him alone? So far he had only seen her employ such tactics for Gregory. "And I thought you must have been laying in wait for Mr. Breedon."

Roxana's head dipped forward. "I was, but I believe he did not walk today, as is his habit."

Tenseness had crept into her voice, negating Max's disappointment that Roxana was not watching for him.

Max reached out and put his arm around her shoulders. She felt rigid under his touch. He told himself he offered her only comfort, but he suspected he sought solace for himself.

"I'm sorry, I did not mean to digress. I did suggest to Thomas that he speak to you himself, but he declined. He said you would not listen to him."

"I listen."

"Yes, I believe you do, but have you given Thomas the full measure of your thoughts?"

"I've told him my intention is to keep him my heir," said Max.

Roxana moved forward and brushed snow from Alexander's tombstone. The snow fell all around her, dusting her blue cloak with white specks. "Do you suppose your father yearned for a military life?"

"Why?"

She turned and looked back at Max. "He encouraged three of his sons to follow the drum, did he not? Would not at least one son normally be encouraged to become a member of the clergy? And a third perhaps encouraged to engage in civil service? Many positions in the government are drawn by appointment, are they not?"

"I do not think he foresaw this outcome. And I think my brother's deaths took the will to live out of him. I will not have this future for Thomas." His own role in encouraging their choices figured more prominently in his mind. They had trusted him. That they had to take employment while he, as the oldest son, had everything was a crushing weight he found hard to bear.

Had his father planted the enthusiasm for military careers in his brothers' minds? Even in his, for even as he knew he was the fortunate one, he'd envied his brothers' carefree military careers.

Roxana turned around and walked toward him. He wanted more than anything to pull her to him, just to feel alive. But that felt blasphemous in this place.

"I suppose it is small comfort to think they are all in a better place," she said softly. Reaching out from under the folds of her cloak, she put her gloved hand on his sleeve.

"Indeed." As far as he could see, the gentle rolling hills and the massive house on the hill behind them was his. There was no place better than this.

Her touch heated him, provided barrier to the chill wind. A snowflake fell on her dark lashes and clung for a moment. The cold had brightened her cheeks and he felt caught in a moment out of time. He could hear his brothers urging him to quit being a stick-in-the-mud and have fun. Kiss the girl.

But his place was to do the right thing. A duke could not go around kissing unmarried girls without them thinking that he would offer for them. After looking at the graves, he knew he could not marry. It was a fleeting fancy that he would not spend the rest of his life alone. His duty lay in grooming Thomas to take over the title and estate.

Roxana deserved better than a dalliance that would lead to nothing. And his behavior in the kissing bower had been beyond the bounds of acceptable. Nothing good ever came from incorrect behavior.

Another snowflake fell on her cheek and he wanted to touch his lips to the moisture. "We should return to the house, Roxy."

She took a step back and smiled. "Ah, but it is so beautiful out here. I love snow. Ah, and there is Mr. Breedon on his constitutional after all. You should of course go back to the house, and I will just say hello to Mr. Breedon."

She skipped toward the gate, excitement coloring her eyes. He watched her run toward Mr. Breedon with all the enthusiasm of a child. She scooped up a handful of snow to throw just before she reached him. And Max was left behind with the dead and buried.

After Roxana's loosely packed snowball hit him on the shoulder, Mr. Breedon turned and scowled at her. With his round face he resembled a petulant child more than an angry man. Hardly the expression to strike fear in a miscreant. She could not imagine a situation where she would ever fear Mr. Breedon.

Roxana had actually meant to miss. She laughed anyway and stepped forward, allowing her legs to slide out from under her. The heavy wet snow was not so deep that it provided cushion for her fall, and she was throwing the game before she even started. She suspected Max would provide a worthy opponent in a snow fight, and she would never have to pull back. That is, if he could be persuaded to relax.

"Do you not love snow, Mr. Breedon?" Her thin cotton dress sopped up the moisture like a sponge.

"No."

Roxana scrambled upright, making sure that Mr. Breedon was allowed a healthy glimpse of her ankles. Did he even notice? He had not stepped forward to help her to her feet.

"I am sorry, then." She brushed snow from his shoulder. "I will contain my enthusiasm."

"My apologies, Miss Winston. I fear that I am quite worried about the snow."

"The snow?"

"Yes, I am afraid this snowfall may make the roads impassable."

Roxana slid her gloved hand into the crook of Mr. Breedon's elbow. Why was he concerned about the snow? "The party has just started. Surely you do not plan to leave soon?"

"I hate feeling as if I am trapped in a place and cannot leave."

"If the snow delays your departure, then I cannot be dissuaded from liking it even more."

Mr. Breedon shuddered. "Well, frozen ground makes better traveling than mud, so it may not be such a bad event after all."

They walked along the snow-blanketed path as the flakes fell all around them, creating a veil between them and the whitening countryside. At least the trees they walked between blocked the wind. Although she was starting to feel the sting of the cold where moisture had seeped through the darned areas in her glove, and holding Mr. Breedon's arm meant her thin cloak was open, allowing the frigid air to penetrate the wet muslin of her gown. Perhaps falling down had not been such a good idea, and it had failed to draw Mr. Breedon closer, as was her intent.

"I think the snow quite beautiful," said Roxana.

Mr. Breedon's lips flattened to that simple slash in his face. "Makes my knee hurt."

"Was your injury from a riding accident?" inquired Roxana.

Mr. Breedon shook his head. "My phaeton overturned."

"It must be perfectly terrible to have such a thing occur. I am not entirely sure those high carriages are safe. You are quite brave to drive one."

"I was not driving," squawked Mr. Breedon. "They must have wanted to cause me injury."

Roxana was not quite sure who they were.

"Well, I am truly sorry for your difficulties. I wish I could ease your pain."

Mr. Breedon stopped abruptly and swung around in front of her on the path. "Miss Winston, are you my friend?"

The question took her by surprise. "I should hope so."

He screwed up his mouth. "My mama thinks you are offering false coin because . . ."

Roxana's heart pounded heavily in her chest. One misstep and her chances of bringing Mr. Breedon to a place where she could ask for a financial settlement would crumble. What if he asked to marry her without compromising her? What if he held himself to the rigid bounds of propriety?

"Because you are well heeled?" She finished for him and looked down at her toes, toes she could

barely feel, which was blessed relief from the stinging they had been doing earlier.

"That is usually why women toss their handkerchiefs in my direction."

"Yes, but I do like you, Gregory. You are very kind
and . . . and . . . gentle. Mr. Scullin and his grace
treat me quite differently. They frighten me at
times. I am very comfortable with you. What proof
could I offer to you my affection is genuine?"
Roxana had a clue, but she could not suggest it.

"My mama says something is havey-cavey about
you being here at the party without your parents."

Roxana took a leap of faith. "Yes, but you do not
always agree with your parents' assessments."

He stared at her as if unable to make up his
mind. Roxana stood her ground although she shivered in earnest. A cold spot grew in her heart. She
feared that self-absorbed Mr. Breedon actually had
started to care for her, and what she intended to
do would wound him. Even though she would
treat a monetary settlement as a loan to be repaid,
he would see her actions as a betrayal.

"I do hope we are friends, Mr. Breedon. I would
not be averse to being more than friends, but I
have been given to understand that I would not
meet your parents' expectations. I quite understand that, although your parents could not find
fault with my lineage or my c-connections." She gestured to the house as the wind resumed and blew
right through her.

"B-b-because I have f-f-four sisters my p-p-por-
tion will be small." Her teeth chattered and she
could no longer stop them. Her portion would be
nonexistent, but Mr. Breedon did not need to
know that.

"Are you cold, Miss Winston?"

Nearly frozen solid, but at least he noticed. She nodded her head.

Max had slid his arm around her shoulders, or he would have seen her back inside. Mr. Breedon stared at her as if he had never been confronted with such a dilemma.

"C-c-could you warm me?" she asked.

He grabbed her arms and began rubbing vigorously up and down. Roxana was impatient with his obtuseness and she stepped forward, touching their chests together. Finally, he wrapped his arms around her and pulled her against his warm body. She settled her gloved hands at his side, barely feeling her fingers.

"Oh, thank you," she whispered. Even through his clothes she could feel warmth. She tucked her head into the crook of his neck, her nose touching his chin.

"You are like ice," said Mr. Breedon.

"I am sorry, although I feel much warmer already."

He rubbed her back fiercely. She would have asked him to be gentler, but she needed him to make an advance before she turned into an ice sculpture, before he realized he should be leading her back to the house, before she began to think he did not like women.

Finally, his stroking changed and Roxana took that moment to lift her head and meet his eyes. Their lips were only an inch apart and he was not so much taller than her that he would have to bend over. Roxana stared at his milky white face and his little eyes and she lowered her lashes for fear he would see her assessment for the coldhearted thing it was. If he did not kiss her now, she knew he would never be persuaded to compromise her.

Finally his lips nipped at hers. Roxana tried not to pull away or resist. And she was acutely aware of her lack of engagement. With Max her heart had pounded and her knees had gone weak; with Gregory she felt only chilled and detached.

She tightened her arms around him and waited . . . waited . . . would he not do it again? Her eyes fluttered open just as Mr. Breedon was plunging forward for another kiss. His face hit hers with the speed of a galloping horse, and Roxana wondered if teeth could bruise. But she had to concentrate hard to keep her teeth from chattering. Lord knew biting him would not further her cause.

Mr. Breedon folded both his arms around her back, and in her half-frozen state she tried to convince herself that his embrace was pleasant even if his kiss was not. Oh stars, Max's lips had felt so much better, firm, where Gregory's were nonexistent. And it was as if he intended to squeeze the life out of her in his bear hug.

Mrs. Porter had told her that men were pretty much interchangeable when it came to matters of intimacy, but oh she was so wrong, thought Roxana as she pushed at Gregory's shoulders.

Max leaned against the wrought iron fence, the cold of the bars seeping through his greatcoat. Yet as he watched Roxana charm and cajole Mr. Breedon, Max knew he needed to keep her in his sights. That was the trouble with having an unchaperoned guest; no mother or father would raise the alarm if Roxana was gone too long.

When Breedon kissed her, Max slammed his hat low on his head and trudged toward them. How could she? When the taste of her burned in his mouth, the feel of her curves imprinted on his brain, and the sight of her blue eyes made his insides turn to mush, how could she throw herself at that overgrown boy?

Because Breedon would perchance marry her, whispered a devil on Max's shoulder, and he could not. Not if he wanted to keep Thomas as his heir. Her scheming and manipulation bothered him, but she seemed to like Mr. Breedon. Had Max not watched her face light up as she saw he was out walking? Could she really care about the lout?

The snow came down in clumps and the wind shifted over it, filling in the indentations of their footfalls, erasing the hollow where she had fallen—deliberately, Max assumed. God, for one of her tricks on him, he'd show her what a real man would do. Yet, Breedon seemed to be giving her a good demonstration of a far-too-intimate kiss, without the thin excuse of mistletoe hanging overhead.

Roxana pushed at Breedon's shoulders and a feeling Max would otherwise call relief surged through him.

"Mr. Breedon, Miss Winston," he called, still a hundred yards away. "I do believe the weather is turning quite nasty."

Breedon did not release Roxana as Max had expected. Instead he clumsily patted her and looked around her. His round face glowed with excitement. "Miss Winston has grown quite cold."

Not the usual reaction of a woman being kissed.

Perhaps Max could garner joy from that. He needed joy to temper the black wish in his soul to offer to meet Mr. Breedon at dawn. Not that he had ever seen Gregory roll out of bed before noon. "I daresay it would be best to return inside, then," said Max.

As he neared them, he saw that the redness of Roxana's cheeks had faded to a pale waxy white. She shivered. "Y-y-yesss," she said, backing away from Breedon.

Max yanked loose the buttons on his greatcoat and shrugged out of it, draping it about Roxana's shoulders. He wrapped the muffler she had given him around her face up to her eyes.

"Oh, I say," said Breedon.

Roxana did not say anything. Max steered her up the slope and over the park, directly toward the house. The footpaths were covered anyway. "Cannot have one of the guests frozen," said Max.

The wind kicked up around them and Max felt the bite of it through his day coat. His overcoat dragged through the snowy ground as Roxana stumbled forward. What kind of footwear was she wearing?

He knew she was warmer when she protested half the way to the house that he should take his coat back. Mr. Breedon trudged along behind them, looking disgruntled.

"I will be fine, Miss Winston. My clothes are warmer than yours."

Finally he whisked her up the stairs and into the front hall. "Fire in the library?" he asked the footman taking his hat and gloves.

"Yes, your grace."

"Stoke it up and send for Miss Winston's maid."

Max trundled Roxana toward the room, paying little heed to her muffled protests.

Roxana drew off the scarf and uncovered her mouth. "Thank you, Mr. Breedon," she said at the doorway. "I enjoyed myself so much."

Gregory mumbled something and headed for the stairs. His face was a picture of surprise, disappointment and excitement all rolled together.

"He lets you turn into an icicle and you are thanking him?" muttered Max. With his hands on her shoulders, he wove her between the leather chairs, sofas and reading tables of the room. Her cloak felt ridiculously thin, and, he could see from the darker splotches of blue, quite damp. Stopping a few feet from the fireplace he turned her and reached for the ties under her chin. After casting aside the muffler, he undid the cloak and then her bonnet, then tossed the items toward a chair.

He stepped to the side, allowing the footman who had followed them into the room access to the fire. The man silently added wood until the small flames snapped and crackled and roared up the chimney with a rush of a large blaze.

Max reached for her hands and stripped off the gloves that clung to her hands with dampness. Her wince made him gentle his movements.

The footman scooped up her cloak and bonnet—a silly little thing that hardly provided protection from the weather, but by the same token did not impede a gentleman's kiss with its tiny brim. "Anything else, your grace?"

"Just send her maid, thank you."

The footman bowed, then closed the door. Max should have told him to leave it open.

Max took her bared hands between his. They felt like ice. He rubbed his hands over hers, trying to bring blood back into them. "For God's sake, do you mean to freeze to death just to be with him?"

"It was the dampness, I think. I had not realized it would snow. And I did not dress properly for the bad weather."

"No, you did not." Max pushed her palms toward the fire.

"I really had not intended to be outside for more than a few minutes."

"But you could not bypass an opportunity to waylay Breedon?" Max shoved a footstool to within a few feet of the fire. "Sit."

She sat on it, her blue eyes following him. "I have been colder before."

He was relieved to see color returning to her face, although she held out her ashen gray hands toward the fire. He knelt down and lifted the edge of her skirt.

"Max!" She drew her feet back under the white muslin of her gown.

"Take off your shoes."

As he suspected, she was not wearing boots, but thin-soled slippers meant for indoors.

Impatient at her silent refusal, he reached under her skirt and slid off her shoes, then reached up to strip down her damp stockings. He swallowed hard as he realized he was undressing her. Her toes were red and adorable, cold but not showing signs of frostbite. Her foot cradled in his hand, he could not bring himself to let go.

"I hope you enjoyed his attentions," Max said.

He looked up at her face and her hair was mussed from his hasty removal of her bonnet, and her blue eyes luminous in her face. She looked like a woman who had been thoroughly kissed. Only not by him.

She shook her head but said, "He was only trying to warm me."

"Roxy, you cannot go about inviting men to kiss you."

"I have only ever invited one man to such liberties."

And that wasn't him. But as he looked at her and continued to hold her foot in his hand, he wanted to be the only man she thought about no matter who kissed her.

He lowered his eyes to her collarbone, right before him. The muslin of her day gown dipped only an inch below the indentation at the center of her throat, yet the sight was obscenely intoxicating, especially since a necklace with a sapphire pendant hung there. He had a vague memory of grabbing for the charm as his mother leaned over him.

Before he knew what he was doing, he touched the pendant. Roxana's chest rose beneath his fingertips. "I'm glad you've worn these."

His fingers slid along the edge of the chain and sparks flew down his fingers, down his arm and spread through his body, like a rich brandy.

He should give Roxana a drink, he thought. That was the right thing to do, but her breast was just below the heel of his hand, and she was breathing so deeply that she just might close the gap between his hand and her flesh. Yet as he thought of curling his hand around her curves, his fingers slid lower on the soft bare skin below her delicate collarbone.

Her lips parted and beckoned him. She had such a soft, welcoming mouth. So sweet, and the space between them was evaporating. His hand pushed closer as if he would make sure one deep heave of her chest would bring them in contact. Her breath wafted across his lips and he could no longer think beyond how he wanted to touch her, hold her, make love to her.

Chapter
Ten

"Do not ever do that again," said Fanny as she glared at Scully.

Scully looked up from the newspaper and realized the drawing room was empty except for the two of them. After the late ball last night, the day had been desultory, with most of the company lounging around. They must have disappeared to dress for dinner. Until this moment Fanny had been distant, as if their kiss had never happened.

"Do what?" he asked calmly.

Anger at least showed a bit of passion on Fanny's part.

"Do what you did last night." She paced away from him.

"What was that, love?" asked Scully as if he'd done nothing of consequence.

Fanny stopped, swirled around and stared at him, blinking as if uncertain if her kiss was so easily forgotten or that he did not understand the implications of kissing a widow so thoroughly or so publicly. Then again, he did not want Fanny ringing a peal over his head.

Scully stood and outstretched his arms.

Fanny resumed her pacing. "You cannot go around doing such things in company. Everyone now thinks that I am your paramour."

"So it is my failure to be your lover in truth that offends?"

"No!"

"Oh, so I should kiss you only in private, love?" There had been a moment under the mistletoe when she sagged against him. If she would just let him in.

"No," she whispered.

"Ah, are you saying, I should never kiss you again?"

"Yes." Her shoulders slumped, but relief ran clear in her voice.

"I cannot contemplate such a desolate future—" He took a long step toward her. "—and deny myself so heady a pleasure. I am afraid I cannot grant your request."

She turned to face him, her hands on her hips. "It was not a request."

He took a determined stride toward her. Fanny's anger crumpled into an expression of alarm. As he neared her, she squealed and ran toward the door. He caught her before she had gone four steps. Laughter bubbled under his breath, but he held back. Fanny was not yet in a state to appreciate the humor of the situation.

He caught her around the waist, and she struggled to free herself, but not with true conviction. She shoved at his arm across her stomach, but did not spin out of his grasp. He did not hold her so tightly that she could not break free if she really was of a mind to. He put his other hand on her shoulder, stroking lightly.

"Come, my pretty Fanny. You would not deny me your sweet kisses. I should pine away and expire without them."

"You destroy my dignity." She stopped struggling.

Scully pulled her tighter against him. He could hardly kiss her when her back was turned to him. "By making a public display of my affection for you?"

She stilled. "Dev, please, I beg of you, do not toy with me."

Scully dropped his arms. "I have never, not now or in the past, toyed with you."

After a moment's hesitation she stepped away, then slowly turned. "I am a duchess. I must behave accordingly."

"You have been listening too much to Max." He stepped forward. "Come, love, do not pretend that I was the only one to feel anything last night."

She ducked her head. "I cannot bear being hurt again, Dev."

He tucked both his hands around her jaw and lifted her face up. "I would do nothing to hurt you, love."

"But—"

"Shhhh. It was not I that hurt you, but our situation. You are free to follow the dictates of your heart now. You are no longer married to an old man."

"I loved him," she protested.

Scully could not hold back his wince. "Yes, but do you feel nothing for your poor Scully anymore?"

Her eyes shut, and she shook her head ever so

slightly. Had he waited all these years for nothing? The looks they'd exchanged across crowded ballrooms and theaters were just acknowledgment of a guilty secret on her part. It was as if an ax had been tossed into his chest.

He leaned forward to brush his lips across hers, just once. The petal softness of her mouth burned into his brain and scorched him with need.

He pulled away before his anguish bled through. It never did for a man to make complaints of pain, and he never did unless they were false. It never did to take more than was offered, and Fanny offered him nothing. He walked to the window and stared out at the falling snow.

"Scully?"

He raised a finger to the frost on the glass. "Ah, I am doomed to ever wait for you. Alas, I had such high hopes when I was installed in your old bedchamber."

"I need to change for dinner."

He swiveled around. "Might I offer assistance?"

She backed toward the door. "No." The look of horror that crossed her face wiped out his hopes.

"You know where to find me if you change your mind," he said lightly, as if he wasn't bleeding inside.

Max's fingers against Roxana's skin made her tremble. His palm was just a hairsbreadth from her breast. He knew how close he was to touching her; she had watched his eyes drop to her heaving breast. Caught in this mesmerizing web of fascination, she did not know what she wanted him to do. Part of her wanted that intimate touch, but she feared it too.

All she knew was that her blood rushed through her veins, making her fingers tingle and heating her more powerfully than the fire. His mouth was nearly upon hers, and the door clicked behind them.

Max released her bare foot and stood, their near kiss aborted. Roxana sucked in air as if it had been in short supply. Max had not even kissed her, yet she felt as if he'd nearly ravished her. She felt on the edge of wonderful.

"You sent for me, your grace?" The girl who had been assigned as Roxana's maid bobbed a curtsy.

"Your mistress needs fresh stockings and slippers, if you would be so good as to fetch them and a shawl for her." Max picked up the stockings he had removed and draped them against the fire screen. Steam rose from the material. "Leave the door open," he said, leaning his arms against the mantelpiece.

As soon as the maid left, Max moved across the room. Roxana stared into the fire, wondering what had just happened, or not happened. Had Max intended to kiss her, or was he just employing a trick to warm her?

He returned with a deep-bowled glass. "Here, drink this brandy. It will help."

"Do you mean to ply me with spirits?" she asked, taking the glass of reddish brown liquid.

He met her eyes then. His expression was that of a man suffering regrets. Roxana lowered her gaze to her drink, but she did not see that. She saw Max.

His hair was damp and disordered from the outdoors; his skin was a pale gold. He stood tall, his strength visible in the breadth of his shoulders. In one sense he made her feel small and fragile, in another sense she knew he could impose his will on her with physical force—but would he?

Roxana took a hesitant sip. The liquid burned down her throat, yet it was not unpleasant. Thoughts of her father's excessive drinking swirled in Roxana's head. Strong spirits could unleash his temper without warning.

She drew her toes back underneath her gown and held out the glass. "Thank you; I do not want this."

"Do you dislike it?"

She shook her head.

"Drink it, then. It will warm you," Max coaxed.

"I am warm enough." Roxana leaned forward and set the glass on the floor. She wrapped her arms under her legs.

Max tossed himself into the chair that he had robbed of the footstool. The leather creaked and the fire snapped in front of her. Any chill she might have felt was long gone, except the chill in her heart.

Out of the corner of her eye, she could see Max leaning forward, his elbows on his knees, and he twisted a ring on his pinkie.

"How well do you like Breedon?" he asked.

"I like him a lot." Actually that was no longer a lie. She recognized Gregory expected to be coddled and his comfort was of paramount importance to him, but unlike her father he would never beat a woman if she did meet his needs, realistic or unrealistic.

"Smashing." Max leaned forward, picked up her glass and drained the liquid.

Roxana could almost imagine the taste of the brandy on Max's lips. Gregory was nearly a perfect man for her: kind, averse to violence, and he did not drink, but Max made her pulse leap.

The heat from the fire scorched through her, Roxana could feel her skin turning red from her proximity to the flames. She wanted to scoot the stool back, but that would put her within touching distance of Max.

"Are you getting warmer?" he asked.

"I am quite warm." The heat of the fire made her skin hot.

"Alexander loved snow. He raved about the snow in New England, that there were drifts taller than a man's head."

Was Max attempting to tell her about his brothers since she had asked at the graveside? Her heart went out to him. "I imagine that if we have this snow at home, my sisters and brother are having snow fights."

"My brothers always had me at a disadvantage. They would pair against me."

"Did they trounce you?" she asked.

"Never. I could not allow it."

"Oh, I always allow myself bested, especially with the younger ones." Thinking of Mr. Breedon's reaction, she imagined he did not have the same warm memories of snowball fights. "Perhaps it is different for men. Mr. Breedon did not like being hit with a snowball."

Max's voice changed, became tighter, less warm. "I can speak with him, if you will."

"And what would you say?" Roxana spun around on the footstool.

"Since he has demonstrated overt familiarity, I would ask his intentions."

Roxana watched as Max plucked at his sleeve,

removing lint that wasn't there. Was he avoiding meeting her eyes?

"To what purpose?"

"Roxy, you are here without a parent or guardian and the responsibility for your welfare falls to me. I would know that he is treating you honorably, and tell him to desist if he has nefarious motives or will object to your circumstances. I can insist that he does the right thing."

Roxana looked down at her stinging hands. Just as her mother had said, the damage to the reputation of an unprotected young woman staying in his house would prompt Max's insistence upon an honorable course.

But she would need Max to save his talking for later, after she had been compromised. And she did not need the added fear of Max's reprisals in Gregory's mind if her plan was to work. "I should rather you did not." She lifted her head.

Max gave her a wry smile. "Do you not trust me to remain neutral in my conversations with Breedon?"

She shrugged and looked again at her hands. She should not have risked her hands. They would be her livelihood, but time was running out for snaring Mr. Breedon in her trap. "I believe you would strive to do the right thing, but I cannot think that Mr. Breedon is yet prepared to make an offer."

Max picked up the brandy glass and stared into the few drops remaining in the bottom. Max tipped the glass and drained the last of the liquid. Then he stood. "Very well, I shall restrain myself. If you are well, Miss Winston, there are guests I need to attend."

He sounded so resigned that Roxana asked, "Do you enjoy having these house parties?"

He paused. "I take a great deal of satisfaction from them."

"But do you enjoy them? Both you and Fanny spend a great amount of time making sure that things go smoothly, that food and entertainment is available every minute . . . saving guests from disaster."

"Only you, Roxy." Max stopped as if he might say more, then thought better of it. He shook his head and left the room as her maid appeared at the door with dry stockings and slippers.

Max ran into Scully as he exited the library.

"I need a drink," said Scully.

"My room," answered Max, clapping a hand on his friend's shoulder and turning him. "Miss Winston is in a state of *deshabille* in the library."

"My, my, you make fast work of her virtue."

"I did nothing to her virtue; she was nearly frozen and I . . . removed her shoes." Oh, God, he wanted to remove so much more. "Her maid is with her."

Darkness crowded Max's soul, but for the maid's interruption he would have leaped over the bounds of propriety. He could not believe he had such a shaky hold on his self-control.

"Her shoes? That's all?" asked Scully. "I do not think you should give her up to Breedon so easily."

"I cannot marry her. I want Thomas to have the title. She cannot stay content with Breedon long." Max was appalled that he'd just voiced an intention to cuckold Breedon. "Forget that."

Scully raised an eyebrow, but forbore saying anything.

"I did not mean it," said Max.

It was too much to hope that Scully would hold his tongue long. "Yes, you did."

"Breedon has what she needs in a marriage and I do not."

"And that is?"

"Blunt."

"You are—"

"Wealthy, yes, but my wealth is in land. You have not been here for many years. Look around, do you see anything the same?"

Scully stared at Max. "Fanny has replaced everything, hasn't she? How much does she spend?"

"Never mind," said Max. It was not just the ornaments of the house that had cast him into debt. Alexander had gambling debts and Samuel accumulated substantial nursing and hospital bills and debts of a rather mysterious sort before dying of his wounds. "Not all of it was Fanny's decorating. My father was a spendthrift too, plus my brothers left obligations. We need to dress for dinner."

"Fanny hates me," Scully said as he ascended the stairs.

"She does not hate you," answered Max.

"Yes, she does. She says I destroy her dignity. I probably cannot afford her either."

"Well, she has never set much store in dignity before now."

Max pushed open his bedroom door and saw red hair. Did Lady Malmsbury know any boundaries?

"For God's sake, what are you doing here now?" he exploded.

"We'll drink later, old boy," said Scully, slinking toward his own door.

Lady Malmsbury turned around and pouted. "I do not understand why you are ignoring me, Max."

He'd had enough. He marched forward and grabbed Eliza's arm and propelled her out of the room. "I have guests to consider, my lady," he muttered between clenched teeth. "I regret that I do not have leisure to be with you now." He shut the door in her surprised face.

Why would she not get the message? He pounded on the connecting door to Scully's room.

Max needed to change rooms, but as Scully opened the door with his eyebrow quirked, Max realized that switching rooms within the suite would not be enough of a move. Lady Malmsbury would figure it out soon enough if she found Scully in his room. Where was the last place she would expect to find him? Better yet, who was the last person she would want to find herself in bed with?

"You are getting a new suite mate. You might want to lock the door." Interesting that the lock was on the woman's side of the master suite. Max had never thought about that before.

"Do not put Malmsy in here," Scully warned.

"God, no." Max had a better plan.

Fanny sat at her dressing table and stared at herself in the mirror. In the lamplight she did not perhaps look so old. The tiny wrinkles at the corners of her eyes did not show and she could not feel them with her fingertips.

Did Scully truly want her? Or was she a diversion because no one else present attracted him?

After dinner, he had stood behind her chair

and put his hand on her shoulder. The gesture was possessive and familiar, the kind a husband would make, not just a lover's caress.

Then he had gone and pulled Roxana from Mr. Breedon.

Fanny bit her lip, feeling the rise of jealousy, but watch as she might she could detect none of Dev's flirtation occurring between the two. In fact, he had been quite sober. Not the animated charmer she knew. She missed his compliments even though she no longer believed them.

Max had watched Dev and Miss Winston take a turn about the room, but had not made any effort to join them.

After dinner, the servants had set out card tables and a token effort at charades for the younger set was made.

Feeling restless, Fanny lifted the shielded night candle from her dressing table and went to the hall.

Her feet, almost of their own volition, followed the familiar path to her former bedroom. She stood at the door and asked herself what on earth she was doing. The wind howled outside and she shivered.

She turned and scurried toward her room. A door clicked behind her. Quickening her steps she headed for the safety of her room.

"Fanny," came the low call behind her. The rough burr of his voice made her shiver.

She spun around. In his shirtsleeves, Scully leaned against his doorframe. He pushed the door of her old bedroom open wide, the invitation clear.

What had she been thinking? The darkness might conceal a multitude of deficiencies, but it provided no barrier to touch. And Scully liked to touch. She took a step backward.

Her dressing gown was voluminous, very matronly. "I need to get to bed. Tomorrow, with Christmas Eve festivities, will be quite busy."

Scully's grin flashed. He walked out into the passageway, just a few steps from her, and whispered, "I have a bed in there."

Joining him was a lovely idea until the reality of it set in. "Sleep. I need to sleep."

"Yes, I am good for that too." He folded his arms across his chest. He swayed toward her, tilting his head down. "If that is what you *really* want."

At one time he would not have bypassed the opportunity to touch her when they were alone. His lack of desire enhanced her fears that she had long past left behind her attractive years. Perhaps the lack of relations with her husband in his later years had not been just because of his age.

She took a step backwards and an emotion flashed in Dev's eyes.

"I would not wish to offend your dignity, your grace."

Fanny looked down.

He held out his hand. "Come, love, the snow is falling outside and the wind is whipping. To have you with me would warm my soul."

As she stared at his bare palm, Fanny felt her heart sinking. He was asking for companionship. Was she no longer a figure for passion and pleasure? Did she want her relationship with Scully to be about calm comfort, devoid of fervor? What would they have if they no longer shared the intense attraction that had prompted her to violate her marriage vows?

"Come, my beautiful duchess, I want to hear you laugh again," whispered Scully.

She detested Max's treating her like a child, yet

she hated Scully for treating her like a mature woman. She wanted Scully to sweep her off her feet as if she had no mind of her own, yet he left the choice to her. He would not push her or use too much persuasion. The trouble was she wanted him to push and charm and convince her that she should be so ridiculously foolish as to sleep with him again.

She wavered, uncertain of which way her feet would move.

After arranging for the snow sleds to be hauled out of the coach house, Max climbed the stairs to the drawing room. As soon as he entered, the Misses Ferris ran up to him, each grabbing one of his arms. "Have you seen the snow, your grace?"

He nodded. The snow had continued to fall all through the night and morning, but the wind had calmed down. Fanny had planned caroling tonight for Christmas Eve festivities, but he suspected they would just have to carol each other inside.

One sister bounced up, while the other tugged him down, skewing him lopsided. "Her grace said you might arrange for sleighing this afternoon," said Miss Ferris.

"Oh, do say you shall," said Miss Charlotte Ferris, the younger sister by six minutes. "It shall be just the thing."

"Of course I shall, if it will please you both," replied Max.

Scully arched an eyebrow at him from where he sat sharing a book with Lady Angela DuMass. Scully did not seem to be reading, but merely waiting for the indication of the time to turn the page, while watching Fanny.

Max let his gaze skim over all the eligible young women. The Misses Ferris were cute enough with their matching button noses and heart-shaped faces. Lady Angela's fortune and breeding were enough to counterbalance the sharp length of her nose. Miss Lambert was demure enough with her doe-like brown eyes and rich chestnut hair.

These young women were the best that Fanny could assemble on short notice. They all seemed so insipid. Then there was Roxana, who could alarm him to no end, yet he could allow himself to relax with her because she had no expectations of him and welcomed honesty. She also welcomed Mr. Breedon's attentions, and Max could not help but think she had managed to force her affections to follow her less-than-noble ambitions.

The Breedons had cash and income; Max had wealth that was tied up in his vast holdings. A blackness curdled in his soul. If he was even to consider marriage, he too needed to marry a woman with a large dowry.

Max glanced over at his stepmother where she sat chatting with the older women of the group. The two Misses Ferris talked across him, hardly needing more than an occasional nod from him. Lady Malmsbury turned in his direction and gave him a dirty look. Had she attempted to find him in his room last night? He tossed a smile in her direction.

"I am sure you will not wish to go sleighing, since you despise the cold, Lady Malmsbury. Breedon, Scully, Lord Hampton, and Mr. Allensworth: are all of you gentlemen up to driving sleighs? Everyone who wants to brave the cold should assemble in the front hall in one hour."

The snow continued to fall as single horses were harnessed to the sleighs. The bells on their reins jingled as the grooms led the animals into their traces. Roxana had not yet joined the bundled and scarfed group of the younger members of the house party waiting for the sleighs by the drive. Max was tempted to send her back inside if she did appear. He did not need her freezing to death, even though the sleighs were well equipped with lap robes and heated bricks for the sleigh riders' feet.

The door opened and Roxana appeared with Julia and Thomas by her side. The three of them scrambled down the newly swept stairs with Breedon huffing down behind them.

As they joined the group at the bottom of the stairs, Max counted heads. Scully was noticeably absent, so only four men were present. Each would have to drive a sleigh continuously.

The Misses Ferris jumped up and down, clamoring to go first.

Roxana knelt at the foot of the stairs, checking the fastenings of Thomas's coat and rewrapping his scarf. Thomas tolerated her fussing with barely contained impatience.

"Do stop. I can barely move," protested Thomas.

"You will be glad of my wrapping when the wind is in your face," Roxana cautioned.

She turned to Julia, who smiled brightly at Roxana's care. Max went still, achingly aware of the loss of his own mother and that Fanny had not been prepared to be a mother to the self-contained boy he'd become by the time his father brought her home. Roxana would make a superb mother when the time came. Unfortunately she'd probably be wiping the noses of Breedon's whiny spawn. Max shuddered in distaste.

"Let us let the youngest go for the first ride," said Roxana. "It is only fair."

"Oh, yes," said Miss Ferris, clapping her gloved hands together. "Then I shall be first to ride with his grace."

"I can take both of you," Max told Julia and Thomas.

"May I handle the ribbons?" asked Thomas eagerly.

"We shall see," said Max. "Let me make one circuit to show the best path, first."

The groom held the horse until the three of them were packed into the narrow seat. Max watched Roxana and Breedon head for the last of the sleighs. Was she dressed warm enough?

A gust blew her blue cloak against her and failed to show the perfect curves of her form. He was as much disappointed as he was relieved that she had layered on more clothing. Had her poverty prevented her from owning a proper winter coat? Or had she sacrificed her comfort for fear of appearing less than au courant?

Then they were off, the horse prancing, the bells on the harness merrily ringing and the horse's snorts lifting into the crisp air in white puffs. Max led the sleigh down the drive, turning off to cross the flattest part of the park. After completing the circuit and starting down the drive for the second time, Max handed the reins to Thomas.

A few of the other sleighs turned off the drive earlier, taking a more daring path down a drainage ditch beside the drive. He could hear the laughter, interspersed with the festive jingling of the holiday harnesses. Lady Angela began to sing a caroling song and many of the others joined in. Their voices lilted over the snowy parkland.

Thomas snapped the reins and Max put a hand on his arm. "Remember, the horse has to contend with snow, and pulling a sleigh can be more taxing than pulling a wheeled vehicle."

Julia looked over her brother's head and smiled. "I am so glad that Roxy thought of us. She promised our tutor that she would supervise extra study so that he would allow us to come out."

As they neared the group of waiting riders near the house, the young women cheered them on. A few of the older couples had joined the crowd on the steps. Max looked back, calculating how many circuits the horses would need to make.

"This should be our last time; we want to make sure our guests are all able to get their turn."

"We cannot stop now." Thomas jerked the reins. The sleigh bumped off the drive down the slope of the ditch.

"Thomas, look out!" shouted Julia.

Max swiveled around to see another sleigh flying toward them. Roxana and Breedon traveled a collision course.

Roxana screamed, "Right."

Breedon jerked the reins hard to his left. The horse's head jerked sideways, its eyes rolling with pain. The bells' steady rhythm clanged with discordant fury as Thomas tried to stop the careen of the sleigh. The horses avoided each other by the narrowest of margins, while Thomas hauled back on the reins.

"Hold on!" Max shouted, fearing the inevitable collision between the two sleighs would send his sister and brother flying.

But the opposite sleigh tilted up on one runner. The slope of the ditch beside the drive provided the coup de grâce. The carved sleigh upended in a flurry of snow and flailing limbs. Roxana squealed and Breedon yelped as they were flung sideways.

His heart in his throat, Max jumped from his slowing sleigh. Was Roxana hurt? He would never forgive himself if she got hurt. It was all his fault. He should never have allowed Thomas to take the reins.

Chapter Eleven

Scully loitered in the passageway, waiting for Fanny to return from her mission to be sure plenty of blankets and warmed bricks were supplied in the sleighs. Catching her alone was so hard. When she had lingered outside his room last night, her candlelight casting odd shadows through the gap under the door, his hopes had soared.

When she walked toward him, he drank in the sight of her. She was beautiful, but her continued wearing of her blacks made him wary of the unspoken message she was sending. Had she buried her high-spirited side when she buried her husband?

"Fanny, love, would you take a sleigh ride with me?"

"Scully, I—"

"Oh, now I am 'Scully,' and no longer your faithful 'Dev'?" He caught her arm before she fled from him as she had last night, and he propelled her back toward an anteroom.

"You can hardly claim faithfulness," she said.

All right, she had a point. He hadn't exactly been faithful in deed, only in his heart. Which was a point he knew he would never win with a female. He opened the door and prodded her inside the room. "Does a sleigh ride offend your station?"

"I am too old to—"

"Hardly so; you are barely a day older than the day I first fell in love with you."

She rolled her eyes. "Another untruth."

Devlin didn't know what he was doing wrong. He had tried to give her space to come to him, to indicate that he wanted more than physical intimacy, although he wanted that more than anything. And damn Max for suggesting he could not invade her bedroom without an offer of marriage, when he did not even know if Fanny had the least amount of interest in continuing their relationship.

"You used to believe my protestations." For God's sake, he had just told her he loved her, and she assumed it was a lie. He did not know whether to laugh or cry. "So you are a decade older and so am I. You are just as beautiful as you ever were."

Her gaze dropped and her arms folded across her middle as if she were protecting herself. "You know that is not true," she whispered.

"More beautiful." He took a step toward her.

She turned and her hand drifted on the air in protest. "I am afraid the bloom is off the rose."

"Hardly so. I'd say the rose is finally in full bloom." He leaned forward and caught her shoulders in his hands.

She made a move to shrug him off.

"Don't, Fanny." He leaned over to brush his lips

against the nape of her neck. "For God's sake, don't send me away again."

He felt her shudder. Sliding his hands down her arms he nuzzled her neck. She tilted her head, giving him access to the strip of skin between the high neck of her gown and her mobcap.

Impatient, he stripped off the headdress. She broke contact, but he could see from her wide blue eyes and her quickened breathing, his kisses affected her. She backed away. He followed until his chest brushed hers. He had a great deal he meant to say, but her mouth beckoned him.

"I mean to have you again, you know," he said as he leaned toward her. "I don't care how long it takes to persuade you."

"But—"

He cut off her protest with a kiss. Oh, God, he loved the feel of her mouth, the taste of her, the lush feel of her curves pressed against him.

She shoved against him. "I am too old for this."

"Fanny, if you feel too old then do something young and rash like go for a sleigh ride with me. I promise you will not feel old when we are done."

She stared at him as if he had lost his mind.

He plunked her cap back on her head, settling it just so over her curls. "Promise me, if you will not go for a sleigh ride today, that you will agree to go for one after your guests are gone, or if the snow has melted, for a wild carriage drive or a mad gallop on horseback. I need to hear you laugh again."

She ducked around him. "I don't understand what you want from me."

"I want to delude myself with the idea that I could make you happy, Fanny."

Her hand on the doorknob, she paused. He was using the words of a formal declaration. Surely, she could give him a hint of her mind.

"I think I did once."

She slowly turned around, "Dev?"

Shouts and screams from outside made them turn to the windows. Dev felt like screaming, he was so close to breaking through with her.

Roxana felt the sleigh tip and tried to lean against the uphill side, but Mr. Breedon had too many stone on her for her weight to be an effective counterbalance. She did not have more than a couple of seconds to react before she cartwheeled over Mr. Breedon.

As her weight landed against him, he let out an *oomph*. Her first inclination was to giggle. Her hands flayed in search of a handhold to grab. She caught Mr. Breedon's coat. Then the stark thought that one of them could be hurt flashed in her mind.

For a second she thought everything was all right, before she realized the horse continued dragging the overturned sleigh. The carved headrest bumped her head, skimming over her. Mr. Breedon's bulk took the brunt of the sleigh's impact. She tried to push up the heavy wood before it injured him. Then the sleigh ripped away from her hands and Max scooped her up into his arms. He cradled her against his chest, one arm beneath her knees, as if she were a small child instead of a grown woman.

His clamp on her was tight and her feet dangled above the ground. That he could pick her up as if she weighed no more than a pillow startled her.

His brown eyes were stark with panic. "Are you hurt?"

"I don't think so." Roxana swiveled. "Mr. Breedon!"

Gregory lay on the snow, crunched up in a ball. Was he hurt? He groaned and rolled to his back.

Max tightened his grip on her, restricting her movements. Panic tightened her throat. She hated to be restrained, and Mr. Breedon could be injured.

Roxana struggled and shoved against Max's chest. "Let me down."

For a second a mulish look crossed his face and he glanced up the drive as if he would carry her away to the house. The thought of him removing her slippers and socks forcefully flushed heat through her body. A primitive look on his face made her feel as if he meant to carry her off, as if rescuing her conferred rights of conquest on him.

As soon as he let her down, she ran toward Gregory. She dropped down to her knees, beside Mr. Breedon. "Sir, sir, are you all right?"

Thomas came up beside her and said, "I am so sorry, Roxy, sir."

Mr. Breedon groaned. "I am killed."

However, he moved every one of his limbs slowly, as if certain one of them would not function properly.

"Where are you hurt?" asked Roxana.

"I am trying to see," said Gregory peevishly.

Roxana studied his face, looking for hints of pain. His moon face was smooth as ever, his eyes closed but not clenched shut. His breathing was easy and not a single wrinkle that would signify a wince was present.

Max gave a hard look at the man lying in the

snow, then tracked after the horse. The animal stood head down, sides heaving, less than fifty feet away. Apparently pulling the upended sleigh required too much effort.

Roxana patted Gregory's shoulder. She supposed he meant to milk this for as much sympathy as everyone could muster. As little as she liked his ploy she leaned over him, cooing softly as she would to one of her younger siblings after they had taken a tumble.

"Do you need a litter?" asked Max.

"They are trying to kill me," muttered Gregory under his breath.

"Oh, I am sure not. It was just an accident." One that could have been avoided if Mr. Breedon had turned the sleigh right instead of left. Not that it had been his fault. Everyone's natural instinct was to yield to the left when meeting another vehicle. "We will get you back to the house and give you"— she would have offered her youngest brother or sister a candy or pudding—"hot soup and tea and you will feel better."

Thomas's lower lip quivered. Roxana put her hand on his shoulder. "Just an accident with no harm done."

Other couples and several of Max's servants had run toward them and arrived at the scene of the accident. Roxana looked up and saw Julia holding the reins of the upright sleigh.

"I need my moth—a physician."

"Can you sit, sir?" asked Lord Frampton.

"Here, put this under his head," said Lady Angela, holding out her fox-fur muff.

Roxana urged Mr. Breedon to put his head in her lap and used the muff for good measure.

Continuing to pat his shoulder, she raised her head. Out of the corner of her eye she caught Max's expression of disgust. He erased the expression before she could be sure of what she had seen.

The grooms and a few of the men righted the tipped sleigh. Max signaled a couple of the men to lift Mr. Breedon into his sleigh. As they settled him, padding the blankets all around him, he moaned and then stared at Max.

"How could you let that infant drive?"

Max watched as the company milled about the drawing room. The night before Christmas, and he was not in the spirit of the season. He blamed it on the idea that his family was no longer intact. Fanny had resorted to building new traditions, insisting he cut down an evergreen and bring it inside, following the Hanoverian custom of a Christmas tree, recently established at court.

In his opinion the tree had been felled far too easily. Scully had told him to quit beating the snow off so hard, before he broke all the branches.

Scully pulled up beside him, a glass of wassail in his hand. "Quit scowling."

Roxana, Fanny and Lady Breedon were all flitting around Mr. Breedon, where he sat with his foot propped on a stool and a blanket draped around him. Nearly everyone commiserated with Mr. Breedon. Roxana straightened his pillows at least a dozen times.

"He doesn't get so much attention often." Scully lifted his glass and took a drink. When he lowered the glass, his eyebrow was arched.

"Stop." Max turned his back on the domestic

scene. If Breedon had more than a bruise or two he'd burn the Thames. Roxana knew it too. She had met Max's eyes with an eyeroll.

"I suppose he should have enough consideration to have needed to take to his bed so that you might have a clear field."

Max looked up and caught Lady Malmsbury watching him. She flipped her red hair and crossed over to sit beside Mr. Breedon.

"Miss Winston, I don't believe we've heard you play the piano. Surely you would like the opportunity to demonstrate your skills," Lady Malmsbury said in a loud voice.

"Malmsy should take to the stage. She projects so well," whispered Scully.

"But she doesn't like her assigned role."

"Ah, well, what woman does not want to be your leading lady?" asked Scully.

"The ones that want to be yours," said Max, looking back at Roxana. When he managed to drag his gaze away, some circumstance always drew it back to her.

She had shaken her head. "I am sure you do not wish to hear my play, it is very mediocre at best."

"Yes, do let us hear you play," echoed Lady Breedon.

Roxana stood slowly and walked across the large room toward the piano. Max met her halfway there. "Allow me to turn your music for you."

It was the move of a gracious host, since the man she was attached to could not move out of his chair.

Roxana looked up at him, her blue eyes wide. She seated herself on the bench, and as she lifted her hands to the ivory keys, he could see them tremble. "I am sorely out of practice," she whispered.

"I shall be vastly relieved to learn you have flaws," whispered Max, hoping to make her relax.

"You know I have flaws," whispered Roxana fiercely.

She was a schemer and perhaps too direct, yet capable of maintaining a polite fiction with Breedon. "Nothing worth noting. Now, what would you like to play?"

He looked over at Lady Malmsbury, who was looking a bit like a cat that swallowed a canary. What was she up to?

"Something monstrously simple." Roxana shuffled through the sheet music.

Max put his hand on her shoulder. She stopped moving all together. He was aware of both the feminine curve of her shoulder beneath his hand and her tension.

"I don't know any of these," whispered Roxana.

"Play anything."

She took a deep breath and started in on a piece he had heard Julia practicing. Roxana's touch on the keys was tentative, but she seemed to gain confidence as she played. She left out a few notes, and other than hitting one wrong note and once two keys together, she played marginally better than horrid.

Max kept his hand on her shoulder the whole time. Her playing would not impress anyone, but he could feel her trembling. Her composure and ability to manage a performance under pressure impressed him. He could not have known her tension if he had only looked at the expression on her face. She managed a cool serenity. Yet he stood steadfastly by her side, refusing to desert her while she struggled to perform.

"Well done, Miss Winston," he said when she finished.

She gave him a tightlipped nod and stood. She did not protest in a way that prompted him to extend false compliments.

Lady Malmsbury drifted closer. "Oh, do play another."

"It would not be nice of me to inflict my poor performance on the others in the room," Roxana said with a curtsy. "I have neglected playing in recent years."

"Perhaps you should play for us, Lady Malmsbury," said Max. "I am sure you can manage to woo us all."

Why had Roxana not played in recent years? Max took her elbow and pulled her away from the piano.

"I see you are anxious to put a great deal of distance between me and that instrument."

"Perhaps you would do better with a harp," Max said, tucking her hand into his arm and heading for the empty corner of the room.

Roxana blanched. "No. I fear my talent is with my needle."

"Yes, I know." Max swung her into the alcove. "Are you all right?"

"That is the question *du jour,* is it not?" Roxana wore a haunted expression as she looked over Max's shoulder toward Mr. Breedon.

"He is not injured."

"Yes, I know, but he . . ." She bit her lip.

As Max stared at her cherry lips, he realized he wanted to kiss her. He wanted more than to kiss her. He wanted to protect her from Lady Malmsbury's attacks. He wanted to shelter her from her family's poverty. He wanted to prevent her from marrying a man who loved himself better than he could ever love her. And he had could have done all that if he did not need to keep Thomas as his heir.

He rubbed his hand against his forehead. His thoughts swirled in a disordered mess. Roxana did exhibit affection for Breedon, and Gregory was rich enough to solve many of her problems. Max knew he should step aside, let Breedon have her. It was the right thing to do. He just wished it did not bother him so.

"I must get back," she whispered. "Before his mama convinces him that I could never entertain him of an evening."

"Never worry, Miss Winston, I am quite sure he is tone deaf."

"Then I am well suited." Roxana smiled, but she feared it appeared more as a grimace.

She drifted back over to Gregory's side. Would he comment on her lack of skill? Thank goodness she had helped Julia with her piano practice the other day. Julia had been frustrated with her ability, and Roxana had sat down to help her. They both ended up giggling over Roxana's poor skill, which had given Julia more confidence in her own playing.

Even now, Lady Malmsbury's hands glided over the ivory keys, playing an aria that showcased her superior skills and belittled Roxana's inferior ones.

"Can I get you more tea, Mr. Breedon?" she asked.

"No, no, I have had enough." He held out his teacup toward her. "I believe I shall retire."

Roxana felt panic rise in her throat. Sleighing

with Gregory had turned into a disaster. He had been cold and distant with her ever since their accident. She had fussed over him the same as if he were her little brother—four or five years ago. "I am disappointed," she murmured.

"Well, I cannot participate in the dancing later. And since you suffered no injury you will wish to dance."

"I shall not enjoy it above half if you are not here. I am sure I suffered no injury because of your thoughtful shielding of me as the sleigh overturned."

Gregory frowned, then brightened.

"I feel ever so guilty that you were hurt on my account." Roxana resisted rolling her eyes. She knew Max was watching her. "Do you need assistance? Shall I have the duchess send for the footmen?"

"No, I think I can manage on my own." He made a great production of struggling to his feet.

How could she get him to compromise her if he did not spend any time with her? Could she use the excuse of concern for his well-being to check on him later?

He hobbled toward the door. Roxana walked beside him. "Here, do lean on me, sir." She held out her arm. "It distresses me to see you in pain."

"Well, never fear, I have discussed it with my parents and we will leave tomorrow."

Alarm shot through Roxana. "But the roads will be impassible."

"Well, we shall have to go slowly anyway and the grooms will just have to walk alongside the horses. I cannot abide staying when my safety is in jeopardy."

She stared at him, her future crumbling like dust around her feet.

"Even if I make it only as far as the nearest posting inn, I shall be more relieved."

Roxana turned toward Lady Breedon, who looked away. Were his parents encouraging his plan to leave for fear she was getting her claws too deep into him?

She looked around, her eyes blurring. "I will miss you," she whispered.

Roxana turned and stared at the dozens of burning candles on the Christmas tree. Her family would be lucky to have one candle burning this night. Little gifts dangled from the tree and were piled under it. At home there would be only the meager gifts she left for them. She missed her family and the idea that she would have to return to them empty-handed tasted like sawdust in her mouth.

She couldn't let them down. She would have to seduce Mr. Breedon. Stealing into his room tonight was the only way.

Max stared into the low embers of the fire, swirling the brandy in his glass. Scully had declined his invitation to drink with him and could not see that Max was only sipping, as he should.

Back in his old room he could pretend his brothers were still alive, that they would come racketing in, boisterous and unrestrained. Fanny would laugh, and his father would grant them that indulgent smile that was never turned in Max's direction when he behaved in a less-than-decorous manner. And instead of acting as if their antics were insufferable,

Max would grab them to him in tight hugs and never let go.

Yet it was not really his brothers that occupied his thoughts. Roxana had appeared crestfallen when Breedon told her he was leaving. She had put on a brave front for the duration of the evening, but Max could tell she'd had the wind knocked out of her sails.

Max unfastened the catch of his dressing gown; the radiant heat of the fire more than kept him warm. He propped his feet on the footstool in front of him and slunk low in the high-backed chair. He should be relaxed, but he was edgy and restless instead. In front of him on the mantel was one of the gifts he'd bought for Roxana.

That she had failed to bring Breedon up to scratch in a little over a week was no surprise, but she should have had the twelve days of Christmas to ply her charms.

The door clicked behind him. Had Scully decided to join him after all?

When the interloper did not speak, Max looked around the side of his chair and saw a white nightgown and a female form scurrying toward his bed. She tossed back the covers and scrambled in, pulling up the bedding and turning her back as if this were her bed.

His first thought was that Lady Malmsbury had discovered his new room, but as he looked he realized the trespasser in his bed had dark hair.

Emotions rolled through him with a tidal wave of force. Overwhelming him was the fast coursing of his blood. The pooling and pulsing in his lower regions reminded him what to do with a desirable woman in his bed. He stood and tossed back the rest of the brandy and shed the dressing gown.

"Roxana, what are you doing?"

She bolted upright. "Oh my goodness, I must have mistook the door when returnin—Max?"

He could tell from the very breathiness of her delivery she lied. Anger flared through him. He took a step toward her. "Did you mean to trap Breedon or was it me all along?"

"I-I-I went to the necessary. My room is the next one. I m-m-mistook the door. I am ever so sorry."

"Don't lie to me," he snarled. He turned and paced away from the bed, trying to restrain his anger, his desire and his anguish.

"The bed is in the same . . . place . . . as in my . . ."

He made a chopping motion with his hand to end the lie.

"What happened to Mr. Breedon?" she whispered. He heard her stealthy slide across the bed as if she meant to slink out. He'd stepped between her and the door.

"He is, I hope, sleeping like a baby in my room." The excuse he'd given Breedon, that his snores bothered Scully, had been accepted and the rooms changed without a hitch.

Good God, had she meant to seduce Breedon, to endure his kisses and poking? Did she know what she was asking for?

"I know this was his room. I saw him leaving it. . . ."

Her voice trailed off as he slowly turned.

Her gaze had dropped to his crotch.

His erection throbbed in his too-tight evening breeches. He strode across the room, slapping the bedpost for emphasis. "Do you understand what a man does when he finds a woman in his bed?"

Roxana kicked at the covers and dove for the far side of the bed. The jiggle of her breasts as she moved fascinated him. Her foot twisted in the bed linens, and she tumbled to the floor between the bed and the wall.

He should take her back to her room before any harm was done, but he knew as he stared at the slim white foot tangled in his sheets and at the slender ankle where her nightgown crept up and the silhouette of her form that he could no more take her back to her room than he could raise his brothers from the grave. At this moment he disgusted himself.

"Do you?" he repeated, hearing the raw emotion in his words.

She tugged her foot, but it didn't come free of the sheets. He grabbed it and put one knee on the mattress. "Answer me."

She looked back at him, through the curtain of her hair, and he could see her glare. "Yes, I know."

God, he hated being tricked and manipulated, but he meant to have her. He wanted every kiss and touch that she would have granted Breedon, and he would make sure she enjoyed every minute of it. "Then you are doing it with me."

Warning bells sounded in his head, and he knew the minute he took her, he had committed himself to a course of action he would have found despicable in any other man. She was still an innocent, and her desperation had forced her to a path he could not like.

"I ought to thrash you," he said, rubbing his thumb along her instep. He leaned across the bed, reaching to pull her up. "I hate being tricked."

But as he leaned over the far side of the bed,

Roxana had ducked her head and put her arm across her face. For God's sake, she cowered like a whipped dog in fear of a beating. How much pressure had been brought to bear on her to force her to this? An urge to protect her and shelter her from all harm overwhelmed him, yet impatience and the desire that burned low in him tore him in a thousand directions.

"Roxy?"

Chapter Twelve

Scully stood outside Fanny's room, his heart thundering. He cleared his throat and then tapped on the door.

Fanny cracked her door. Her hand clutched at the neck of her blue dressing gown. At least she did not wear her weeds to bed.

"Hello, beautiful." He raised one arm up above his head and leaned against the doorjamb, knowing the stance made his coat hang wide open. He raised a deck of cards in his other hand and flipped over the top card. "Care for a game of piquet?"

"Scully, I . . ." She stared at the knave of hearts on top of the deck.

He leaned closer. "*Vingt-et-un?*" He needed to get in her room.

Her luminous blue eyes widened. "What are you doing here?"

"I want to give you your Christmas gift." He leaned his hand in and brushed his fingers against her cheek. "Let me in, my pretty Fanny."

"You can give me my gift tomorrow with all the others."

"Oh, I hardly think that would serve, not this gift, anyway." This afternoon they had been on the verge of reaching an understanding when the shouts from the accident outside had interrupted their tête-à-tête. So long after midnight, they were unlikely to have any interruptions.

Her eyes narrowed. "What do you mean to give me, a deck of cards?"

He smiled, sensing victory. Her curiosity was his best ally. "I have it right here." He patted his breast, frowned and then patted his hip pocket. "No, here."

His gesture drew her gaze down to the falls of his unmentionables. He'd left off his waistcoat and consigned his cravat to the floor of his room. Heat built in him and he began to swell as she stared.

"That too."

She blanched, her expression turning uncertain, her eyes still cast down. "But it's Christmas."

One-handed, he flipped the card on the top of the deck back over. If his arousal alarmed her, the movement would distract her attention. "You used to enjoy playing cards with me, love."

She continued to stare below his waist. He pushed on the door and she looked up, alarmed, but she had forgotten to hold it tight. "Do not be afraid, love. I'll leave if you insist."

He pushed around her and drew her into the room, shutting the door. He pressed a kiss to her lips. Moisture collected under his arms and the sooner he was rid of his clothes the better.

He dropped to his knee. "Fanny, love, you would—"

"What are you doing, Dev?" she asked, alarmed.

"Trying to present my gift." At least he was back to "Dev." That was a good sign. "You may not want it."

"Of course I should want it. You are being very odd. I am not a queen requiring genuflection for presentation of a gift."

"You are near enough to a queen. It is the only higher rank. I know that I have no title or no expectation of one, since I have five older brothers." He was perspiring in earnest and botching his presentation. "You should not have interrupted me. I had this all planned."

He tossed aside his coat, then had to pick it up to retrieve the ring from the pocket.

"For heaven's sake, just give it to me," whispered Fanny. "You are behaving too strange."

Scully closed his eyes and drew a deep breath. "Fanny, dear heart, you are the most beautiful woman in the world."

"Hardly," she snorted.

"To me, you are, and—"

"Tomorrow will be quite busy, Dev, and I—"

"Stop interrupting."

She shifted. "Dev, what are you doing?"

"Stop talking. I have never done this before and I'm sorry if I'm making a hash of it. You would make me the happiest man if you would agree to be my wife." The words came out in a white-hot rush, not at all the smooth proposal he planned.

Silence was his answer. Fanny had gone quite still.

He held out the ring, needing to fill the gap. "It was my grandmother's ring. I know it is old, and you like new things, but we could have the stones reset. The sapphire reminded me of your eyes."

The ring was extravagant, the huge blue stone encircled by diamonds.

Another gap stretched in the room. He needed to fill it. "You could give me an answer, you know. There are twenty diamonds. I have been assured they are quite fine specimens." And he'd told himself he would not insist upon an answer right away.

"I did not expect this," she whispered. Her voice sounded tearful. "Why would you . . . you . . . now?"

"Max said I must," he answered, and then cringed. Of all the things he should have said that was not it. He stood holding out the ring and feeling like an idiot. Perhaps if he kissed her and did not allow her the breath to answer, he could salvage this miserable effort.

Yet her eyes filled with tears and she stared at the ring in his hand almost as if it were a snake that might bite her.

"For God's sake, Fanny, do not cry. You can refuse me."

Roxana slowly lowered her arm from where it shielded her face; She saw Max's extended hand, palm up. Her nerves were shattered, and she was shaking. She stared at his hand, distrusting the offer of assistance.

She had steeled herself to invade Mr. Breedon's bedroom and tell him that she had mistaken her way back from the necessary. She'd rehearsed the lie a dozen times in her head. She'd thought it sounded plausible.

But Max was not so easy to fool. His anger charged the air. His edict chilled her heart. Did he really intend to have his way with her or was he just trying to scare her?

His hand moved from her foot to curl around her ankle. His other hand grasped her upper arm, and he dragged her back up on the bed.

He unwrapped her ankle from the tangle of bedding and lifted the covers for her to settle underneath them. She stared at the tented sheets and blankets.

"You're cold. Cover up," he said brusquely, as if she was being a ninny. As if climbing into bed with him were normal. As if she were not in a gnarl of nerves.

She wasn't so much cold as frightened, and apprehension made her shake. "I can leave now."

"You're not leaving." Max grabbed her legs under her knees and thrust her under the sheets. His motion made her nightgown ride up to her thighs, but the covers landed over her, hiding any indecency.

"Not until we settle this," he muttered. Kneeling on the bed, he drew off his shirt and undershirt.

Roxana felt an involuntary gasp leave her lips. She had seen a man without his shirt before. She had seen laborers, but Max had none of the burliness of them. He had more the physique of a statue of antiquity. His musculature stretched smooth and long. His skin fairly gleamed pale gold in the firelight.

His hands landed on the buttons of his falls. Her gaze jerked to the upside-down horseshoe of his flat stomach, and the line of dark hair that ran down under his waistband. Heat mingled with fear stabbed through her.

He struggled with his buttons as if they were too tight to wrestle free of their moorings, and Roxana clenched her eyes shut. Other parts of her body clenched, and she drew up her knees. Clearly, Max meant to take advantage of her mistake.

Her thoughts flew at lightning speed. Max was not whom she intended to trap, but he didn't want to be married. He was wealthy. Could her plan work with him? He was her friend and she did not want to betray that. And his burst of anger alarmed her.

Her mouth went dry at the thought of what he would do. That he would do anything surprised her. She had been told of, nay he had demonstrated, a certain correctness in his behavior—although not always with her.

And a part of her, a sick, depraved part of her, wanted him to kiss her again.

The mattress lightened, and she peeked one eye open. Max stood beside the bed. He slid his unmentionables down, and the only covering remaining on his body was his thin cotton drawers. They rode low on his hips, the ties dangling over that incredibly large bulge.

Seemingly unconcerned about his near-nakedness, he crossed the room to the chair where he had been sitting. After draping his clothes over the chair back, he picked up his dressing gown. Then he walked to the fireplace, where he removed a ribbon-tied box from the mantel.

She should have made a dash for the door, she berated herself.

He returned and tossed the dressing gown across the foot of the bed. His nearness made her heart gallop. She shut her eyes again.

The box landed near her face and she flinched.

"You might as well open that. I had meant to find a private moment to give it to you. Now is as good a time as any."

He was giving her a gift? Now? She did not move.

"Would you like me to open it for you?" he asked.

She nodded.

He sat on the bed, picked up the box, untied the ribbon and folded back the tissue paper. She could only look at him and the smooth muscles flexing under his skin as he moved.

"Roxana, shan't you look?"

She tried, but as she lowered her gaze to the box, she saw past it to his lap and she couldn't look away.

He tossed the box to his nightstand. "They're kid leather gloves. You can try them on later."

Had he bought her gloves because he had seen the darning on hers? That touched her in a way she didn't expect. She brought her gaze back up to his face. His anger was no longer visible and she searched his eyes for a sign that he had hidden it away to let it fly later, but he watched her with a patient concern.

"Thank you," she mumbled, and her voice was strange, breathy and raspy.

He smiled slowly and she felt his smile in every corner of her heart. She closed her eyes, trying to block his effect on her.

A cool breeze from the covers lifting made her shudder. Then Max slid in beside her. He pushed her knees down and brushed his legs against hers. His body pressed against her side and the heat rising off his skin made her want to push close, except she lay frozen on her back, the blankets wadded in her hands. How could her plan have gone so terribly awry?

His bare chest touched her shoulder and her skin tingled. His silent nearness forced awareness through her pores. His fingertips grazed her face as he lifted a strand of hair away. His hand cupped around the side of her head, smoothing her hair away from her face. He shifted up and pressed a kiss to her forehead. "Relax. We shall be married."

No! She did not want to be married. Her eyes flew open. "But—"

"Which is more than I can say that Breedon would have done."

Then Breedon would have been happy to buy her silence. Roxana bit her lip. She had to salvage her plan. Her dreams of an autonomous future with no man to control her and the ability to support her family were on the line. How could she convince Max to give her money? Thinking clearly when her body was coming alive with sensations was impossible.

Max's hand skimmed over her hand, urging her to loosen her death grip. He would be furious with her when he learned she wanted only compensation for the loss of her virtue. But what choice did she have? She had to pretend that she wanted him to marry her, and then deal with asking for money in the morning. He would hate her for her trickery.

He propped his head on his hand, his arm folded beside her head. His gaze weighed on her.

Why hadn't he kissed her or touched her or done any of the things Mrs. Porter suggested would happen? He'd taken off most of his clothes, which made her breathless. But then he just lay beside her, doing nothing.

Or, well, more than nothing. The heat from his body so close to hers chased the chill from her. She could not continue being frightened of his anger, when it had disappeared. She searched his expression for any sign of resentment, but his rage was gone, replaced by a lazy confidence.

As he stroked his hand over hers, tingles danced over her skin. How could such a circumspect touch make her melt?

"Are you quite sure you do not need explanation?"

She shook her head tightly. Mrs. Porter's explanations had been detailed enough that they shocked her. Yet as her mind raced over the idea of that portion of his anatomy inside her, a shiver rushed through her.

He smiled slowly. "You are incredibly beautiful, but this notion you have of being a sacrificial virgin shan't suffice for long. Let go of the covers, Roxy."

She forced herself to let go of the covers. "I'm not—"

"You are. You cannot have expected Breedon to make every move." He picked up her hand and laced his fingers with hers. "You did expect to have relations with him, did you not?"

"I thought if I put myself close enough that he would need no more encouragement." Her voice sounded strange, breathy and thin.

He brought her palm to his lips and pressed a gentle kiss there. Nipping at the inside of her wrist, he shifted his fingers between hers as if exploring her fingers was more important than holding her hand. "Mayhap you have not put yourself close enough to me. You could touch me."

"I know that." But she did not reach for him.

"I'd like you to. Come, Roxana, I am not the only one unduly affected when we are alone together." He put her hand down to her side, then moved to her other hand and lifted her arm above her head. "There is heat between us."

There was more than heat. She had been aware of him in that way ever since the first time she laid eyes on him. But she did not want to taint her desire with the knowledge that she was betraying him. He was the first man she had ever felt a bond of friendship with. She did not want him to hate her, and she did not know that her emotions would survive what she needed to do.

She wanted to touch him. She wanted to bring her elbows together and shield herself. Caught in a horrible place of indecision, she did nothing.

Max put his hand in the center of her chest, over her racing heart. "You know, Breedon would not have cared if you found pleasure."

Max expected her to take pleasure in their congress? As her chest rose and fell, he traced lazy circles over the upper curves of her breasts. She could have pretended whatever she needed to with Mr. Breedon. But nothing would be a pretense with Max. Her emotions rolled too close to the surface.

His fingers drifted to the ties of her nightgown and he pulled the bow's string. "Do you have any bruises or injuries from the sleigh accident? For if you do, now would be the time to tell me."

She shook her head.

He touched the bared skin at her collar and slid his fingertips under the edge of the material. "Did you like the Christmas tree? It is a new thing for us, but I saw one at court last year."

She was turning into a quivering mass, and he had not so much as kissed her. And he wanted to talk about the Christmas decorations? Perhaps she had misunderstood how this worked.

When she did not answer, he continued. "Finding a tree of the right height that had grown evenly was harder than I expected. Of course the snow made it difficult to assess." His thumb brushed over her breastbone, exploring her cleavage. "Your heart is racing, you know."

Roxana removed her gaze from the tester above her and looked at Max. His face was so close she could see every dark eyelash around his warm brown eyes. The hint of his beard showed below his firm jaw. His lips parted and he breathed more deeply than normal, although he managed to carry on a one-sided conversation.

"We have always had a Yule log, though the servants complain it is difficult to keep lit. But then, split wood burns so much better."

"Max?"

He pushed up on his elbow to lean over her. His eyes were dark and heavy-lidded. His breath brushed across her lips. "Yes, sweetheart?"

Sweetheart? "Do you mean to talk to me all night?"

"If that is what it takes," he said, but then he brushed his lips across hers. His touch was light and altogether unsatisfying. She wanted more.

"What do you"—his hand curled around her breast—"oh!"

A jolt shot from his hand to the damp place between her legs, and his mouth covered hers again. She lowered her arm around his neck.

He kissed her languorously as if in no hurry at all. Her bones were melting and a building urgency made her arch into him. His thumb skimmed over the tip of her breast, and pleasure rippled through her, traveling directly to her womb.

He ended the kiss as if reluctant, his lips clinging to hers. "Are you done being frightened, pet?"

His voice was rough and low. He hovered above, waiting for her answer, with his mouth a mere hairsbreadth from hers.

She raised her other hand and covered his bare shoulder.

He kissed her again, lightly, teasingly, and she found herself following him, her head lifting off the pillow as he drew back. His lips curved in a smile before they entirely left hers. "Now is the time for plain speaking, my adorable Miss Winston."

His hand skimmed over her breast and she wondered how he could speak at such a time, when she felt as if she were unraveling.

"I'm not so frightened," she managed to whisper.

"Good, for I am deuced tired of this restraint." He shifted his body over the top of hers and nudged apart her legs with his knee. His weight pressed her into the mattress as he kissed her again with more purpose and intensity.

His hands drifted over her, exploring and alternating between places that prompted a slow swell of heat and places that sparked and tingled with an instant fire. Each time he touched her in a new way, he paused, giving her time to react and absorb his possession. And as his caresses dropped lower and became more intimate, everything seemed to spiral and pool in that secret place.

He moved to nuzzle her neck and Roxana stared at the tester, so aware of him, so hungry for him, her body wanton and waiting and her heart breaking, because she knew with each low moan and cry she was betraying him. She gripped his shoulders, her fingers aching to explore his firm golden skin, yet restrained by her double crossing.

He whispered sweet things to her—commands, coaxing, and compliments. He touched her with such a mix of reverence and patience that she knew he made love to her. It was more than a simple seduction to him. And it was more than that to her.

"I don't want you to hate me." A sob cracked her voice and she blinked hurriedly. She bit at her lip, trying to keep her confession of her whole nefarious plan held inside. She could not tell him or she risked failure, and she was out of time. But not telling him made her feel that she was holding herself apart in this moment that was about sharing everything.

He settled himself on his elbows as he stroked her hair. "I could never hate you. Do not worry. I promise all will be well." He kissed her face, trailed little nipping kisses down her neck.

"I think—"

"Try not to think so much, pet. Just feel."

His head dipped lower until he caught the material of her nightgown and her nipple in his mouth.

The hot wet heat of his mouth through the cotton of her gown shot pleasure through her body, and every sensation echoed in her woman's core. She felt too much.

He shifted back up to kiss her lips again. She abandoned her fight of reluctance and gave over to the tightening and tingling cascading through her body.

He tugged up the hem of her nightgown. She

hardly noticed except when his bare skin landed against her breast she felt a new spiraling of vibrations. Her insides tightened and held as if waiting for something to happen. Yet she was aware that there were more steps to this intimate dance.

"Roxy, darling, am I to assume you want to be caught *in flagrante delicto?*"

"Caught?" she echoed dimly, his words not penetrating her focus on exploring the contours of his firm body. And his hand. Oh stars above, he touched her intimately, his fingers sliding along the cleft between her legs.

"Clothes off?" he asked.

"Mmmm," she managed.

He lowered his head to her other breast, his mouth no longer impeded by material.

His slipping fingers found a spot that thundered sensations into her body in a way that she could not even call it pleasure. It went beyond pleasure. His tongue swirled against her beaded nipple. She was coming undone.

She moaned and tossed her head side to side, as Max's magical touch brought her into a dangerous swirl of unimagined yearning for something just out of reach. She searched for relief, yet holding on to him, knowing he guided her to deliverance. Finally the first swells of a wave of pure bliss broke over her, drowning her in a mind-numbing pulsing paradise.

Max's weight and the pressure of his hand against the throbbing of her body soothed her, while the tenor of his kisses changed, as if he were now exploring her body in a way that was less about her response and more about his interest. She struggled to swim out of the fog of repletion.

She grew aware of the nightgown bunched at her shoulders, that she held handfuls of his hair. She relaxed her grip, hoping she had not hurt him in her frenzy.

He lifted up, tugging her nightgown over her head. "How much time do I have before we are discovered?"

"Discovered?" she said, as she was suddenly bare. Worry tapped at her complete state of contentment. She shoved it away, preferring to linger in the afterglow.

He pulled the covers over his shoulders, although not before his gaze had swept over her naked figure. "Roxy," he urged.

She could hear the strain in his voice. Tension was palpable in the tautness of his muscles under his skin. He reached for those ties on his smallclothes.

"Roxy, how long do I have?"

She brushed her hand over his chest, pleased that the gap allowed her to explore more, but missing the skin-to-skin contact with him. He groaned. With his hand at the nape of her neck, he brought her up for a deep kiss. His hunger was unmistakable and she wanted to ease him, to give him every measure of the pleasure he had given her. Oh God, for just this moment she wanted to love him as if tomorrow would never come.

"How long?"

"All night?" she whispered, knowing she was missing a matter of import in his question. Or perhaps he just liked to talk of nonsensical things like Christmas trees when he made love.

She slithered down, pressing her lips to his chest. Could she bring him to the place she had been?

He pushed her away while moving to his knees on the bed. "What?"

Had she done something wrong?

He gathered the covers, piling them not so they covered her, but so they were in between her and the door.

"Bloody hell, do not tell me you neglected to plan a timely interruption."

"A what?" Had she not understood completely the way to go about being compromised?

As if he could not help himself, his hand stroked over her curves. "How the hell did you plan to force an offer if you did not arrange to be discovered?"

"I was to go to you," she said in a small voice.

"Roxana, if no one witnessed your disgrace, then I could do nothing to insist—Oh Christ, you are so beautiful."

He put his hand over his face, raking into his disordered hair. "Bloody hell, we cannot go further. Damn!"

Roxana saw the heaving of his chest as he breathed heavily and cursed. She twisted so that she could reach the laces of his small-clothes.

As her fingers brushed against the heavy length of him, a shuddering groan left his mouth. He had not had any qualms about touching her private parts, and she wanted to touch him. She paused to run her fingers over his length. The leap of his member under her ministrations pleased her. Anticipation began a slow build in her again.

"Oh hell, you'll have to scream."

Like hell she would. "I will not."

But then, she didn't have to as the door clicked open and Roxana caught a glimpse of satin, lace, and white, white skin before Max threw the covers over her head, muffling the words that were said, but not diluting the scream of rage and mortification.

Roxana struggled against the covers, but Max pressed down as if he intended to suffocate her.

Chapter
Thirteen

Fanny drew away from Scully. Her heart pounded madly. He had proposed and she had not expected it or been prepared for it. She had barely allowed herself to think that he wanted to sleep with her.

He listed his shortcomings so fast—his lack of title or prospects, his modest income, his small estate, his work for the foreign office that took him away for long stretches. Did he want her to refuse? Yet all that really registered was that odd knee-jerk response of his when she had asked him why. Anger and hurt burned under her breast. "Max said you must what? Offer to marry me?"

Her voice squeaked. Since when had Max interfered in her love life? Since he became duke. He had that right. And to be precise, she had no love life.

"Forget I said that," said Scully.

If she accepted the ring, perhaps she could console herself that everyone would understand her foolishness. "The words are said; you cannot unsay them."

"Then allow me to explain." He cupped his hands around her shoulders.

The ring dangled beside her face, pinched in his thumb and forefinger. It was undoubtedly the most precious thing Scully owned. While his grandmother had been a countess, Scully was a younger son of an earl with several nephews between him and the line of succession. If Fanny took it from him, he would regret the loss of a bauble so valuable.

"I cannot think it should matter." She turned and held out her hand. "I want the ring."

"Fanny?" He stepped forward, a smile breaking across his face as he lifted her left hand. "I had thought you would need more convincing."

She snatched her hand back, suddenly thinking she had made a grave miscalculation. The disappointment she expected on Scully's face was not there. "I will consent to a private engagement, nothing more."

His smile faltered. "If that is all you can agree to right now, then I will be glad of it."

His dark hair dropped across his forehead as he reached down for her hand, lifted it and slid the ring on her finger. "With this ring, I plight my troth," he said solemnly, unlike her carefree Scully.

He lifted her hand and kissed the back of it, turned it over and kissed her palm. Then he reached to cup her face.

She spun away and tugged at the ring, which refused to leave with the ease it had slid onto her finger. "I did not think you were serious. You are never serious."

"Men never jest with proposals, Fanny." He caught her hips, her more-than-ample hips.

She twisted and backed away from him.

"I love you," he said quite firmly. "I have loved you for fifteen years."

He would not love her when he realized she was not the same woman she was ten years ago. Why had he said fifteen?

He closed the gap between them. Fanny spun around again and found herself confronted with the wall of her bedroom. The toile de Jouy wallpaper greeted her. She slapped her hands against the wall, which seemed to approach with dizzying speed.

"Interesting position, Fanny. But I am game." He pressed his erection against the curves of her derrière and slid his hands around her waist. "Although I have to wonder if you will complain about your dignity later. Mind you, I shan't care if you laugh a little."

Did he really want her? The evidence of his body would suggest so, but she clenched her eyes shut, waiting, fearing his interest would fade when he felt what deficiencies a middling-aged-woman's corset could conceal. He had to have felt the extra padding around her midsection.

Instead he shifted, rubbing against her in such a suggestive—lewd—manner. Her breathing quickened and her blood thickened. Heavens, could she not restrain her response? How could she be aroused by such coarse bawdiness?

He slid his hand up and cupped her breast. "Quite clever of you to realize that you would do well to avoid touching me, my hunger for you is so near out of control."

She heard the catch in his voice with disbelief. And as he'd distracted her with fondling her breast—which quite shocked her—he pulled her hips back tighter against his. Then his hand dropped quite blatantly to cup around her woman's mound. In spite of the shocking manner of his seduction, if one could call it that, tingles raced along her spine, under his hands, in her woman's core.

"Oh, Fanny, this might work quite nicely, but in front of your looking glass, so I might watch your pretty face."

She squawked. The idea of his watching her reflection as they made love appalled and titillated her. What a horrid person she was to want him after such crude suggestions.

His hands smoothed over her curves, then he backed away.

Heavens, she felt a fool. The burn of humiliation stung her cheeks. The betrayal of her body was clear.

"I think I should want to kiss you awhile first, Fanny. I do not think I would rush this moment. I have looked forward to it so long. I would have you disrobe and kiss every inch of your fair flesh and feast my eyes upon your loveliness." He stroked her hair. "I want your sweet honey hair across my pillow, your—"

"Stop it, Dev." She pulled her hands down and began to tug on the ring. With every word he reminded her of how dowdy she had become. "You can leave now. Your games are done."

His hand closed around hers, stopping the removal of his ring. With his other hand he produced the deck of cards. "These are for games, love. What I do with you is real. If you would prefer we play games, I will deal the cards."

He flipped over the ace of hearts. How had he managed to change the top card from the knave to the ace?

"I would beg that we play for kisses, my pretty Fanny."

"So much for your lack of control," she said bitterly.

"I have never lacked for control, love. It took me three years to seduce you before. If it takes me as long again, I shall relish every moment."

"Your math is sadly lacking, Dev." She turned and leaned against the wall. She again tugged at the ring. Damn the humidity that made her knuckles swell so that a ring that fit was near impossible to remove. Her hands had not become grotesque, the swelling noticeable only to her with certain rings that no longer fit. How long before they would become gnarled and ugly?

"It was ten years ago, not fifteen, and . . ." She had fallen into his arms with so little provocation and prompting on his part she was ashamed. He had not campaigned for her seduction for three years. He was Max's friend from Eton, often underfoot, always begging her to join them at cards or riding, archery, picnics, facilitating the friendship she had finally formed with her stepson, who had been too self-sufficient to accept her as a mother when she arrived at the age of eighteen. Being maternal to his nine- and seven-year-old brothers was much easier than forging a relationship with a rigidly correct eleven-year-old Max.

When Dev had been here every school break, and months at a time after he and Max finished school, Dev had made her laugh, reminded her she was still young, although her husband's years were wearing heavy on their marriage.

He touched a finger to her cheek. "And?"

She stared at him, wondering if she had misconstrued the past, if she had not recognized when his offers of friendship had changed to more than a harmless flirtation. And God forgive her, her husband had allowed it and interfered only after she begged him to ban Dev from the house. Tears burned at her eyes.

He leaned in and pressed his lips to hers, gently, persuasively. "Your lips are a taste of heaven." He touched his finger to the bow of her lower lip. "So soft and sweet. Always the ones I've wanted, even if only for conversation."

She closed her eyes. "So you would offer marriage for companionship?"

"For that, but for everything that comes with marriage. Most of all I dream of having you in my arms every night."

She could not give him everything he should expect in a wife. Her age may preclude children. And she was tired of all the time involved in managing a large household, and with Julia's debut in a few years that was likely to get worse. She opened her eyes and found Scully's intense blue gaze and a cocked eyebrow.

"What am I missing, Fanny? What constrains you? Why are we not in yonder bed, finding heaven?"

"I'm fat."

He laughed. "You cannot expect that I am disappointed that there is more of you to love."

She pushed him away.

He caught his arm in her elbow and swung her around. "Ah, Fanny, love, I am well aware of the lushness of your womanly figure—I look upon it every day with lust in my heart."

"Do not jest so."

"Lust in my loins, then. That should be obvious to you. I have changed in ten years too. I think I may have a little paunch." He made an effort to stick out his flat stomach.

"You have not changed."

"I have so. No one ever calls my shoulders puny now."

She took a hard look at him. The changes in him had been gradual, but he was no longer the boy of one and twenty who had cajoled his way into her bed. He was a man who had made it to the ripe old age of thirty without marriage or even the hint of particular notice to any young woman. Why, when he could have any fresh-faced young misses such as Miss Winston or Lady Angela, would he want her?

He leaned his forehead against hers. "I am sure we should have many discussions, but I really would like to make love to you now."

But that was not to be, as a screech split the night. Fanny jumped and Dev winced.

"Did you hear that?" she asked.

He groaned. "Leave it be."

But a primal scream followed, long and loud and unignorable.

What did Lady Malmsbury plan on doing? Max wondered. Standing there and screaming all night? Eliza picked up a book and launched it at him.

Max deflected the book. Roxana struggled against the covers he had yanked over her head.

Two naked women in his room, every man's dream and Max's worst nightmare.

Lady Malmsbury had appeared in his room, opened her filmy lacy robe and said, "You cannot ignore this."

Actually Max probably could have ignored her;

he wanted Roxana more than anything he'd ever wanted in the world.

Color and the seductive expression drained from Eliza's face as she saw he was not alone in the bed. Her eyes widened and then narrowed as her face contorted with rage.

"For God's sake, do you mean to bring the whole household upon us?" he hissed.

"Who is it? What whore do you have in your bed?" Lady Malmsbury stood, bare chest heaving, unmindful of her lack of covering.

"Just a maid," answered Max. It wasn't exactly a lie if he used the word to mean maiden.

Lady Malmsbury picked up his brandy glass and hurtled it. He ducked and the glass smashed on the wall behind his bed. Then she charged toward him, claws bared.

"For God's sake, Eliza, do you mean to be found intruding in my bedroom when I have another woman in my bed?" He wondered what was the point in trying reason when he had a madwoman on his hands. "What will your husband say?"

He grabbed her wrists before she could do damage, and he was not entirely certain she was not going for Roxana, who had pushed the covers down and then pulled them back over her head.

"I hate you!" she screamed, then sobbed. She bucked and twisted, whipping her head around. Her red hair stung his eye as it lashed across his face. She reached for his washstand and grabbed his folded razor, although how she meant to use it while he still held her wrists he did not know.

His door clicked open and Scully stood there, his eyebrow cocked. "Exactly how many women do you have in here?"

"One too many," grunted Max, holding his

stinging eye closed. He slammed Eliza against the wall, trying to make her lose the blade.

"No need to wink, old boy."

Fanny peeked over Scully's shoulder and blanched at Max's state of undress, the wrestling match or perhaps Lady Malmsbury's best imitation of a wild woman from the Amazon and clapped a hand over her eyes.

"Quite a conundrum you have here," said Scully.

Max slammed Eliza's wrist against the writing desk and succeeded only in knocking a stack of papers to the floor.

"Do help me, and for God's sake we need to get her out of here," Max said in an as evenly modulated a tone as possible. Lady Malmsbury had the worst timing in the world.

Or he supposed it could have been more ghastly. Two more minutes and he would not have been in any state to defend himself.

"Scully!" hissed Fanny, pushing him into the room, removing her voluptuous dressing gown and shoving it toward him. "Do something."

"Ah, what fetching nightclothes, dear. Are you quite certain you wish me to do something here? There is an awful big audience. I am thinking of your dignity."

Fanny snorted.

Max continued wrestling with Lady Malmsbury and he could see Roxana squirming under the bedcovers. Please let her be pulling on her nightgown. "Scully!" he whispered with as much force as he could. "She has my ra—"

Eliza screamed with frustration. Max refused to let her go, fearing she'd slash him anyway. He wrapped his leg around hers, forcing her toward the floor. They bumped into the washstand and he knocked his razor out of her hand. He lifted and swung her away.

Fanny reached in, grabbed the doorknob and closed the door while remaining out in the passageway.

"Perhaps you would like to use this dressing gown, Malmsy. But I have no objection to you not," said Scully. He approached, holding the blue robe open. He cocked an eyebrow and looked his fill, then tossed the dressing gown over her head. "There is a side door that the servants use."

"And a stairway," added Max, getting a better handle on his grip of Eliza. That took care of one woman, but what about Roxana? What was wrong with him?

Max let go of Eliza'a arm, and she stripped the dressing gown off her head and lurched for the razor.

With lightning speed, Scully caught her free wrist and twisted her arm behind her back. "I say, that is not in the Christmas spirit, Malmsy."

She yelped.

But Max was beyond caring if she was in pain. Max folded her other arm up behind her back. Scully added his grip around her wrist.

She screamed. Max clapped a hand over her mouth.

The murmur of voices outside the room alerted Max to further crisis. He'd meant for Roxana to scream to raise the hue and cry. He did not want it sounding as if he was murdering a woman.

Together they propelled Malmsy to the servant's door.

"Might be best to gag her, before we let her go," said Scully.

Max only grunted as he opened the door. "If

she wants the entire household to see her like this, by all means let her scream."

He abandoned his hold, seeing that Scully had her controlled. Malmsy struggled and Scully pushed up her arms behind her back. She yelped and went still. Dodging around the pair of them Max opened the door to the narrow and dark wooden staircase leading up to the attics. From there she could find her way to her floor and bedroom.

Scully shoved her in and quickly whipped the door closed, taking care to close it softly only at the last minute. Then he leaned against it as Malmsy pounded on it. "She's like a rabid dog. You might want to get dressed, son. Sounds like a bit of a crowd gathering. I'll guard the stair door."

Max nodded, swirled around and ran back into his room and grabbed his dressing gown, pausing only to retie the ties on his small-clothes before they fell off. "Roxana, come with me," he whispered.

She had pulled her nightgown back on and knelt on the bed. He bit back the surge of disappointment. Compromised was one thing; her reputation entirely ruined and everyone in the house knowing was another. Why the hell did he think he needed to be caught, when he would do the right thing no matter what?

He stooped to grab Fanny's dressing gown from the floor and wrapped it around Roxy's shoulders and shoved her toward the servants' door. A matching door opened into her room too. He took her elbow and guided her through the narrow passageway.

Scully nodded and mouthed "Miss Winston" as if it were normal to be running women through the servants' doors.

Max opened her door and leaned close to whisper in her ear. "You had a nightmare."

Pressing a kiss to her neck, he wanted to hold her. He did not have time. She stared up at him, her blue eyes wide and not quite focused. Heat stabbed low in his gut. He had no time to lose, and he gently pressed her into her room. He consoled himself with the thought that there would be plenty of nights in the future.

He ran back through his room and threw open his door. Along the passageway doors opened and heads popped out. People milled around him in various states of undress, their faces masks of curiosity and anxiety.

"I heard breaking glass. Did you hear breaking glass?" said Lady Angela.

"Oh, I'm sure not," said Fanny.

"I only heard a woman screaming," said Sir William Breedon.

"I say, Trent, do you have a woman in your room?" Sir William asked.

Fanny cast a desperate look at him. "What is going on, Max?"

"I think the screaming was coming from Miss Winston's room," he said.

Fanny stared at him as if he were half crazy. He strode quickly to Roxana's door and pounded on it. "Miss Winston, are you all right?"

Roxana opened the door, looking dazed. Her hair was tangled and mussed, and she clutched Fanny's dressing gown to her neck. He wanted to kiss her and hold her and reassure her that everything was all right. Instead he repeated, "Are you all right, Miss Winston?"

She stared at him.

"Did you hear the screaming?" asked Fanny gently, moving between Max and Roxana.

She swallowed hard. She lied all the time; surely this one little falsehood was not beyond her.

"I had a nightmare," she said woodenly.

"Did you scream?" asked Fanny.

Roxana broke her gaze away from Max as if it required monstrous effort.

"I dreamed that Lady Malmsbury was trying to kill the duke." She shot Max an angry glare. "Or he was trying to kill her. I could not be sure." Then she closed the door.

Max winced.

The chatter around him turned to Lady Malmsbury's welfare, as if Roxana's dream indicated harm befalling Lady Malmsbury.

"What is behind this drape?" asked Mr. Breedon, who had managed to walk out of his room without assistance.

"What is?" echoed Lady Angela, reaching for the drape.

"Just the servants' stair," said Max.

"I say we need to have a look-see in your room," said Sir William.

Better his room than discovering Scully guarding the servants' stair. Max gestured that way. But Lady Angela was busy pulling back the drape.

Roxana stared at the door. Why had Max put her back in her own room, when he had been so adamant about being caught earlier? Or was Lady Malmsbury's intrusion enough? Roxana wasn't even sure Lady Malmsbury had known whom she was.

Had he rethought his decision to marry her? No problem there. She did not want to be married, but, oh stars, she had not expected to feel so wonderful. And then be reminded so cruelly of the male species's propensity for violence. He had tossed and slammed Lady Malmsbury as if she were a rag doll. He had forced her to her knees at one point. Roxana remembered too many times the same sort of display between her parents.

Was all that necessary? Once Max held Lady Malmsbury by the wrists, surely he did not need to toss her all over the room. His superior physical strength should have been sufficient restraint until Lady Malmsbury's anger played itself out. But he had seemed determined to force his will on her when she did not immediately comply with his request to stop screaming. Roxana stuffed a fist in her mouth to hold back the sob that threatened to break out.

She crossed her room and sat on the bed. She heard the activity in the hall, but stared at the wall. She closed her eyes, not knowing if she had failed in her mission or succeeded. In any case, she needed to leave soon. She crossed to the wardrobe and removed her clothes.

She had not expected to get so swept away. No matter how wonderful she felt she could not live with the idea that if she crossed Max he would explode in the same physical violence her father used to cow her mother. For a few minutes she had thought maybe she could just give in and marry him, but her dreams of a life plying her needle had sustained her too long. Emotions threatened the sensible plan that had sustained her for years.

Roxana ignored the tapping on her door. The door opened. Roxana did not know whether to expect Max. She found herself shaking.

"You better get dressed and come down to the drawing room. I've sent for your maid to attend you." Roxana turned and saw the duchess standing by her door, looking as regal as one could in a fussy, furbelowed nightgown. With a wince, Roxana wondered why women who had full figures thought that ribbons and bows would do anything beyond call attention to the fact.

Then she knew she was only setting her thoughts on fashion and gowns because that was much more comfortable than thinking about what would happen with Max.

"You might wear something modest, Miss Winston."

"Yes, your grace," said Roxana.

Fanny crossed her arms and looked at her. "Are you all right?"

"Yes, of course, I'm fine." But she was anything but fine. She was shaking and the knot in her stomach made her woozy with illness.

Leaning against his bedpost, Max tried to get control of his wayward body. He had been so close to sinking into Roxana, to releasing his heart and soul to her, to that physical act that would bind him to her and her to him in a union more sacred than marriage.

He would have thought that the interruption would have lessened his desire, but now he just plain ached for her and had had time to recognize that this act that he had engaged in many times before had transcended just the bodily pleasure. Good God, had he fallen in love with her?

Instead of the anguish of fearing for Thomas's future, he felt relief, relief that he could feel so deeply about a woman, relief that he could relax around her and did not need to be ducal every second, and relief that he would no longer feel so alone. He would work something out for Thomas, refuse to give him the money to buy a commission, find a way to purchase a property for him. The only thing Max wanted was Roxana.

His door opened, then clicked shut.

"What on earth were you thinking?" asked Scully.

"I told her I would marry her," Max said, pushing away from the bedpost. With luck, enough of the night would be left to have her return to his bed or go to hers.

Scully had his arms folded and leaned back against the door. "It is not like you to allow your peccadilloes to become such a public spectacle. You have upset Fanny."

"I had no way of knowing that Lady Malmsbury would—where did you go, anyway?"

"Malmsy was sobbing rather loudly on the stairs, so I escorted her to her room. I also told her that I expected her to leave at first light or I would go to the sheriff's and lay down a complaint against her for attempting to kill you."

Max shrugged. The worst punishment she would face would be a fine and the public humiliation of explaining why she was in his bedroom in the middle of the night. When the crowd intent on learning her welfare reached her room they found her pretending sleep in her bed.

"I told her to keep her silence or I would carry my tale to her husband."

"I ended my affair with her months ago because of her jealousy. I told her I would no longer call upon her." Max explained. "I cannot imagine that

I was the least bit unclear, and I have not offered her any encouragement here. I have only strived to not be rude."

Scully made a toss with one hand. "Malmsy is married and her own woman. What on earth were you doing with Miss Winston, son?"

"I was seducing her, of course." Max let the "son" go. "Lady Malmsbury's interruption was ill-timed."

"I have no sympathy; the timing was ill for me too. Bloody hell, I don't know whether to call you out or thrash you. I suspect I would do both, but it is unlike you to behave so badly." Scully stared at him, his blue eyes for once quite serious. "You have nearly destroyed her. Why would you have her in your bed?"

Max straightened, unwilling to be taken to task even though he knew he had taken the wrong path. He should have escorted Roxana back to her room, kissed her good night and sat her down in the morning and explained he was willing to re-consider his stance on marriage.

"We are talking about my future wife, Dev. I think that is enough."

"Yes, we are talking about your future wife. Fanny is fetching her. Get dressed, and we'll witness your formal application for her hand down in the drawing room."

Max had no objection to making the whole thing official, even though to do so in the middle of the night had the ring of unsavory scandal about it. "I'll announce it to everyone over dinner."

"You'll do no such thing," said Scully. "She has been chasing Breedon about for the last week. You'll wait until everyone leaves, then post the banns."

He wanted her his wife before six weeks had passed. "I won't risk a seven-month baby as heir."

"Is there a chance of that?" asked Scully sharply.

"No." They had been interrupted.

"Then you keep your hands off of her," said Scully.

Scully's silent rage penetrated his brain. "Why are you so angry?"

Scully shook his head and opened the door. "Come down to the drawing room when you are dressed."

Max felt his heart leap at the idea of claiming Roxana as his own.

Chapter Fourteen

Devlin poured himself a brandy as he waited.

Roxana sat with her hands twisting in her lap and her gaze down. She did not look like a woman happy with the outcome of this evening's events. She should be; Max was so much better a catch than Breedon.

Max had not shown up yet, and Fanny had gone to get dressed. Miss Winston wore a green velvet gown with Juliet sleeves and a rather more-opaque-than-normal fichu filling in the neckline. Her hair was arranged severely in a smooth topknot. The cascading curls were all tucked in and restrained. And the dazed look of a night creature mesmerized by a lantern's light was replaced by a look of worry. How had she ended up in Max's bed?

Scully wondered if Fanny had asked about her well-being. He knew from his sisters' tales that initiation into the bedroom rites was not always so easy for women. When he returned from settling Lady Malmsbury into her bedroom and whispered

in Fanny's ear that Miss Winston had been in Max's
bed, Fanny had stared at him.

"I cannot believe it," she repeated again and
again.

Scully could hardly believe it either. He'd never
known Max to disregard propriety. He sipped his
brandy and had a bad taste in his mouth, not that
anything was off with Max's brandy.

The door opened and Max walked into the room.
There was a spring in his step and an expression of
happiness that Scully had not seen on Max's face
in years. Not since before the news of his brothers'
deaths had reached him.

From the minute Max entered the room, his
focus had been on Roxana, but she kept her gaze
down.

Fanny slipped in the room and came over to
stand by Scully. He reached out and put his arm
around her waist.

Max cast a look in their direction as if they were
intruding, but his offer needed to be witnessed.
He knelt on one knee in front of Roxana and
reached for her fidgeting hands. She let him take
her gloved hands, but Scully could see her reluctance.

"Miss Winston, would you do me the great honor
of becoming my wife?" Max reached into his pocket.

Scully had the sense he was watching an execu-
tioner's blade fall with the stay of execution in his
pocket and unable to reach the scaffold in time.
Max had used the formal, correct words, but Scully
should have warned him to speak of love. Christ,
they were both horrible at proposals.

"Thank you. I am mindful of the honor you do
me," said Roxana in such a small voice Scully had

to strain to hear her. "But I do not wish to marry, your grace."

Scully watched the joy and excitement drain from Max's face. Scully took a step forward.

"We have to get married. I've ruined you," Max said.

"Yes, but no one knows. You've taken great pains to make sure of that, and I am grateful for your care." She withdrew her hands.

Max stood and for a minute looked bewildered. Then he leaned down in front of her and thumped his fist on the table beside her. "You have to marry me, Roxana. It is the right thing to do."

Roxana winced.

"Max," warned Scully in a low voice.

Max kept his back to them and said in a low voice that radiated with emotion, "Could you give me and my bride-to-be a moment of privacy?"

"Miss Winston?" Scully asked.

She looked up and nodded almost regally.

"We'll be just outside," said Scully, shepherding Fanny toward the double doors.

He moved out in the passageway and pulled Fanny toward him.

"I cannot believe she refused him," Fanny whispered. She looked over her shoulder. "Perhaps we should not leave them alone."

"Perhaps she has had too many shocks this evening. Perhaps she is just insisting he give his heart."

Fanny looked toward the door. "But no one refuses an offer from a duke."

"So do you admire her for it, or hate her for it?"

"Neither. It just makes me question myself," whispered Fanny.

Dev suspected that was a close as Fanny could come to admitting her marriage was not a true love match, at least not on her side. "Love, I think now would be as good a time as any to discuss our own future."

"I can't marry you, Dev."

Scully groaned.

She tugged at the ring on her finger. "Although I cannot seem to get this ring off. I will have to use butter on it."

"Fanny, we'll settle this later. Don't fret about the ring."

"It is too valuable for me to keep."

"It is safe where it is, and I'm not leaving any time soon."

Perhaps a misalignment of the stars caused all offers to be refused this night. Only how could that be on Christmas morning?

As soon as Max walked away from her, Roxana stood. Her stomach hurt. He stood on the far side of the room and raked a hand through his hair as if needed distance to get control of his anger. She moved to the window to look out on the clear moonlight reflecting on the crisp snow. It looked cold outside, but Roxana suspected it did not compare to the coldness in her heart.

Max's shock had surprised her. She had expected signs of relief.

He walked up behind her and she could feel his approach with every fiber of her being. Her body begged her to turn and throw herself into his arms. Her mind warned her that her emotions and the pleasure he had prompted from her body were too intoxicating and would tempt her. Her heart she ignored.

"Roxy, you have to marry me. I can give you time to adjust. I know you are fond of Breedon, but he would never suit you."

"I know," she answered, looking up to see his reflection over her shoulder. His image in the window was faint, as if he were a ghost, but she knew he was all too real. Solid flesh and tender touches, heated kisses and compassionate embraces—she fought back the memory of being in his bed. She hated that he was reduced to a pawn in her plan. She could see his consternation.

She understood now why her mother had said she needed a champion to take care of this ugly business. She tried to prevent her trembling from betraying her anguish.

"You know? Did you not expect Breedon to make an offer?"

"I hoped he would not. I want only compensation."

"What?" Max raised his voice. "What are you talking about?"

"You have, as you said . . ." The words were like sawdust in her mouth. "You have ruined me." She straightened her shoulders. "I would like a settlement. I am told a girl in my position may demand money in lieu of an offer."

"Marriage will repair any damage to your reputation, Miss Winston," he said stiffly.

"Yes, well, I would prefer money. It should make me feel much better."

"We're getting married," he said grimly.

"What about Thomas? I thought you wished to keep him as your heir."

"I cannot now."

"Yes, you can."

"I never, never would have done what I did if I had any doubt that we would be married at the first possible opportunity. I thought I made that clear."

"You made it clear that you expected us to be married, and that I could not leave." She pushed her hand against her stomach, trying to mitigate its churning.

"You were willing. I made sure you were willing. You accepted my touch and experienced pleasure. No woman being assaulted does that."

Had he forgotten her reticence? "I am certain we were both overcome by . . . by passions."

His voice was full of venom. "I would not have touched you if you did not want me."

Roxana spun around, unwilling to let an attack come from behind. The fury in his voice made her fear that he would strike her next.

He took one look at her hand against her stomach and his eyes narrowed. His brown eyes were as hard as granite. None of the warmth that she was used to seeing there was at all reflected back. Was this the man who had an hour ago treated her with reverent patience?

"Compensation is granted to a woman who is carrying a man's bastard. You, I assure you, are not with child." He folded his arms tightly, as if he were restraining himself from striking her. "Your virtue, while muddied, is still intact. I have offered marriage. I owe you nothing more."

He stared at her and she glared back, but inside she was crumbling. Her dreams were folding in on each other. She knew only how to strike back to hold her little piece of ground. If she bent to his will now, she would never ever be able to hold her head high. She would be just like her mother, forced to acquiesce to everything her husband wanted.

"Now, say you will marry me," he demanded.

"I know you are used to having everything you want, and that you decide what is best for everyone without consideration for what they might desire, but I cannot imagine anything worse than a marriage based on this coercion." Her voice was breaking. "I am sure on calmer reflection—"

He growled and turned away from her, striding toward the fireplace. "Damn it, Roxana, I have to marry you."

"I'm sorry."

He slapped a clock from the mantel.

As the chimney clock crashed on the floor and splintered into a thousand pieces, Roxana yelped.

Max stared at the splintered mess of the clock on the floor, the inner workings spewed like animal guts on the carpet. He could not believe he had killed the clock. Never had he allowed himself to vent his spleen so destructively. It was not proper behavior for a duke.

Nothing he'd done tonight was proper behavior for a duke. Nor was this ravaging pain tearing apart his insides proper emotion for a duke. He was supposed to be above it all, impervious to the lower emotions, his dignity and comportment perfect.

Scully opened the door and looked in. "I think that is long enough, son."

"This is my house," yelled Max, and he felt like a tempestuous child. The kind of child he abhorred. The kind of child he never was.

His gaze swung to Roxana, and she was backed against the moonlit window, one hand still pressed against her stomach and the other hand clasped her arm, her fingers squeezing hard.

He hadn't risked touching her, because he feared his control. He wanted to pull her to him and hold her, but he could not, not with Scully and Fanny watching.

Max wheeled about and headed for the door. He did not know where he was going until a sleepy footman chased after him with his overcoat and scarf, the scarf Roxana had given him. He stopped and put the garments on; no need to lash out at a footman who did his job.

The cemetery gate clanged, and he walked back to the fresh graves. He felt more dead than alive, but then he had to believe that being dead would remove all pain. As he stared at his brothers' markers he could not understand why they, who had been so alive, were dead, and he, the wooden stiff one, was the remaining brother left alive.

A movement caught the corner of his eye, but he dismissed it. Who would be in the cemetery on Christmas morning besides him? His eyes were blurring anyway and it must be only an animal.

Roxana thought she might shatter if she moved. The cold glass at her back was support for her weakened knees. He would not give her the money she needed?

Scully moved over to where she stood against the window and took her elbow.

"Fanny, she's shaking like a leaf."

The duchess followed Scully and wrapped her arm around Roxana's shoulder. "Come sit down."

Amazingly, her legs worked as she moved across to the sofa where she had sat before.

"Are you very sure that you do not want to

marry Max? You will not get a better offer," said Fanny.

Roxana pressed her lips together and shook her head.

"Might I inquire why?" asked the duchess gently.

Roxana searched for an excuse. The truth that she could not contemplate marriage to any man would be scoffed at. "I am sure I am not good enough for him."

Scully stood in front of her, his arms folded and for once his flashing grin absent.

"Well, in matters of birth there are those that would say I was not good enough for his father, although there was no real danger that my children would succeed to the title," said Fanny.

"But Max would have Thomas as his heir."

"Oh, Miss Winston, there is no chance of that." The duchess's arm stiffened against her shoulders. "He will . . . he will have his own children."

Roxana did not answer. There was no guarantee that Max would have a son to succeed him.

"Your birth is better than mine. Your father is a baron. My father was a just a commoner." Fanny waved her hand in the air. "All that is neither here nor there."

Scully's attention shifted between the two of them, but his gaze seemed to harden as it returned to Roxana.

She tried to draw in a calming breath, but she continued to shake. She looked at the broken clock on the floor and felt chilled again.

Scully met her eyes as she turned back forward. Empathy flashed in his expression before she lowered her gaze.

"I am sure this is all my fault. I could not watch

over you every minute and Max offered to help and I am sure that too much proximity breeds familiarity . . ." Fanny seemed to run out of energy. "This is so unlike him."

"It is not at all your fault, Fanny," said Scully. "Max knew the line and jumped right over it. His behavior is at issue here, not yours."

Fanny seemed more distracted than not. Roxana stared at the floor. It was clear that the duchess and Mr. Scullin cared about Max. While they were attempting to do right by her, their concerns were for Max.

"He has made up for any breach of decency with his offer. And I have refused. There is an end of it," said Roxana, searching for dignity.

Oh God, what had she done? Her family was counting on her, and she should have accepted his proposal when he would not give her the money she needed. But the dream of her dress shop had sustained her for a long time and she could not abandon it.

A duke would not let his wife's family starve.

"Miss Winston, I have known Max a long time. I can assure you that his heart is at stake in this matter," said Scully.

"Is it?" Roxana asked sharply. She could not stand more guilt. Her family depended on her, and Scully intimated she had wounded Max. She knew that she had betrayed these people, intending to use them ill from the very minute she walked into the house, and that was burden enough.

Her stomach churned, and she feared she would be ill. "I have to go," she whispered.

She had to leave before she agreed to become his wife. His heart was not engaged, she told herself. He just . . . just lusted after her. Mrs. Porter had explained how that worked. And damn it to hell, her heart had turned traitor to her because she wanted to believe that Max would never hurt her, not as her father had. But she had seen evidence of his violence, in the killing of the fox, in his destruction of the clock, and in the way he had made Lady Malmsbury shriek in pain as he tossed her about.

Scully sighed as he watched Fanny lead Miss Winston off to bed. He would not be able to settle things with Fanny this night. He rather thought it would behoove him to keep Max company, at least until Malmsy left the house.

He went to Max's room, but it was empty. He wondered if he had gone down to the library for a drink. As he crossed through the entry hall a footman leaped to attention.

"Have you seen his grace?" asked Scully.

"He went outside, sir."

"Do you have any idea where?"

"He appeared to be heading for the family plot, sir."

Scully had the footman fetch his coat and followed Max outside. He turned up his collar around his ears and hiked across the snow. The surface crunched under his feet. And Max's footsteps where the surface had broken showed his path.

The gate clanged as he opened it.

Max stood still and solitary. His scarf was fisted in his bare hands.

"Drink?" asked Scully, holding out the flask he had taken the liberty of filling while waiting for the footman to bring his outdoor wear.

"I did not force her."

That might explain Roxana's fear. "Did she say you did?"

"I told her she couldn't leave. I did not mean that she . . . that we . . . that she must submit."

"It's a fine line," said Scully, and he took a drink.

"I am not used to dealing with virgins. I told her to scream and she refused. She was not averse to pleasure."

Scully lifted an eyebrow.

"Yes, I'm sure. We had intimacies enough that I could tell it was new to her."

Which wasn't exactly the question Scully meant to ask, but he could tell Max was searching for the exact moment when things had gone wrong.

"Why would she not scream if she felt I was abusing her? A scream would have settled the matter of her being compromised before it had gone so far."

"Compromised?"

"She meant to catch Breedon," Max said bitterly.

"Ah, but you had switched rooms with him."

"For God's sake, what did I do wrong?" Max bent his head and held it in his hands.

"Did you tell her that you loved her?"

"I—no." Max frowned. "She's not interested in love."

"On the contrary, all women are interested in love, especially from a husband." Scully took another drink.

"No, she wanted money. I can only comfort myself that she wanted money from Breedon."

Scully choked on the brandy and coughed.

Max took the flask from him and drained it.

When Scully could breathe again, he asked, "Did you agree to give her money?"

"No, I thought to force her to marriage, by refusing it." Max handed back the empty flask. "Despicable of me."

He moved away from Scully. "I don't have the ready to spare anyway."

Scully put the information in the back of his brain. He'd sort it out later when he was less wrapped up in his own pain. "You know, you are not the only one who has been refused this night."

Max paused and then looked over his shoulder.

"I mean to try again, though. My ring is stuck on Fanny's finger." Scully barked a laugh. "Some justice in that."

Max returned and threw an arm around Scully's shoulders. "Fine Christmas this is turning out to be." He gestured toward his brothers' graves. He started to speak, but was unable to get the words out.

Funny, Scully had not thought Max would take the death of his brothers so hard. Scully had thought himself closer to Samuel and Alexander than Max. When they had asked him how Max would deal with their deaths, he had not realized how deeply it would wound Max.

"Do not give up just yet." Scully tossed his arm around Max's shoulders so they could toddle along like two peep-of-day boys who needed to lean on each other to stand. "She is terrified of something."

"Who, Fanny?"

"No, Roxana." *Well, possibly Fanny too,* thought Scully, but Fanny tended to be more dependent.

Max snorted. "Do not be absurd. Roxy is afraid of nothing. That is one of the things I admire about her."

They took a few steps toward the house, then

Max stopped. "The only thing is, I believe she was put up to coming here and being compromised by the richest man here."

Alone in her room, Roxana finished packing. Her shaking hands hardly allowed her to complete her task. Her mind was swirling with condemnations of herself.

She would have to find another way to get to London and open her dress shop.

Stay with the duke.

The thought kept intruding.

Marry the duke.

No, she could not give him control of her.

She feared if he approached her, she would fall apart. When the girl assigned as her maid appeared at first light, she had her summon footmen to take her trunks down. Perhaps the Breedons would allow her to ride with them to the next town.

But as she descended to the front hall to see what she could arrange to transport her trunks, the footmen were carrying her bags out of doors and lifting them onto a carriage.

She took a step toward the door.

Scully walked through the hall, brushing his hands. Roxana drew up short. Were they sending her away? Had Max decided he could not tolerate her presence? If so, that would solve the problem with transportation. Except they would send her home instead of to London.

"Miss Winston, might I have a word with you?"

She nodded, swallowing hard.

He led her into the library. He gestured for her to have a seat. She noticed two empty glasses and an empty decanter on the table between the two easy chairs.

"Merry Christmas," he began with his easy smile.

"Merry Christmas," she managed her voice croaking.

"Are you all right?" Scully asked. He leaned forward and studied her.

"I'm fine."

"Are you quite certain?"

"I'm fine," she repeated.

"Max did not injure you in any way?"

Roxana met his eyes firmly. "Not in any physical way."

Scully's eyes narrowed. "Max said you asked for money."

Her ability to stand her ground dissolved, she looked down at her clasped hands. Had her behavior been dissected and the entrails read? Her skin heated.

"For the damage to my good name?" She had not meant to sound uncertain.

"Why do you need money?"

"I cannot say."

Scully folded his arms. "So was your plan all along to come here and blackmail a man?"

Roxana refused to answer. She stared at her hands. Scully stood and she clenched her eyes closed. Something landed in her lap; she opened her eyes and saw several bank notes.

"You don't deserve it."

Had Max changed his mind? "Did Max . . . ?"

"Max loves you, whether he knows it or not."

Roxana felt hot tears sting her cheeks as she gathered the funding for her dreams, and an amount that would keep her brother and sisters fed and warm for years. "I'll repay it all."

Scully went still.

Max must have changed his mind. Either that or the light of day had returned reason to him and he remembered he did not intend to marry.

"I am ever so grateful for your intercession." She sprang out of her chair and headed for the door. Now she could follow her dream and open her dress shop. And if her heart ached at the thought of leaving, she told herself she was doing the right thing. She would never give a man the rights that marriage conferred upon a husband. Therefore she could never give Max what he wanted. And he would realize that her leaving would be best for both of them.

Chapter
Fifteen

Max woke late in the morning. His sleep had been late in coming and fitful. Desire tormented him all through the night. He had been so close to burying himself in Roxana's willing body when they were interrupted. He could scarcely think of anything else. Never had he anticipated with so much intensity the joining with a woman. He had gone past want. He *needed* her.

He shoved down the throb of his body. Just because he was more than ready for lovemaking did not mean she was as prepared. He might have ruined everything with his impatience. His gut twisted and his head ached. That she might have interpreted his unwillingness to wait as a lack of concern about her disturbed him.

The copious amount of wine he and Scully drank last night did not help his pounding head, but that did not mitigate his desire for Roxana. Yet, a certain optimism coursed through his blood.

Roxana had been confused, upset and overwhelmed by all the events of yesterday. If he just restored their friendship, gave her time to become used to the idea that they had to marry, she would come around. He would invite her up to London to stay for the season. Her whole family could come. He could afford to feed and house them, at least. He would tell her if she still did not want to marry him at the end of the season he would bow out of her life. But he had no intention of letting that happen.

In their heartfelt discussions last night, he and Scully had come to the conclusion that women much preferred the courtship to the engagement. Surety was more of an attraction to men. He would court Roxana and make her acknowledge that she enjoyed being with him.

When he thought of her response to him in bed, he knew her resistance was naught but a paper tiger. When he convinced her to come up to town, he would have to book lodgings or stay with a friend. And if Fanny could not cope with shepherding Roxana about, he could have one of his aunts come and stay too.

He growled at his reflection in his shaving glass as he realized he would have to restrain his physical desire. He would have to wait for marriage, to demonstrate to her that he could control his urges. That would be the hardest part, but dear God, madness had overtaken him last night. It was never well done to ignore the rules.

He knew that.

Finishing his ablutions and patting dry his freshly shaved face, he took an extra minute to put his razor in the cupboard.

He rushed downstairs, only to be waylaid by Fanny outside the breakfast room.

"Is Miss Winston with you?" she asked, her face puckered in worry.

"No, of course not. Is she not in her room?"

"No, she is gone and her things are gone, and what am I to tell her mother?"

"She can't have vanished into thin air." Panic crashed over Max like a rogue wave that would drown him. Had his actions of the night before prompted her to run away? He could not believe she had disappeared.

He took the stairs two at a time and threw back her door. The room was neat; the bed already made or never slept in. The cupboard drawers were empty, the wardrobe was empty; no sign of her occupation remained in the room. It was if she had never been. Yet he had not dreamed such a perfect, irritating creature.

Also missing was the pouch of his mother's jewelry. Anger clenched at his guts. She was not only an extortionist, but also a thief? He shook it off. It was his fault. He had not listened when she said she needed money. He bent his head and raked his hands through his hair.

A paper peeked out from behind the writing desk. Max shifted the desk from the wall and retrieved the letter. He skimmed down the contents, reading the reports of health, the loss of tenants because of a raucous party, a great deal of focus on food or the lack thereof, and then the instructions for compromise, disjointed and vague. A tear stained the page.

Hellfire and brimstone, here was the proof that Roxana's plan was not her own. That she had been forced to . . . but the letter writer clearly wanted Roxana to accept marriage.

Max stared at the tiny crisscrossed writing and the tear that blurred the words. Had the tear been Roxana's?

He had to go after her.

Desperation made strange bedfellows, thought Roxana as she looked around the building she had just leased. The storefront downstairs would allow for her shop. The attic above provided a long work area complete with skylights to take advantage of the sun, and the storage room behind the shop would provide fitting and changing rooms. And she would make her living space in a far corner of the attic.

Her breath hung in the air. Water had run in from the windows set in the roof and stained the ceiling, but she was excited. The money she had saved hitching a ride with Lady Malmsbury would help her fund the necessary modifications to the building.

She hadn't intended to ask the woman who had made an enemy of her for a ride, but when her trunks accidentally got carted out with Lady Malmsbury's baggage and stowed on her carriage, she'd bribed her ladyship's coachman to let her ride on the box with him to the nearest posting town.

At the coaching house, when Roxana had not moved off the box fast enough, Lady Malmsbury had spied her and then said, "You were the one in his bed. I saw dark hair, and I have not seen a maid of the house with hair so dark. Nor would he have made such an effort to conceal the identity of a servant."

"His grace has treated us both ill," answered

Roxana. "I apologize for stowing away on your carriage, but I wished to get away quickly."

Lady Malmsbury's green eyes flashed, but then she asked Roxana's destination and agreed to carry her to the city. Other than listening to Lady Malmsbury's rants Roxy had tried not to think about Max. That he had been the woman's lover made her chest ache, and while she did not believe above half of what Lady Malmsbury said, that half hurt.

Still, that was in the past, and Roxana had her seed money for her business and she'd found a great location. Max had given her the way to pursue her dream, and for that she would be ever grateful. If her money seemed to be disappearing a little faster than she wished, she would open her business soon and earn it all back. And as soon as she knew her father had left home and could not abscond with it, she would send money home.

Max knocked on the door of Wingate Hall and waited patiently. He was astounded that a footman failed to open the door when he approached on horseback. His carriage was a day behind him; he had ridden on ahead, hoping to run across Roxana. He could not believe he had not encountered her on the road. He'd even followed a mail coach for several miles, checking the passengers when it stopped at its posting inn.

Where the hell was she?

He fisted his hand and banged on the door, but as he looked around, the Hall had the signs of abandonment about it. The drifts of snow in the corners of the stairs indicated they had never been swept clean. The windows were streaked with dirt and the pleasure gardens to the left of the house appeared terribly overgrown.

He backed away and saw not one puff of smoke from any of the chimneys. Were they away?

Max pulled out the letter and reread the postmark. It had come from this county and this was the return address.

He scanned the horizon. The smell of wood smoke hung on the air. Once he spotted the column of smoke he followed it down to the small cottage. He led his horse toward the signs of life.

He knocked on the weathered wood door and a girl with blond hair and freckles and Roxana's blue eyes opened it. She stared at him while wiping her hands on her apron.

"I beg pardon for my interruption. I am looking for the Winstons." Max had the horrible suspicion he had found them.

She looked over her shoulder and then dipped her gaze to the floor. "Won't you please come in, sir?"

"I'm Trent," he began.

Her gaze shot up and he was again reminded of Roxy. Yet this girl was younger and less self-assured. He could see from her startled reaction she recognized his title.

"Let me get my mother, your grace," she said with a curtsy. "Jonathon, come take the duke's horse."

"Is your father home?" Max removed his hat.

She shook her head and then scrunched her nose. "Is Roxy with you?"

Max paused in looking around the tiny parlor crammed with broken and worn furniture.

A boy scrambled by him, coughing.

Max stopped him. "Tell me where I might put him up, and I'll take care of him. You go back inside."

The girl pulled her threadbare shawl tighter around her narrow shoulders. Max was suddenly aware that he was letting out the heat and it was undoubtedly a precious commodity for a family living in complete poverty.

No wonder Roxana had asked for money. Seeing this wretched existence, he marveled that she had not stolen his mother's jewelry. Instead she had entrusted her maid to return it to him with Roxana's thanks and an apology that she had not had time to write a proper note.

Where the hell was she? Fear gripped his heart and squeezed hard.

Fanny dismissed her maid and settled into bed. Scully assumed Max's duties as host after Max left, telling everyone he had to escort Miss Winston home. It was as if a new outburst of the plague had begun, the exodus of people needing to leave because of sick relatives on Christmas morning had been so massive. Other than the insatiable curiosity of the remaining guests, Fanny was relieved.

She was glad of Scully's support, but she did not think she could put him off much longer. He was growing increasingly impatient with her unwillingness to change her mind or discuss why she did not want to marry him.

Yet she could not believe he really wanted to marry her, and he had dropped off to a campaign of hand kisses and touching the small of her back in a way that made her shiver, although she had to think it the grossest overreaction. He was probably counting the days until he could leave and forget that he had made such a rash offer.

For several nights she had stayed awake waiting for him to come to her room, but he had not. And she was too old to make do on so little sleep.

She hovered in that land of nod.

Suddenly she startled awake. Had she heard a tap on her door or only dreamed it? Her body didn't differentiate. Her flesh came alive, hungry for Dev's touch.

The door opened and Dev came in holding a nightlight. He bent and put the candle on her nightstand. And she was still not sure it was not a dream.

"Sleeping, love?"

She struggled to sit up in her bed. She bit her lip, fearing to say anything that might make her wake.

Dev flopped onto the bed beside her. "I am exhausted. How does Max manage all this host duty stuff and nonsense?"

All right, she was awake. If she were making this dream he would behave like a lover, not an overgrown boy. "Dev, you should not be here."

He toed off his shoes and they thumped on the floor. "I'm tired of trying to court you gently. I want more than that."

Had he been trying to court her gently?

"You want me too, Fanny. You know you do. I have seen you watching me across the room. I shall be glad when everyone is gone and I can be free with my affection."

He scooted up on the bed and raised himself on his elbows.

"I was not aware you were using—"

With hardly any warning, he kissed her.

"—any restraint."

He kissed her again as if he meant to devour her. After a whimper of surprise she kissed back with the hunger she had been trying to hide. Every pent-up emotion she'd felt for the last ten years came out in her response. The taste of him swirled in her mouth, and he breathed harder and faster.

He pushed her nightcap off and slipped his hands through her hair. He eased back, nibbling at her lips and murmuring, "So sweet, love. You taste so sweet. Let me stay with you tonight."

He stared down at her, his blue eyes begging.

Fanny did not know if she could fight herself any longer. She found herself shivering with longing every time he drew near to her, every time he tossed his smile in her direction, and his touch made her mindless.

"Put out the light," she said.

His grin flashed, and she closed her eyes, fighting back the urge to treat this too nonchalantly. This was too rare an event for her to partake lightly. Letting him stay the night in her bed would change her life forever.

His weight shifted away from her and her eyes popped open. Fear that he might leave made her heart choke.

He slid off the bed and shed his jacket and unbuttoned his unmentionables. His urgency to draw his shirt over his head and step on one pantaloon leg to draw off the other leg made him tip and hop sideways.

A giggle bubbled up from deep inside her and the sound startled her as it left her mouth.

"Ah, there is the Fanny I know and love."

His small-clothes dropped and her giggle ended.

His male member jutted proud and erect in front of him. He stood still for a minute as if letting her soak in the sight of him naked.

When she was finally able to draw her eyes away from the thick length of him, rising from that dark thatch of curls, she noticed other things. She drank in the strength of his thighs, and the rippled expanse of his stomach—so much for the paunch he had claimed. Her gaze forayed up his lightly furred chest, with the whirls of hair around his flat dark nipples. Every change to his body marked his new maturity and his strength. Her mouth watered.

Dev watched her patiently. He had not been near so patient the first time, the only time they made love. He reached over and slowly pulled back the covers. He slid in beside her and rolled to settle on top of her. His weight pressed her into the feather mattress, and she noticed the care he took to mount her gently.

His body had changed, but the changes marked him as more mature. His shoulders were broader, and she thought he might be bigger in other ways.

He nibbled at her lips and she felt a sigh leave them. She wished the changes to her body had been improvements.

"Fanny, love, as you can see, I am ready for you, but there is no hurry."

He was clearly no longer a boy and she was no longer dealing with the play of an impatient young man.

He shifted to nibble at her neck. As his body slid along hers, she felt his hardness pressed into the juncture of her thighs. Through her nightrail, she felt the probe of that part of him. She turned her head to the side to allow him to taste her neck.

The candle flame flickered in front of her, too bright.

"You forgot to blow out the light," she whispered.

"I didn't forget," he said, and then he kissed her deeply.

His hands dropped to her shoulders, and she winced. Fear gnawed at her stomach. She wanted the light out so she did not have to see him gulp down disappointment. His hand slipped lower and he eased her nightrail up her legs. She reached to hold it down.

"Fanny!" he protested.

"The light," she whimpered.

"You would starve me of this pleasure? I want to see you. As you looked your fill of me." He tugged at her nightrail, but she refused to lift her hips.

"Please, Dev."

He straddled her locked-together legs, and pushed up to his knees. "Are you still scared of me seeing you in the altogether?"

His hands made a leisurely tour of her body before slipping to the neck of her gown.

"Please put out the light." She might be able to tolerate his touch, but his looking upon her naked was too much. Her anticipation cooled.

"I love you," he whispered. Then he ripped her nightgown down the center.

A squeal left her mouth, and she lurched upward. A burst of heat scorched through her body.

He pushed her back down into the bed. Peeling back the fabric, he let it skim over her skin with a teasing stroke. The shock of cool night air against her heated skin raised gooseflesh.

"Dev!" She did not know if she protested the

way he made her melt or the destruction of her nightclothes.

He grinned. "I'll buy you a new one. I'll buy you a whole new wardrobe. I'm tired of seeing you in black." His eyes roved over her flesh, and he brushed the scraps of her nightgown away. Yet as she watched him, the warm twinkle did not fade from his eye, nor, more importantly, did his erection wither.

She fought for bravery, to rise above the flush that heated her cheeks. "I'll have you know that black is quite slimming."

He laughed. "Ah, there is that hidden practical streak in you." He cupped a hand around her breast. "I shall call you my baroque beauty."

He skimmed his fingers down over her midsection. "Look how lovely and soft your skin is."

She put an arm over her face. She wasn't that brave.

He pulled the edges of her ripped nightgown over her flesh and waited until she lowered her arm. Then he pushed them away again, taking special care to tease her skin with the frayed edges of the gown. His eyes sparkled like fine crystal and he leaned over and brushed his lips against hers.

"How could you ever think I would not savor looking upon you? You are so beautiful, my heart is full."

"Hush," she whispered, and decided to believe him.

The increasing hitch in his breathing poured faith through her. And his touch was so slow and thorough she could not doubt him. He lowered his head, nipping at her flesh, molding her with his hands, and touching the tip of his tongue to her nipple. But then his head sank lower and he tasted her navel and dropped lingering kisses all across the quivering flesh of her belly.

He seemed determined to look at every inch of her as he urged her legs apart.

Then his head dipped lower, and he had not lied about kissing every inch of her, only she was lost to everything but the gluttony of pleasure.

Max stared at the ceiling of the cottage. He lay in the bed in the single bedroom. Lady Wingate insisted he sleep here. She took Roxana's bed in the attic. He would have refused, but with Jonathon sleeping in the parlor on a sofa too short for the growing lad, no other space was available for Max. He could not force the girls out of the attic. He would have slept in the stables with his coachman and accompanying outriders, but the idea of it mortified Roxana's mother.

What would he do with them?

He had bought them food and supplies, and then a letter from Roxana arrived with a ten-pound note in it.

Where had she gotten that kind of money? And why was she in London? Lady Wingate seemed as upset and surprised as he was that her daughter had not returned home.

Did she still intend to catch Breedon? Alone in London, all the care he had taken to preserve her reputation was for naught.

His offer to take the Winstons back to his home had met with a refusal. "Lord Wingate would not like that," said Lady Wingate primly.

Max hardly cared what Lord Wingate liked, since

he had provided so ill for them. As he stayed longer he learned that the family had moved to the cottage so they might let the main house and dismiss all the servants.

Brought up to believe that the lord of any county had an obligation to keep the locals employed, Max could not understand their philosophy to economize. Besides, without proper upkeep a house like Wingate Hall would deteriorate and could not fetch a decent rent.

If he had the money, he would turn Fanny loose on renovations for their home while he concentrated on maximizing production of their farms and fields. But he suspected they would balk at the idea of charity, especially since he had no claim to them.

Roxana had refused him. The thought stabbed through him. She did not want to be married to him, not even to be free of this poverty and to rescue her family from it.

As he stared into the dark he made plans to install caretakers in Wingate Hall and convince one of his outriders to stay behind and take care of the work they needed a man to do. He felt an obligation to be sure that Roxana's family was cared for. He had ruined her, forced her to flee to London, and he could not leave her family to suffer on in this pitiful existence.

Still, the ache in his chest spread until he wished only for oblivion to ease the pain. Not even her dire background had prompted Roxana to think that marriage to him would be better than whatever life she could have with so little in the way of family fortune.

What could he do but honor her unspoken plea to stay out of her life?

* * *

Scully resisted the temptation to complete the union of their bodies. Fanny whimpered as he teased. He had brought her to the edge of satisfaction and then moved away to kiss her belly and breasts, then her neck. Her hands slid to his hips and tried to draw him in.

"Say you love me, pretty Fanny," he whispered.

"Dev, please."

"Say you love me," he demanded again.

"Please, I need you," she moaned.

Her hips swiveled and he could not wait for her to say the words he had waited half his life to hear from her. But then as he buried himself into her dewy body the rapture of the moment had control of him. She moaned, and the spasms of her release brought him to heaven and he followed her down in the fall back to earth.

"Don't move," she whispered.

Of course he moved, just slightly in and out, one stroke.

Her heavy breathing hiccupped.

Another stroke, before he lost all the firmness, then another, and he suspected he had no need of a recovery period.

Fanny moaned and twisted and then her body filled with new tension, and she clutched at him as he moved with a slow easy glide. He kissed her slowly, deeply and she began to strain against him. He stroked her full breasts, tugging at her tightening nipples. Her moans, sighs and expression guided his kisses and caresses until he could feel her loss of control.

Then, as she shuddered and whimpered, he heard the words he'd been longing for. "I love you."

They brought with them such a rush of emotion he shuddered into a new peak.

As their bodies thrummed and pulsed and their panting slowed to sighs, he lay on top of her, relishing the cooling of his skin, the warm damp places he was still connected to her.

Fanny whispered, "Really, do not move. Or I shall have to kill you."

"I could not move. Marry me, Fanny." He leaned up on his elbows, careful to keep his lower body motionless. "Marry me, tomorrow."

She stared up at him, her blue eyes blinking.

"No secrets between us now, love. Is it that I am not rich enough to buy you curtains and cabinets and paintings and sculptures?"

She shook her head.

"That I don't have a title?" he asked, pulling her hand up and kissing her palm.

"What, then?"

"I am too old; I might not be able to give you children."

"You might be carrying my baby now. Fanny, I don't care. I have no title to pass on. My estate is small. A lot of children would bankrupt me. I shall have Thomas and Julia and dozens of nieces and nephews who would treat me as their favorite uncle if I do not have children. If I have you, there will be enough people in my life to love."

"I cannot abandon Max," she whispered. Tears filled her eyes. "He is so alone, and I am sworn not to tell him. His brothers made me promise."

"We would never abandon Max. He is my closest friend. But he will marry Roxana. I am sure of it."

"If he does marry her, then I will marry you," she whispered. "If you still want me to."

Scully groaned, but it was a better answer than what he had before. "Or if I do get you with child, Fanny. I must insist and Max would expect it."

Now Scully wanted to plant a child in her womb.

Chapter
Sixteen

November 1805

After the seamstresses left for the day, Roxana straightened the workroom and picked up a garment to finish sewing. She stretched the tired muscles in her shoulders.

"Pardon, Mademoiselle?"

Roxana turned to look at the woman she had hired to provide a face to the world for her shop. Although the front woman claimed to be a member of the French nobility, Roxana guessed she had probably been a lady's maid in France before fleeing from the terror. Her manner toward their patrons was properly deferential without the haughtiness Roxana might have expected from a woman born to be served. But they had both made a silent pact to not ask about each other about their pasts.

"Is everything locked up below?" asked Roxana.

The other woman, known as Madame Roussard,

nodded. "Do you think it ez possible you will be able to pay wages this week? Some of the girls have talk of leaving."

"If anyone pays us." Roxana shrugged. "I have plans to show you, if you would like a cup of tea."

If she went by the number of orders she received, Roxana was doing all right. If she went by the amount of money she'd actually collected, she was failing. Miserably. She had not been prepared for her clients' disregard of her tickets. Then half of society disappeared from London after the season, leaving their accounts unsettled.

With the social season months away, Roxana had decided to concentrate on capturing the business of the ladies of the evening. Mrs. Porter and her girls had always paid promptly. Apparently they possessed a better appreciation for a working woman's need for solvency.

Roxana pulled the ever-present kettle off her stove and poured hot water into her teapot and carefully measured in tea. She could not offer milk or sugar, but Madame Roussard would not complain. Her stoic acceptance of the hardships made Roxana feel worse.

After they settled into two chairs dragged over from the work area, Roxana opened her sketchbook.

Madame Roussard put a hand to her chest and said, "Mon Deus, these are, how you say, risqué."

"Yes, well," Roxana rubbed her face. "I need to do something."

Madame Roussard reached over and put her hand over Roxana's. "These are for you?"

"No. Oh, no!"

Madame Roussard's dark eyes for once shined

with hope. She had seen too much and her eyes were normally flat. She turned away, then took a sip of her tea.

"You must think things are very bad indeed," said Roxana, startled by the idea that Madame Roussard thought Roxana might be contemplating supplementing their income with money gained from harlotry.

"There was that gentleman—"

Roxana made a chopping motion with her hand. She did not want to talk about Max, think about Max. If only she could quit yearning for Max.

Madame Roussard was under strict orders to not reveal Roxana's name to anyone, and especially not to any man, but Roxana feared her father learning her whereabouts more than she feared Max finding her.

That he had come looking for her had not surprised her. That he had visited her family and offered to take them in had. Between that and his searches for her, she felt a sick sense of guilt and a wish that she could include him in her life. She had so little connection to her family and none to anyone she could call friend. A wave of longing so strong it made her sway slammed over her. Oh God, she missed Max, but he would never understand her choices.

Madame Roussard stood and went down the stairs and a few minutes later returned with the ledger book. As they looked over the figures, Roxana knew that drawing in new clientele would not be enough to save her business. If she did not send home money to her family every month, she might have been eking by. If she did not have to pay Madame Roussard to provide a face to the world, she might be able to pay the seamstresses. If Max had not given her the money, she would not have come this far.

"Ah, it is time you let me go, n'est-ce pas?"

"No. I won't do that."

Madame Roussard had been more than a manager; she had guided Roxana in decisions that running a business required. She had insisted on the seamstresses when Roxana could not sew fast enough to keep up with orders. She had steered Roxana through the pitfalls facing a young woman alone in London. She had become the closest thing Roxana had to a friend. Yet a wide gulf of experience and years separated them.

"We only have need to survive until the season, non?" Madame Roussard shifted in her chair. "I leave France with nothing or I give money to you." She looked down at the sketches of the revealing dresses.

Madame Roussard suddenly looked as old as Roxana felt. What would happen to her if the shop closed? Not only was Roxana's family dependent on her, but also Madame Roussard had often hinted that Roxana had saved her from a life of prostitution. A middle-aged French émigré with few marketable skills, no friends and a questionable past could expect little in the way of employment opportunities.

"I'll find a way to make this work," Roxana vowed, even if that meant she had to apply to Max. God knew how much she already owed him. But before that she would see if she could induce her first clients to return to the fold. If Mrs. Porter and her girls were back in business, perhaps they would commission new gowns.

* * *

Max shook off the cold as he entered his home, but nothing thawed the frost from his soul.

"Brandy?" asked Scully from the library door. "Take off the chill."

"Don't you have a home?" asked Max, not at all surprised to find Scully in the Trent library. But he took the proffered glass just the same.

"You did not bring back Miss Winston?" asked Scully, standing to the side of the roaring fire.

Max stared into the glass of reddish brown liquid. He remembered bringing Roxana in here to warm her, handing her the glass of brandy and nearly having his way with her in front of the fire. At first he had been relieved that he had not taken her virginity, but now he only regretted it.

"She's not there." Max had just returned from his fourth trip to Roxana's home.

"She's not at her home?" The smile faded off Scully's face and, as happened more than not lately, it was replaced by a look of concern, almost pity. Max downed the brandy in one gulp. He hoped it would remove the burr of pain, but he knew it would not.

At least Scully had given over telling him he did not know how to drink properly. Only the rising cost of French brandy kept Max from bathing in the stuff.

"Where is she?" asked Scully cautiously.

"Somewhere in London." He had only told them he went to visit the Winstons, but Max could no longer keep the secret.

Scully looked blank. "Where in London?"

Max threw his glass at the hearthstones. The sound of shattering crystal gave him only a small measure of satisfaction before shame at his child-ish tantrum smothered the relief that he got from any release of anger. "I don't know."

"That is why you have been to town so much," said Scully as if a puzzle had finally been solved.

Max had been to London dozens of times. It was if the last ten months were a blur of traveling and searching for her and not knowing how she would respond if he found her. "I cannot find her. She never went home, and she sends her family money on a regular basis."

"Then there is a return address on her money letters, is there not?"

"The Lombard Street post office." Max had wasted hours there hoping he would catch her in-quiring after her mail, but the letters were ex-changed infrequently and with no regularity.

"Oh." Scully sat down in the nearest chair, a sick look on his face.

"She's not with her father. Nor was he easy to run to earth."

"Does he know she is missing?"

"I take it he has not been informed in so many words." Max did not know what to make of Lord Wingate. The man had been quite animated talk-ing about his schemes to win back his fortune. Max's gentle suggestion that he might be best served by repairing his estate was met with a blank look.

"I have recently learned their tenants were a certain abbess and her girls. I hope that they did not give Roxana a misguided perception of that life."

"She would not have chosen to become a whore," said Scully quietly.

Max just didn't know anymore. Was the idea of

marriage to him so repugnant? How could she come apart so blissfully in his arms, and then repudiate everything that had gone between them?

"She already sent money home before I left the first time. Did she think that I would not honor my offer to marry her if she sent word to me?"

Scully swallowed and waited for him to continue.

Max stood and paced the room. "I thought mayhap she tried her hand at dressmaking, but I have been to every mantuamaker in London. I have begun looking in brothels. What else could she be doing but working on her back? How else could she have sent money home so soon?"

"I gave her money," said Scully, so low that Max was not sure he had heard him correctly.

"You did what?"

"I gave her a monkey. She was upset. I thought it would calm her." Scully walked to the brandy decanter. "Then she started talking about it as a loan and assumed you had given it to her. I didn't think it would hurt for her to think you had given in to her request. I had no idea she would disappear."

"You gave her five-hundred pounds?"

"If one is very frugal one could live quite a while on five-hundred pounds."

Max stared at the fire. "Perhaps you would have done better to just shoot me."

Scully turned slowly and looked anguished. Max felt remorse; he had no right to destroy his friend's happiness just because he was miserable.

That she had not left completely destitute offered a dram of relief, but where was she hiding? "It seems she would choose anything rather than marry me. I am off to find this Mrs. Porter first light."

* * *

"Mademoiselle, there ez a gentleman below. He will not leave until he speaks to you."

From where she was using the last of the fading light from the setting sun, Roxana looked up from the worktable. She stitched a ruche on the bodice of a garment ordered by one of Mrs. Porter's girls. In the end the working girls had driven a hard bargain, but Roxana had agreed to their price if they promised to pay promptly.

Roxana's first thought was that she wanted to finish the piece before the light was completely gone, but she put down the garment. She often dealt with suppliers and weavers, taking on the ordering of fabric, pins and needles, while Madame Roussard dealt with the clientele. "What gentleman?"

Madame Roussard looked round-eyed. "He say, he ez a duke, *mon chere*. And he say he knows you are here."

Roxana's hands shook, and she could not identify her emotions. Anticipation curled around a feeling suspiciously close to happiness.

She stood and removed the smock that covered her plain green gown and moved closer to her living area. "Send him up, then."

Max entered the attic and Roxana felt light-headed. As he cleared the last step, he stooped, missing the sloping roof. His hat in his hand, he walked forward until he could stand upright. Neither she nor any of the women working for her ever needed to bend to clear the eaves. He seemed large and imposing in her female sanctuary.

"Miss Winston," he said, and she had forgotten how low his voice was and how the timbre vibrated through her.

"Your grace," she answered as calmly as she could manage. Inside she was in turmoil, but, thankfully, her voice did not betray her.

Madame Roussard hung back on the stairs, waiting.

"Thank you, Madame. You may leave us."

Madame Roussard nodded and descended the stairs. She would lock up and leave.

Max looked behind him at the empty stairs. "Are you sure that is wise?"

Roxana paused in moving toward the stove. She chose to ignore the jibe. "Would you like tea? I am sorry there is no sugar or milk."

"Please."

She could feel his gaze on her, like being watched by a wolf. Max seemed rangier, leaner and harsher. An undercurrent of anger hung in the air and made her jumpy. Had he searched for her only to satisfy his sense of honor? Oh God, she had missed him.

"So you have found me," she said as she poured water into her teapot and added tea leaves. She also lit the lamp with its precious oil. She could not skimp while he was here.

"Yes," he answered.

She turned and realized he still wore his caped greatcoat. Was it the same one that he had thrown around her shoulders when she had chased after Breedon in the snow and grown too cold? "May I take your coat and hat?"

He handed her his hat and slid off his greatcoat. He looked around as if he had not even noticed his environment before now. Her heart beat madly as she stood close enough to smell the cold on his skin, the hint of bay rum and just him.

She stood clutching his coat to her, afraid to

move yet drawn close as if he were a warm fire in the middle of winter. Her body remembered his touch with every fiber of her being.

His exploration of the room stopped on her iron bed. She had curtained it with heavy velvet to keep the warmth in as she slept, but the curtains were drawn away from the foot to allow the heat from the stove to enter the enclosure.

He turned toward her as if aware of her reluctance to move away. "Roxy?"

She forced herself to draw back and cross the room to one of the work tables, where she laid his greatcoat and placed his hat. "As you can see, this is my workroom. I have four seamstresses who work for me during the day, and of course Madame Roussard provides a face to the world, so no one of consequence knows I am here."

"I take it you did not want to be found."

Roxana bit her lip. Did he appreciate anything of her efforts to start her business and make a success of it? She turned and leaned against the work table. "I am glad *you* found me."

"I came to take you back home."

She turned her back to him and leaned her hands on the table. "I am happy here. Well, mostly happy here. I confess to occasional loneliness. I miss my family, but I do not wish to return home."

"Not there. Not your father's home. I wanted you to know that my offer is still good."

He was still talking of marriage? She looked down at the table. "I have no wish to leave here."

It was a lie, in some ways. At times she wanted to be with him much more than she wanted to be here, struggling to make her business work. But turning over control of her life, mind and body to him, to any man, terrified her.

"Roxana, marry me."

"I'm a woman in trade, Max. A duke cannot marry a person like me. I won't give this up. I have worked too hard for it."

Could they not have closeness without marriage? Many women took lovers and Max was already that in her mind. He was her lover, the man who made her come alive in the night, the man whose touch made her shiver, the man who had woken her to a side of life that offered so much more than she expected.

Max crossed the floor behind her, his footsteps solid thuds on the floor. He reached around her for his coat and hat. "I don't know why I came here," he said.

The idea that he would leave so soon, before she had a chance to tell him that he had changed her, had woken her to the joys of pleasure. That she wanted him to stay. That she thought about him every minute that was not filled with work and many times when she sat sewing or listening to the seamstresses gossip or when she lay alone in bed at night. Especially when alone in bed at night.

She turned, caught between him and the table. Her breasts brushed against his chest and Roxana and Max both went still. Under her bodice her breasts tingled, ached. Her blood rushed to her nether regions.

"I do not want you to leave," she whispered, breaking the charged silence.

He looked down on her, his brown eyes searching.

She put her hand on his chest, then the other hand, and she slid them up to his neck.

"Roxana." His voice was anguished.

She pushed closer to him. "I want you to stay," she said with more surety.

"You don't know what you are saying," he said. As he looked down at her his breathing quickened and his nostrils flared. He felt the burst of passion too. She knew he did.

"I am a woman grown now. I know what I am saying."

He winced as if she had struck him.

"I am not quite as naive as I was at your house," she said urgently. She had grown up and gained confidence in her ability to make her way in the world.

"And that is my fault."

She heard the heaviness in his words and did not know how to make him see that she did not regard maturity and knowledge as a burden.

Roxana stretched up on her tiptoes, sliding her breasts against his chest. And he kissed her. He kissed her like he was starving, and she was glad the desperation was not all on her side.

She pushed up into him, relishing the feel of his arms around her, his hands against her back, fingers splayed. He held her tight with hunger, but also with a gentleness, as if he meant to treat her like a precious and rare treasure.

She threaded her hands in his hair, feeling the strands curl around her fingers and holding his head down to hers as their tongues swirled in an age-old dance.

She could barely think; her thoughts became just a jumble of disordered sensations of his solid strength, his probing kiss, the taste of him and his cradling hold. Her body, so long deprived, came alive, quickening and melting. Heat swirled and simmered below her skin and sparks shimmered along her spine.

She wanted more, and she tugged at the knot of his cravat. He yanked it free and the ends dangled. She eased around toward her living space and, pulling the ends of his neck cloth, she tugged him toward her bed.

As if with great reluctance, he ended the kiss, but then nibbled at her lips. "Roxy, we cannot unless . . ."

"Hush," she murmured. "I know what I want."

He dug in his heels, and she let loose of his cravat. Instead she backed toward the bed, pulling out the beaded pins that held her bodice closed. As the material loosened and slipped, Max's gaze dropped to the falling material. As Roxana remembered how she had felt watching Max undress in front of her, she wondered if she could manage to be that brave.

"Christ, you would be wearing that," he said as if she had played unfairly.

She glanced down at the red silk of her shift. She had forgotten she had worn the nearly sheer undergarment. But as her clothes wore out and the likelihood of her ever wearing her red silk ballgown again faded, she had begun wearing the two silk shifts in the normal course of the week.

Then he had closed the distance between them and lifted her off her feet. He kissed her again, and she could feel his restraint dissolving.

"Are you certain, Roxana?" he asked.

"I am certain. I have missed you so much more than I ever would have thought."

"Then you will—"

She cut off his words with a finger across his lips. They would have to settle many things, but she did not want that to intrude now. "Not now, Max. Please, not now."

She told herself that he understood she wanted him in her bed. That she was no longer the semi-innocent young lady of the ton, but a working woman of a different class and station. "If you must talk, talk to me of Christmas trees and such nonsense."

"Roxana, that night I wanted to calm you." He stroked the side of her face.

"I know." She reached for the buttons of his coat. "You did. I was frightened."

"Odd—you seem fearless."

She paused for a moment. "I was afraid you'd stop searching before you found me." She had not realized how much she hoped and yearned for him to find her. She knew he would eventually succeed. She had been counting on him coming to her. "Will you forgive me for being so foolish as to run away?"

"I would forgive you anything," he said, but he shook her shoulders back and forth as if he would punish her instead. Then he kissed her.

She pushed her dress down and shivered as the cold air of the room encountered her heated skin. Or she shivered because even though he said he would forgive her anything, he made a mocking gesture of punishment. She was not so certain of his reaction when she stood in the way of what he wanted.

Yet, sometime in the last months, as he searched for her and her family's sparse letters reported his kindness and offers of support, she realized she had slipped over the edge into a commitment of her heart. She might not be able to tell him, because he would expect her to marry him, but she had fallen in love.

Chapter Seventeen

Of everything Max imagined when he found Roxana again, this was the stuff of dreams, not the small hopes he had held. As her plain green gown slipped to the floor and exposed the bright red of her sheer shift, he wondered if he had died and gone to heaven.

But then, heaven probably wasn't located in the corner of a cold attic workroom above a dressmaker's shop. He did not want to let her go, for fear she would evaporate into thin air. Yet she felt real to him. Her skin soft and smooth, her body warm and pliant, her kiss as welcoming as any man could want.

Roxana had changed into a woman in the time they had been apart, and the thought broke his heart, yet he knew it only made him want her more. He could make love to her without restraint. Before, he had been constrained by her innocence and the fact that she needed instruction. Still, his thought was to treat her with reverence. And this

time, they would be married. He could not bear
the thought of it any other way. If she had any fears
that what had gone on in the last year deterred him
in any way, he would set her mind at ease. They
were meant to be together, even if she had not realized it. But she must know it now.

He kissed her and allowed his emotions free
rein. His heart galloped and his blood coursed
through his body, journeying to his lower half. He
leaned down and caught her legs under her knees,
lifted her and carried her across the room to the
bed.

The cold sheets jarred him as he placed her on
the bed. He would take her out of this place and
show her that she deserved to be pampered and
surrounded by comforts. He only stripped off his
coat and waistcoat and dumped his Hussar boots
before he slid in beside her. She caught him to
her, and he found her lips again.

As he ran his hand over her ribs, he suspected
she might have lost weight, weight she did not
have to lose.

"Have you been eating?" he asked.

"Hush," she said with a slight laugh. She trailed
her hand down his front to find the buttons of his
falls.

His heart pounded and he slid his hands over
her curves. For the next few minutes he was lost in
the feel of her, and their clothes were pushed off
in frenzied haste. He tried to pause to be certain,
but she writhed under him, urging him with her
kisses and eager touches.

He had so much to say to her and so much they
needed to settle, but he had wanted her too long,
wanted her with an aching hollowness since the
morning after she had crawled into his bed. In the

back of his mind was the fear that he would be cut off before he could complete this union with her. When he tried to speak, she would press her mouth to his, touch her tongue to his lips, sigh into him.

And he had one burning thing he needed to tell her, that she needed to know as he nestled between her legs, prodding her woman's core with his male member. She needed to know how he felt before he made them one in body, because for him it would be more than just a physical union.

He held the reins of his urgency. He needed to make her understand. He cupped her face and stroked her hair back, holding her down, impeding her efforts to keep their mouths locked together in one endless kiss. "Roxana."

Her blue eyes opened and she looked sultry and dazed all together. She made a slight moan of protest and shifted against him. The rush of heat nearly overwhelmed him. His hips rocked forward, probing that warm wet entrance to heaven.

For a second all he could think of was the feel of her skin against his, the taste of her, her scent. "I love you," he whispered, and then again louder. "I love you more than anything."

He eased his hips forward and encountered the resistance of her body.

He reached to check his position, not fully comprehending the impediment.

A look of determination crossed her face. Roxana slid her legs up and folded them across his hips and added pressure. Then with a jerk, as if he had broken through a barrier, he slid inside her. Her body gloved him like a tight sheath. She whimpered and shuttered her eyes.

That he had hurt her tore at his heart. He had thought she had gained experience to match her confidence. He had accepted that she was no longer chaste in his mind, had thought that was one reason she did not want to talk, but his every thought was shouting that she had been a virgin. "Sweetheart, look to me."

She blinked her eyes open. They were glassy and tear filled.

He shuddered. Holding his desire in check made him quake. "I'm sorry. I've hurt you." His voice broke. He kissed her cheek. "I'll stop."

He said the words, but he did not know where he would find the strength to withdraw, and she needed to loosen her legs. His mind swirled in confusion. He reached up to pull her leg away from his backside.

Instead she slowly rotated her hips and a rush of heat burned through him. She held his gaze. Her eyes were like sapphires, glittering in the low light from the single lamp.

"I am given to understand that it won't hurt again." Her voice was breathy, yet sure. "Please, I want you. I have wanted you forever."

He heard "forever," and that was all he needed. He loved her forever too. And she was his in every possible way. He began that slow slide in and out, watching her for any indication that she was in pain. When she met his thrusts with eager moans, the thread of his control snapped. Then he was lost in the blue of her eyes, the warm heat of her compliant body, the magic of her sighs.

The butler leaned in the London drawing-room doorway. "Should I hold dinner longer, your grace?"

"You have not heard from the duke?" asked Fanny.

"No, your grace," answered the butler.

"This is not like him," she muttered. "Very well, serve dinner. If the duke returns please inform me at once."

"Very good, madam," said the butler, closing the drawing-room door.

Fanny turned to Scully. "I'm worried about Max. He always sends word if he does not plan to eat dinner here."

Scully stood and offered her his arm. "He is out looking for Miss Winston. Perhaps he has found her."

"He would have sent word about dinner. He is always proper when it comes to these things."

"When it comes to Miss Winston, all bets are off."

In spite of his nonchalance, Fanny knew Scully was worried about Max too. He had insisted they accompany him to London to be there at the town house with him. He had confided that he had seen Max behave in unexpected ways that were quite alarming.

"I never should have let him take responsibility for her well-being. He feels he has failed and must make amends."

"Ah, well, if he brings back Miss Winston as his bride, you shall have to marry me, you know. I want to take you home with me. I have to go home sooner or later."

Fanny had resisted Scully's repeated requests for marriage. She was worried about Max. He had changed so much from the time the caskets came home. It was as if the tight control he kept on his emotions had broken. Then the whole affair with Miss Winston shattered him, turning him sullen and angry, snappish, unlike the Max she had known.

He had always been so easygoing, well mannered and perfectly behaved; she had thought he no longer felt the emotions of a normal person. She had done him a terrible injustice. "I think we need to tell him about Alexander and Samuel."

"It is not up to us to decide," said Scully.

"Yes, but I thought it would be a few months, but it has been three years. What will Max thinks when he hears the truth?"

"He'll probably forbid you to marry me, so we should hurry up and do the deed, love."

Fanny shook her head. It had been months now that Scully shared her bed, yet her womb had not quickened in pregnancy. He might protest all he wanted, but she knew denying him children was wrong.

Roxana relished the feel of Max. His skin was warm against hers. His breath rasped into her mouth and his hands were magical as they coaxed her body into new heights of rapture, and then that male part of him filled her, stretching her so much she did not think it possible to contain him, but as he drew back and forth nothing had ever made her feel more complete than him inside her.

He groaned and pushed deep inside her, and then wracking tremors shuddered through his body. She could feel the throbbing pulse of his release deep within her. Her heart pounded against his and she felt filled and complete, connected to him in a way that was beyond the physical. This joining of their bodies was as close as they could come to marking their rapture. Yet she was disappointed it was over so fast, disappointed they would need to talk, that she would again hurt him with her need to be independent.

Yet as he rolled to his back, carrying her with him and then pulling her up, she protested the breaking of the connection between them. But then his mouth closed around her beaded nipple and spark after spark flew to the fire still smoldering in her woman's core. His tongue rolled and teased her to a new tenseness that could be ended only with a release.

He moved to her other breast, nuzzling and sampling as if she was a tasty treat to be savored. Then, his hands at her hips, he drew her up as he scooted down the bed, his kisses trailing down her belly. Her shock and surprise was soon replaced by raw pleasure at the wicked ministrations of his mouth on that most sensitive part of her. Then she was coming apart and falling all at once, and Max was there to catch her.

He settled her against him, drawing the covers over her and settling one hand over the curve of her bottom, the other holding her head to his chest. He pressed kisses on her forehead and crown as she drifted down through the glow of completion.

She was nearly asleep when he said, "You need to get dressed."

She shook off the fuzziness and raised her head. He slid her to his side and scooted to the edge of the bed, leaning over to retrieve his clothing.

"My carriage is outside, and I'm taking you away from here."

He handed her shift to her.

Roxana clutched the red material to her breast.

He'd heard nothing of what she had said. Her breath snagged as she shook her head. But his back was to her as he drew on his underclothes and he did not see her refusal. "I'm not leaving. This is my life."

He turned toward her as he buttoned his unmentionables. "Roxana, you have to marry me now."

She shook her head. How many times did she have to refuse him?

"You could be carrying my child." He reached for his shirt.

Roxana backed off the bed, still clutching her shift to her, feeling naked. Her feet encountered the cold bare planks of the floor. Their unpolished worn feel was familiar to her, comforting because this was her place. Yet the floor was frigid against the bare soles of her feet, as if to mark her step into a separation from him and the bliss they had shared.

"I'm sorry, I do not want to marry you, Max." It hurt her to say it.

He stared at her as if she were a foreign creature. He bunched his shirt in his hands. "My honor demands marriage, Roxana. I cannot live with knowing I have ruined you. I thought . . ." He shook his head. "You have given me no reason to refuse that makes sense."

He might be standing there barefoot and shirtless, but he was every inch the imperious duke. And she hated to defy him, but . . . "If I were to marry any man, it would be you, Max. But I shall not marry."

"You are mine, now, Roxy." He pulled on his shirt. "You will marry me."

"You do not own me," she said in a low voice. A

wife was a possession, which was why she would never marry.

He bent and picked up his socks and sat in the chair to tug them over his feet. Even his feet were beautiful, long and masculine. "I want to take you away from this miserable place."

Anger sparked in her. "This miserable place is my business that I have planned and saved for for years, and I have struggled to make my dress shop successful. I know I have not paid you back yet, but I will. I have clients, and for God's sake can you not see that I am proud of this?"

His brown eyes turned stony. The warmth that had been there as they made love was gone. "Why do you feel you must struggle? I can take care of you. I can take care of your family. You do not have to work so hard to live. I *want* to take care of you."

"I do not think you know me, if you cannot see how important my dress shop is to me. Please, Max, I do not want to fight now. I cannot marry you. I just want to be with you."

He stopped in drawing on his low boot. "Then marry me, Roxy."

She took a step back, biting her lip. If he said the right words, she feared she would say yes. And then she would live in a perpetual state of fear, waiting for the day she pushed him too far. "I think you should leave now."

"What was this, Roxy?" He stood and gestured to the bed where the evidence of their lovemaking was clear. "What did you intend when you invited me into your bed?"

"I wanted money," she meant it as a jest, but it petered out when she could not add the smile.

"Bloody hell!" He tossed his boots aside and thundered toward her.

His boots thudded against the floor. She spun away. The wall stood in front of her and there was nowhere for her to go. Memories of her beatings when she defied her father flashed like lightning strikes through her head. Max did not like being defied.

She dropped to her knees and wrapped her shift around her hands. She needed to shelter her hands; they were her livelihood. He would beat her into submission. It was just like her father beat her mother, beat Roxana when she was defiant. A husband had that right. A lover might assume it. How foolish she was to think the distinction mattered.

He stood over her; she could feel him towering above her, his shadow completely enveloping her, and she waited for the blows to come. . . .

"I think you should go look for him," said Fanny, putting down her napkin.

Scully continued with his soup. "Not, yet, love. I do not mind having you all to myself of an evening. Do you think you could forget about Max for a moment and concentrate on me?"

Fanny suddenly burst into tears. Scully stared at her, wondering what devil was in it now. He pushed back his chair and moved around to her chair.

"My pretty Fanny, whatever has distressed you so?"

"I cannot marry you, Dev. I know I cannot give you children, and I cannot do that to you."

Scully sighed. "I do not need children, Fanny. Am I not child enough for you? Or am I too much a child in your eyes?"

He had hoped for a smile through her tears, but she turned away.

"I have decided it will not do. I have kept you from your home too long. You should be free to marry a young woman who will be your companion forever."

Perhaps he had been too indulgent with Fanny, letting her decide when she trusted his love was strong enough, when she believed enough. "Fanny—"

"You have been disappointed every month. I have seen your reaction, Dev."

"Of course I am disappointed that we will wait another month to be married or that I must restrain my ardor for an entire week or more." A thought knocked at his brain. "How can you think that I do not remain steadfast in my love and devotion?"

Fanny blushed.

There had been plenty of laughter and times that he chased her down the walking paths at the Trent estate and she had giggled, running away, but always let herself be caught in the most secluded arbors or in the artificial grotto that seemed to have been built for their private picnics. He had played the game, stashing blankets and wine and strawberries. Other times he included her children, teasing them into laughter and teaching Thomas the finer points of piquet and crabbo, and telling Julia she was growing into quite a beauty. He had given Fanny the idyllic courtship any woman would beg for, and more.

But ever since they had arrived in London, following Max on his quest to find Roxana, she had been a bundle of nerves and exaggerated emotions.

"I am applying to the archbishop for a special license tomorrow. We will be married by week's end."

Fanny raised her tear-filled blue eyes to his. "Dev," she whispered.

He was tired of hearing her protests. "What date is it?"

"December tenth," she said, and then her eyes widened.

"Special license, Fanny. I am done trying to convince you of my love."

"Dev?" Her expression was uncertain, not daring to hope. "Do you think I have—"

"Yes, your French friend is late."

She smiled, and for once her smile did not warm his heart. That she would consent to marriage only when she was with child bothered him. Did she not love him? Or was he still only a playmate to her? Or just a means to an end?

He had to get away. He had gotten what he wanted; he should not be so bitter about the method. He was sure that when he had time to reflect he would be glad that she might be with child, but he would have much preferred that their marriage had come first.

"I'll go find Max," he said.

Max stared at the bony knobs of Roxana's spine and the ripples that marked each of her ribs beneath the lily-white skin of her back. But most of all he noticed the long pink welts of scars crisscrossing her back. He touched a finger to one long thick ridge. How had he not noticed these before? But as he trailed his finger down the pink strip, the texture of her skin was still soft and silky, only slightly marred to the touch. Would he have even noticed the slight change from undamaged skin to the healed marks?

She shuddered.

Her dark hair was still in a low twist at the base of her skull. The knot had loosened and hung down, but that they had not unpinned the dark masses of her hair was another reason he could see the scars now.

"You have cowered like this before. Do you think I would ever raise a hand to you?" He hunched down behind her, his fingers still tracing the lines and patterns of her disfigurement, as if he touched her gently enough, soothingly enough, he could heal her. But Max's anger and disappointment had stilled. Did her refusal to marry have to do with this?

Roxana's spine straightened, and she seemed to be trying to unwind her hands from her shift. She was not a woman who was meant to cower, and it tore at him to know that there were times when fear overtook her so powerfully. She shook her head and her long dark hair swung down over his hand, covering the secret and the gooseflesh that rose on her back. "You did not throw your boots and cross the room so quickly to . . . to . . ."

"To kiss your scars. I did not see them before now." He shifted her hair out of the way and pressed his lips on the trail of abuse. "Who did this to you?"

"It does not matter." She leaned forward to her knees.

"This is more than one thrashing." Her father? Surely it could not have been the weak down-trodden woman who was her mother. He remembered the tiny cottage where her family lived and the strange man who was her father, the man whose permission he would need to marry his daughter, and understanding clicked into place.

"It does not matter," she repeated.

He pressed his lips against her nape. He wanted more than ever to protect her, to take her away from the horror she had lived in her life. "I crossed the room to wrestle you into clothing because if you keep prancing around naked, I will end up back in your bed and my poor coachman is waiting outside in the cold."

"I don't believe you," she said wearily.

"This is why you refuse to marry me, Roxana?"

She turned slightly. "A husband has the right to discipline his wife."

"Not to do this, Roxana." He brushed his palm over her back.

She grabbed his thumb, circled it with her finger and thumb, and then pulled it off and held the circle in the air. "You could beat a wife with a rod as big as this. I will never marry, Max."

Max felt sick as he recognized that the law allowed a man the right to control his possessions. And a wife and children were considered his possessions. He struggled against his own need to claim her as his own and protect her.

"At least let me take you home. Fanny has probably held dinner for me. You have not eaten." He pulled the wadded mess of red silk from her hand and searched for the hem to position it over her head. She shivered. The room was cold and he wanted her again; scarred or too skinny, she was still everything he wanted in a woman. Yet she did not trust him. She tarred him with the brush of a man who had beaten her.

He shook his head. Who was he fooling? Men

made laws that gave them the right to bend women to their wills.

"No, Max, go home."

He pulled the shift over her head and lifted her long silky hair free of the material. He pulled out the few pins that clung ineffectively to the strands. Piling them in his palm he reached around and handed them to her. "I'm not leaving you alone this night. If you will not come home with me, then I'll stay here."

"I have work to do. Go home, Max. Go have your dinner."

He lifted her into his arms, standing and carrying her over to the chair he kicked directly in front of the stove. How could he win her trust if he insisted on going against her expressed wishes? "You are intent on breaking my heart."

He sat her down in the chair and said gruffly, "Get warm."

Collecting his boots and the rest of his clothes, he drew them on and looped his cravat around his neck. He drew on his overcoat and hoped that the capes would disguise the disarray of his clothing, although his coachmen and the accompanying footmen would not have any doubt about his purpose in a dressmaker's shop well after it had closed for the evening.

As soon as Max left the room, Roxana stood and found a wrapper and scuffs to put on her feet. She would need to go lock up after him and set the bar across the door, but she wanted to be sure he was gone before she went down to the shop. She leaned over the table to blow out the lamp, saving the precious oil, and opened the door of the stove. The dim orange glow from the coals provided enough light for her to sew.

She heard the door below and knew she needed to go downstairs and throw the bolt. Her eyes blurred as she crept toward the stairs and found her way down them in the darkness. She had not thought he would leave so easily. But he had gone, and she felt even more acutely alone.

As she made her way among the wire frames displaying her creations, her chest began to ache. A sob broke free as she approached the glass door at the front of the shop. She could see, outside, the tall form of him standing in the recessed doorway. He turned and she did not know if he saw her or had heard her in the clear silence of the moonlit night, but he reached for the knob and stepped back inside her shop and gathered her to him.

A starkness in his face hit her much harder than she expected. She buried her face against his coat.

"So you wanted to become my mistress only?" he asked.

She nodded, relieved he understood.

"You know I cannot live with that, Roxana." He kissed the top of her head. "I cannot stomach the dishonor." Then he backed away from her, reached for the door, then stepped outside into the cool night. She saw his crested carriage pull up, and he swung inside.

Why couldn't he?

As she watched his carriage drive away, she felt as if she had severed her last link with the world. She had told him to leave and he had honored her request. She pressed against the glass and her sobs broke free.

As she bolted and latched the door she saw a man

move on the other side of the street. The street was fairly deserted, but London never slept and even though all the shops were closed, people still traveled the street.

Chapter
Eighteen

Max pressed his palms against his temples. What was he to do? He wanted her. He owned her. He could not own her. His thoughts swirled and he came back to the realization that he had again behaved with dishonor. He had convinced himself that she was no longer an innocent, so there was no harm in bedding her. God, he knew better, but he could not think clearly around her. Nothing good ever came of violating the tenets of his upbringing.

His carriage drew to a stop and the door opened. Scully swung inside.

"Where have you been?" asked Scully.

"Are you my keeper now?" asked Max, wondering how Scully had come across him.

"Forget that. Did you find her?"

Max stared at his hands.

"Fanny is in a fret about you," Scully said.

A sharpness in his voice made Max look up at his friend. "What is wrong?"

"Offer me your congratulations, son. She has finally agreed to be my wife."

Pain shot through Max. Roxana would never agree to be his wife, and he finally had a glimmer of an understanding why. She was wrong, but how could he expect her reason to be balanced with those scars on her back? "Good, then."

"I suppose we shall have to draw up a settlement." Scully turned toward the carriage window and stared out. "You are the head of the household."

"I need to draft a piece of legislation before the next Parliament."

Scully turned toward him and stared. "Did you find Miss Winston?"

The carriage pulled up in front of his town house then. As Max alighted, not commenting, he stared at the ornate limestone and tall windows. He was a man who had so much, but he would trade everything he had for the chance to hold Roxana.

He entered the marble-floored hall and stared at the gold-plated girandoles, the gilt mirrors and expensive paintings. Did Roxana truly prefer her bare wood floors in her drafty attic above her dress shop?

The butler reached for his coat and Max shrugged out of it, forgetting the disarray of his clothing. He headed for the library and sat down to draft a bill to prohibit violence against women. He knew his chances of getting it passed were slim, but he had to try.

Fanny's knees were shaking as she stood in the drawing room and recited her vows. Scully stood beside her and solemnly repeated the minister's words. He seemed quite subdued, but he had done

as he said and obtained a special license so they
might be married right away.

Her French friend had visited this morning with
a vengeance. She only hoped she did not soak
through her rags and stain her amber gown. That
it was not too late to tell Dev that she was not pregnant and end this before he was bound to her for
life tormented her.

She had been presented with plenty of opportunities to tell him, but had kept her mouth shut. On
one hand she was relieved she was not with child,
but disappointed too. She feared her soon-to-be
husband's reaction. Would he hate her? He had
insisted on marriage only when he thought she
was with child. She had wanted him to insist, and
he had left the choice to her.

All her life, men had told her what to do when it
came to marriage, love and relationships. Her father had insisted when the over-fifty-year-old duke
began courting her that she must dismiss her other
suitors. And she had. When the proposal came,
she accepted it, as she knew she should. Her husband and then Max had made all the decisions
about the upbringing of her children. She did not
know how to make decisions for herself. She could
furnish a house or arrange a party, but she had
never decided her own fate.

And she feared Dev would be angry, feared he
would be disappointed and she feared that she
had finally done the thing that would make her
content at the cost of everyone else's happiness.

Max stood stoic and silent, his face betraying no
emotion. Would he hate her for abandoning him?
Would he look for a wife? Would he allow her children to live with her and Dev, or would he insist
they remain in his home? He had that right.

The ceremony ended and Dev turned to her and tilted her chin to press the sanctified kiss on her lips. His lips were dry and the kiss quick, as if this was too dignified a moment to ruin with passion.

Julia clapped her gloved hands together and Thomas stepped forward to kiss her cheek.

Scully kept his hand under her elbow as if he could steady her shaking. He cast her a skeptical look as if uncertain why she was exhibiting such a fit of nerves. She had to tell him that she had tricked him. She could only hope that he would not hate her for it.

The packet of papers arrived just a few days before Christmas. Roxana had hung red ribbons around the shop windows and splurged on candles to burn late into the evening. It was an extravagance, but it drew customers' eyes to her windows in the short dark days before the holiday. She had been lighting the fat candles as the darkness fell, when the footman entered her shop.

She had not heard from Max. She had thought she had seen him standing in the street in front of her shop, but he had not come inside.

As she took the packet of papers upstairs and unbound them she began reading. At first she was confused, but then she began to understand that it was legislation drafted to make it illegal to beat a woman to the point her skin was broken. As she drifted in and out of the legalese she frowned. The last paper was a letter and at the bottom of the page was his signature, "yours forever, Maximilian Trent."

"Mademoiselle, there is a gentleman to see you," said Madame Roussard.

If she had been paying attention she might have heard the unease in her manager's voice, but her heart was soaring believing Max was below.

"Please would you lock the shop, then send him up to me."

"Yes, Mademoiselle."

Hearing the footsteps on the stairs, Roxana turned and expected Max, but instead her father stood there with that look in his eyes. Her fluttering heart came to a dead stop, and the raw metallic taste of fear filled her mouth.

"Hello, Papa," she said.

"So this is how Trent keeps his whores?" he asked.

Roxana didn't answer. Nothing she could say would dispel his anger.

"How much does he pay to keep you?"

"Nothing. This is all my doing. I pay for this." Roxana winced. Why couldn't she keep her mouth shut?

"Anything my daughter owns belongs to me. Where is the money?"

Roxana closed her eyes.

"I saw you lighting the candles. I saw Trent leaving here at night. I know there is money."

"There is no money for you."

The first blow across her cheek whipped her head around. The next knocked her to the floor. And then she protected her hands.

Scully entered Fanny's room, his room now too, without knocking. Fanny had behaved strangely for a bride, shaking and jumpy. Or perhaps not so strangely for a bride, but for a woman of middle years who had been married nearly twenty years before and had been his lover for the last year, she was extraordinarily skittish.

She had disappeared before the wedding breakfast and then several times throughout the subdued celebration of the day. Perhaps the pregnancy made her ill, but she had seemed unwilling to be alone in his company.

She stood fully dressed in front of the fireplace. "Ah, there is my beautiful bride."

"I have done a dreadful thing," she whispered.

He walked to her and rested his hands on her shoulders. "Yes, you have become too slender. All that play, Fanny." He shook his head as if he regretted their days of laughter. In truth, he would regret giving them up during her confinement. "We shall have to take care that you grow fat and round as a dumpling, my darling."

She turned, her eyes huge in her face. "But that is just it, Dev. I'm not with child."

He pulled her to him and offered comfort. "I am sorry, love. I am so sorry."

She struggled away from him. "I knew I was not when I married you. I am so sorry to have tricked you. Can you forgive me?"

Dev felt the side of his mouth twitch. "So are you saying that you wanted to marry me anyway?"

"I am so awful, I . . . Yes. I knew I was only a little late. I have always known when I was pregnant because everything smelled like fish and I could not eat a bite of salmon with getting sick and I had salmon that night that you said we would be married. So I knew right then I was not with child."

"Fanny, darling—"

"I should have told you then, but you had sent for Julia and Thomas and I did not want to tell you. I think I might have confessed if you had stayed for the rest of dinner, but by the time you returned with Max, I decided I would not." She burst into tears.

He laughed.

She stared, her blue eyes swimming.

"I'm sorry, love. I cannot but be relieved."

"You are not angry with me?"

"No, you silly pea-goose. All I ever wanted was for you to decide *you wanted* to marry me."

"I wanted you to tell me to."

"Yes, well, we should both be happy, then."

"Max told you that you must propose," she said skeptically.

"Max is my friend, not my father, and his condition was imposed only if I knocked on your bedroom door, love. I chose to knock. I love you, Fanny, darling. You are everything I need to make my life complete."

"Yes, but what are we to do about Max?"

Madame Roussard knocked on the door, speaking in a jumble of French that Max's servants didn't understand. She'd finally passed a bloody piece of paper to the butler, who had recognized Max's signature.

He barely remembered shouting for his carriage to be sent round to Roxana's shop, before running out the door, unwilling to wait while the horses were harnessed and maneuvered through the crowded streets.

"I should not have let him in," muttered Madame Roussard, trotting along beside him. "I think she think it ez you."

Madame Roussard gathered the hem of her

gown and skipped to keep up with his long-legged
stride. He just wanted to get to Roxana.

"He look so like her, I think he ez a relative."

Chills shot down Max's spine. If he had been
there, he could have protected her. It wasn't safe
for her to live alone in the heart of the city, although he suspected nowhere had ever been safe
for Roxana.

"He knows her name, *comprendez-vous?*"

"I understand," he answered.

He entered the shop and barely noticed the
candles that had been allowed to burn to pools of
wax in the windows. Without waiting to be shown
back, he wove through the back rooms and noticed
the disturbed bolts of fabric with gaps between
them. He took the stairs two at a time, barely remembering to duck as he went under the eaves.

While the workspace was hardly disturbed,
Roxana's living corner was a mess. Her table had
been turned over and the chunks of her teapot
along with clumps of wet tea leaves were scattered
on the floor. The way the bloodstained pages of
the bill he had written were strewn about made a
mockery of his paper-tiger efforts. Bills and laws
would not protect her from the irrational acts of
what must be a madman.

Roxana sat backwards in a chair, her head
slumped forward over the back. A group of women
milled around her, dabbing at the wounds on her
back. They dipped bloody cloths in a bowl of water
that had turned pink.

As he moved forward they parted in front of
him, but then one put a shawl over Roxana's shoulders to cover her bare back. Her head jerked, but
she did not make a sound.

He crossed to the other side of the chair and knelt down in front of her, pushing her tangled hair from her face. She blinked her blue eyes open.

"Roxy, you are coming home with me."

She flattened her mouth and shook her head slightly. "I cannot. There are dresses to be sewn and cut and . . ."

"They will wait or Madame Roussard will handle everything until you are well."

Tears welled up in her eyes. "He took my best silk."

"Has anyone sent for a doctor?" Max stroked her hair, seeking to soothe her.

"No doctor. I cannot afford . . ." Her voice trailed off and then she began to cough.

He could see that coughing hurt her. He stood and looked at the women standing around her as if they had lost their guiding star. "Are there gowns to be completed? I see cut pieces over there." He pointed to one of the long worktables. "One of you clean up the teapot and papers."

He looked at Madame Roussard. She nodded and began setting the seamstresses to their tasks.

Roxana tried to stand, but she leaned heavily on the chair back while holding her gown so it wouldn't fall. "I need to get back to work."

"Roxana, I must insist that you come home with me and allow me to take proper care of you until you are healed." Her skin would mend as it had before, but would she ever be truly healed?

Max took a step closer and caught her elbows. "Even if I have to carry you out of here."

Her eyes rolled up and he caught her as she collapsed. The women around him wailed collectively, but Roxana was silent and far too pale.

* * *

Roxana woke on her stomach in a bed with several pillows under her. Her back ached and she suspected she had a cracked rib or two. Her wounds were damp, her back exposed and she wondered if she was still bleeding.

As her senses slowly returned to her, she realized the room was much warmer than her attic and the sheets were quite luxurious. She flexed her fingers and was relieved they were fine.

"You're awake."

She shifted too quickly and fought a wave of pain, but Max sat at a writing desk in his shirtsleeves. His coat hung on the back of his chair. He set down his pen and moved closer to the bed.

As she started to rise up and then realized she did not have anything on, at least not on her torso, she sank down into the pillows. "Where am I?"

"My bedroom, where I can watch over you." He knelt down beside her so she did not have to strain her neck to see him. As he did, his gaze traveled down her bare side and then returned to her face. He touched her cheek, gently.

Warmth curled in her belly.

"Am I wearing anything?" she asked.

"Salve on your wounds," he said with a slight mocking glance.

He stroked her hair behind her ear, although she could see it lay in a braid beside her. Her hair had been combed out and plaited. She could not picture Max being the one to do that. Perhaps he had assigned a maid.

"Your workers are making you a dressing gown with padding on the shoulders that they are convinced will keep the material from touching your back, but I'm afraid it hasn't been delivered yet. And as soon as you can sit, the doctor says we need to bind your ribs. We can put dressings on your wounds, but you seem to find that distressful, so I thought it better to leave them off until the bruising and swelling eases."

"How long have I been here?"

He pulled his watch out of his waistcoat pocket and flipped open the gold cover. "Five hours. The doctor thought it was best to let you sleep. Since you pulled away when we tended your wounds he thought your sleep was not too deep, but perhaps borne of exhaustion. Madame Roussard confirms that you often work all day and all through the night. Although the doctor did give you laudanum to ease the pain."

She closed her eyes. Her father had taken what money she had in the till and several bolts of her most expensive fabric. Without his stealing her goods, she had been barely scraping by. She might as well consider her business a failure.

"Could you eat?" he asked.

Life went on.

"I don't think so." She turned her head away.

His hand curled over the top of her head. "We have many things we need to discuss, but you need to know that I have insisted that your father be arrested."

She stared at the far wall, at the rich paint above the layered wood panels on the lower half of the walls. A carved wardrobe of rich mahogany stood screaming Max's wealth and standing in the world.

"Roxana, he is a madman and I cannot allow him to roam the streets."

"You know from the bill you propose to put before Parliament that he did not break any laws."

"He can be held indefinitely on debts, and I swore a complaint against him for theft."

She snorted. "I am his chattel and what I own belongs to him."

"I claimed a partial interest in your business, since Scully's five-hundred pounds founded the enterprise, and I have assumed your debt."

So she had a failed business, a loan she could never repay, a criminal madman as a father and Max knew her as a liar and trickster as well as less than virtuous. What would she do now?

Would she have to marry Max now? Did he even want her to, now?

"Sleep, then. Try not to worry. Madame Roussard is minding your dress shop and your father cannot get to you here."

Max stood and backed away from the bed. "I'll have a maid come and sit with you. If you need more laudanum, let her know."

Roxana did not answer, and when Max left the room she mulled over the conversation. Other than a hint of flirtation, he had been matter-of-fact.

Not like a man in love, not like a man who would pledge his life to her, but a duke who had for a moment lost his bearings but was back on track with his plans to leave Thomas his heir.

She'd failed and she could not in good conscience accept marriage as a means to bring her back from the ruins of her life, but stars above, she'd marry him if that was the only way she could keep him in her life.

Max left his bedroom because he could no longer contain his anger and anguish. What good was his power if he could not protect the ones he loved?

As he stormed through the house, he wanted to break things, to destroy everything in his path. Mostly he wanted to kill her father, strangle him until the breath left his body. He had never felt such a murderous rage before in his life. His brothers had occasionally gone at each other, throwing punches and wrestling each other to the ground until they ended up with torn clothing and bloody noses and Fanny had fretted over them and sent them to have baths. Max had never joined in their fracases. He was expected to control his temper. A duke-to-be couldn't go flying off the handle. Only lately had Max ever felt in danger of losing control.

Roxana was overly affected by displays of temper. He could not let her see his rage.

That she had not mentioned his letter that he had included with the draft of the bill was telling. He had poured out his heart in that letter that had been in Madame Roussard's hands, then in his butler's hands. He'd sworn he would never raise a hand to her, no matter what provocation, and that he still loved her and wanted her as his wife.

Since she referred to the bill, she must have read his letter. Clearly she'd had the packet opened.

Then, as he walked through the streets, needing to keep occupied, he headed for her dress shop. If he could make sure her business was maintained until he returned, he could at least serve her in that way. He passed a shop window that displayed china. He stopped, thinking of the broken chunks of pottery lying on her floor.

Then he bought her a new teapot.

Chapter Nineteen

Roxana woke in the darkness. Sleep, laudanum and the heat of the room left her groggy. Hands stroked a soothing salve on her back. The touch was familiar.

"Max?"

"Shhh. Go back to sleep. I didn't mean to wake you."

She leaned up on her elbows, scrunching the pillow under her chest.

He wiped his hands on a towel, then hung it on the washstand.

"That packet you sent was legislation you plan to present to Parliament, I trust?" she asked.

"It won't pass," he said quietly.

She twisted to look at him.

Running a hand through his hair, he turned and sat in the armchair that had been positioned by the bed. She drank in the long length of his thighs encased in doeskin breeches and the white of his shirt. He leaned forward and placed his elbows on his knees.

"No one I've talked with shall support passage. I don't have enough leverage to get the bill through."

"So it is too late to help me."

"It already was too late to help you," he said.

"Why did you write it, then?"

"Because it needs done." He stood. "Are you hungry?"

Roxana felt a surge of disappointment that he would leave the room. He seemed intent on stuffing her with food. She shook her head.

Nearly every time she woke, he was there, but then he would leave as if he did not want to be with her. Had she ruined everything between them?

"I'll bid you good night, then." He walked toward the connecting door.

"Max, would you stay awhile? I don't want to be alone."

"Neither do I," said Max as he shut the door between them.

She found the padded dressing gown and slipped her arms into the sleeves. Moving gingerly, she pushed open the door separating their rooms.

He stood at the window, leaning on the sill.

"Max?" Her hands were shaking and she did not know what she would say, but she hated the distance that had sprung up between them.

"It's almost Christmas," he said.

So it was an anniversary of sorts for them. "You shan't have the house party this year?"

He turned and looked at her, folding his arms across his chest. "Not without a hostess. Fanny has married Scully. They have gone to his home."

The coolness of Max's room made her senses spring alive. She could hear her heartbeat, the breaths they took. The faint scent of bay rum from him and sweet basil from the salve he used on her hung in the air. "Why do you leave when I wake?"

He turned back to the window and looked down. "It doesn't do for you to see me angry."

She sagged against the doorjamb. "Are you angry now?"

"Every time I see your wounds, I am livid."

He sounded weary and resigned.

"They'll heal," she said. No bones had been broken. It wasn't like the time her father had broken her mother's fingers.

"I don't know what to say when people ask about you. There are rumors that I keep you in a cottage on my estate. Rumors that I ruined you, that I raped you."

"No!"

What was that like for him? The exemplary duke who had broken all the bounds of acceptable behavior and now wore a huge black stain on his reputation. Then she had in effect made the truth closer to that when she welcomed him into her bed.

"You accused me of it yourself," he said in a low voice.

"I'm sorry." She could feel his anger now. It hung in the room like a noxious, sulfurous cloud. Her legs trembled and she had to fight to stand her ground. She wanted to flee.

"Then you just disappeared, Roxana. I had no idea if you were safe or well."

All the time he searched for her had he feared finding a broken woman? Did he start to believe that the gossip about her being ruined was true? She should have let him know she was well. But she hadn't because she'd been afraid he'd find her and persuade her to become his wife. In the beginning she had been too fragile, too uncertain of her ability to make it.

"I never intended to damage you," she whispered.

"No, you managed everything to a T, did you not? You got your money and your dress shop. What I don't understand is why you would not want this." He waved his arm to take in the room. "Why you would not want what protection I can give you?"

"My father broke my mother's fingers when she tried to protect me from him. They never healed right. I have an aversion to anyone trying to protect me. I have an aversion to anyone having rights over me. I have an aversion to depending on anyone besides myself."

But she had learned in the last year that she needed other people. She depended on her seamstresses, her suppliers, her clients, and she needed him, but she was a burden in his life. She was not something he could set to rights or demand conform to his world.

"I've always thought I had everything. I have power and influence and wealth. It is all tied to the dukedom, but I find I have lost the only things that really matter to me. My influence has dwindled to nothing since I am now thought a blackguard. I would give it all up in heartbeat to have the people I love back."

She took a tentative step into the room. "Max."

"I've tried to live within a code of behavior that all this responsibility confers. But when you are around I step outside everything I know is proper."

He seemed so alone.

"I was never part of your world. The same rules don't apply."

"Go to bed, Roxana. If you feel well enough, I'll take you home to your shop in the morning. Fanny and Scully will be back any day, and it will be better for them not to find you here."

She wanted to cross the room, but his anger was like an invisible wall that she could not penetrate. She had not understood how important his ethics were to him. How much had asking him to violate his tenets hurt him? She had not thought beyond what she wanted, and what she did not want.

"Now, go before I do something for which I cannot forgive myself."

Cold hands clutched at her heart. What did he want to do to her? Her knees felt weak and she backed into the bedroom. She had not thought of what she was doing to him. All she had known was that falling in love was not part of her plan. She sank into the soft featherbed, feeling bleak and so alone.

Max stared at the door, wanting to go through to her, but he had promised himself he would not pressure her while she was wounded and vulnerable. He would not ask her to marry him again. But in the past few days he had been to her shop. He'd looked at her creations. He thought of the tiny cottage where she'd grown from a child to a self-sufficient young woman. She made beautiful things from scraps and discards.

He did not know that he would have fared as well under such circumstances. She was strong-willed and fiercely independent and incredibly talented. Perhaps she did not need anyone to make her life complete.

He needed her, and he had to consider that he

might never have her in the way that was right. She had offered only to become his mistress.

The door slowly swung open.

"Max?"

She stood silhouetted in the doorway, backlit by the roaring fire he kept going in his bedroom while he slept in the more temperate lady's room of the suite. God, he wanted her.

"What?" His "what" came out surlier than he'd intended.

"I'm sorry I've hurt you. I'm so sorry for letting you befriend me when I knew it could never be. I'm sorry that I cannot be what you wanted me to be."

"Roxana." Anguish poured through him. He had never meant for her to feel any less than she was.

"I just wanted you to know that all I ever wanted was to be able to build a small business so I could support my brother and sisters. I had planned this course since I was twelve. I allowed myself to think only on it."

"But, Roxana, it was not the only course open to you."

She shook her head. "I knew I would never truly be a part of the ton, as I never wanted to marry. But maybe my sisters could. I am ashamed that I misused your generosity so brazenly, but I had already thought myself so far out of your world that I could not allow myself to think I could be a part of it. I thought that you would forget about me once I left."

"Would it have made any difference if I were like Breedon, without a title?"

She tilted her head sideways.

"Not a duke?" he questioned.

"I don't know, maybe, but you are a duke. And I had to come to London and try to follow my dream."

"You do not know what agonies I suffered believing I had forced you into a nefarious life."

"I should have sent you word."

"Yes, you should have."

"I was afraid my father would find me."

"Which he did, because of me."

"It's not your fault. He would have noticed I sent money and come looking for me sooner or later. He was bound to think he could invest my earnings in some worthless scheme. I know that I have failed."

"You haven't failed."

"I cannot afford to pay my seamstresses."

"I paid them, Roxy. It was a trifling amount."

She winced, and he realized the amount was not trifling to her.

"They would have stayed anyway. They adore you and what you do."

He closed the space between them and brushed her long dark hair back from her face. Her braid had come loose again. He could blame only his poor skill at plaiting her hair, or perhaps it was because he tied the bow near the end; he knew it would be just a matter of time before he would have to weave the silky strands together again.

"Roxana, I took the liberty of going over your accounts, and you have a lot of money on the books. Your dress shop is doing remarkably well. You just need to dun people more. There are many unscrupulous sort who will flock to a new business with the hopes that it will go bankrupt before they have to pay."

"You want me to succeed, then," she asked in a tiny voice.

"I would not wish you to fail." Although he had to admit a tiny part of him did want her to fail, so she would have no choice but to turn to him for rescue. But that was not who she was. She did not look for, want or expect rescue. She took on the world. If that was what made her happy, then he wanted her to have success.

She turned toward the bedroom, away from his touch. He knew he should let her go. She was still weak and sore. But letting her walk away was the hardest thing he'd ever done.

Roxana moved gingerly toward her living quarters. It had once been her home and felt safe to her, but she no longer felt safe anywhere other than in Max's bed. She had avoided that part of the attic as she worked catching up with the things only she could do at the shop. Patterns needed to be cut in muslin and guides for lines of beading or embroidery chalked onto finished skirts.

In her absence a partition wall had been erected, separating the spaces. Her stove had been moved to the far side of the attic, making the work area warmer. The seamstresses told her Max had ordered the changes and paid the workmen.

He had left her at the door of her shop this morning and promised to return, but would he?

She sank down at her table, exhausted. She leaned forward and put her head on her folded arms. She wanted to cry, but she felt too empty to produce tears. Instead she let sleep take her into oblivion.

"So, what do you think?" asked Max.

"Think of what?" she asked.

He moved forward and set a basket on the table. She blinked at him and then realized she smelled roast beef and potatoes, and hunger pains gnawed at stomach. He lifted dishes from the basket.

"The changes? More like a home, is it not?"

Roxana looked around and stopped staring at a large Rumford stove that had replaced her little potbellied stove. How much coal would that take?

She noticed a large, full coal bucket beside the stove. Where had that come from? How would she ever afford the coal for two stoves? The bare floor had a rug too. On the far wall were shelves stocked with dry goods.

"You have not opened your gift."

"Is it Christmas?" Was she dreaming?

"Not yet, but you will want to use it."

She looked and saw nothing. Max pointed around the corner of the bed; behind the curtains stood a little tree with unlit candles on the limbs. A large box tied with a gold ribbon sat under the tree.

"That was the only place I could find with enough space for it," he said.

She stared, her eyes blurring.

"Roxana, I wanted your place to feel like a home."

She wanted to protest that ornaments and Christmas decorations did not make a home. But that he had even thought that she might feel ill at ease in her little room counted for something, didn't it?

She woodenly walked toward it and knelt to open the box. She slowly untied the ribbons and peeled back the paper. Inside was tissue. She lifted the contents and unwrapped a cup, then a saucer and then a lid.

A tea service. As she stared at it she knew that he meant for her to stay here. She had refused him one too many times.

"Thank you," she said around the catch in her throat. "It is lovely."

He placed plates on the table and then served food on them. Gravy slopped over onto his finger and he licked it off. "Not used to serving food. I suppose I'll have to learn."

She stood feeling remiss. Feeling like she should be more grateful for a practical gift that would be so useful.

"Come eat. We can light the candles later," he urged.

She tried, but the meal tasted like dust. He watched her as she struggled to hold back tears.

He reached out and touched her chin. "Roxana, what is wrong?"

"I have ruined everything between us," she whispered. "You are so kind and generous, but I cannot afford the coal for a bigger stove."

"I can for now and you will." He slipped his hands under her elbows and lifted her from the chair. "What would you say if I stayed here with you?"

"Tonight?" Her heart fluttered.

"Tonight, tomorrow, the next day and night for as long as you can tolerate me."

"I would be your mistress?"

"More than that, Roxy. I want to be with you. If it cannot be in my world, then let it be in your world. Let me live with you."

She stared at him, thinking of his huge estate, his town house with the ornate plaster ceilings, marble entry hall, and fireplaces in every room. "But you're a duke."

"I'm abdicating. Thomas can have the title."

The room started to swirl around her, and she could not believe what he was saying. "But, Max, you cannot. You would never be happy living like this."

"I admit, I am used to being waited upon, but could we not find some common ground? I have a few investments that I shall have a little income from, and if I can restore your father's estate so that it supports your family, perhaps in a few years we could purchase a modest house."

She grabbed his lapels, needing to support herself. "Max?"

"I swore to myself I would not pressure you until you were well." He caught her hips and pulled her against him. She knew his low hold was to save irritating her back, yet her blood began to simmer anyway. "I just want to be with you. If you must have your shop, then you must. I want you to continue making beautiful clothes. If I cannot have you in my world, then I would join you in yours."

"Max, stop talking."

He stood still as she tried to absorb what he said. "You have this all planned out?" she asked.

"As you lay in my bed all I could do was think of how I could be with you. I know you don't want to marry, but Roxy, I will never be happy living without you. I love you."

A dam inside of her broke. "You love me?"

"I think I have loved you from the moment you turned to me and said you would curb your disagreeable tendency to speak directly." He stroked her hair back from her face. "Or perhaps from the moment I learned you wore scandalous red undergarments."

How had he known about her red shifts? "I thought you had changed your mind."

"How does one change one's heart?" he murmured against her hair.

"Max, this is more than I can take in."

He kissed her forehead, then pulled her head to his shoulder. "Ah, well, you will need me to apply your salve for the next few days. So shall we see how it goes?"

Was he really willing to give up everything to be with her? Live in a tiny attic corner, when he had a manse with at least a hundred rooms? How would he make do without servants when he employed scores of them?

"Max, the thing is, I have given my heart to a duke and I think I want to marry him."

"Roxy—"

She cut him off, putting her fingers to his lips.

"Our worlds do not overlap much, and it will present many challenges, and unfortunately time apart will be inevitable. But I have been gone near a week and my workers have been able to keep my dress shop thriving. Perhaps I do not need to be here every minute. And I do think it would behoove me to spend more time in society. I had so many ideas for dresses after the house party. With a few supplies I could design anywhere."

His lips curled up under her fingers.

"What?" she asked, curious as to what made him smile in the middle of a serious discussion.

"You absolutely beam when you talk of designing dresses. You should be wearing your creations more often. Besides, I've already consulted a barrister about relinquishing the title."

"Yes, but you see, there is this one thing I want that you cannot give me as a commoner."

He frowned. "I've rather thought it might be a relief to be rid of the burdens. There is so much debt and I do not know that I could find the time to repair your father's estate when I have so much to manage now."

He might think so now, but she knew Max would never be satisfied being idle. Roxana leaned and picked up the papers that had been folded and placed on a shelf. She handed the bill he'd drafted to him. "I want this."

"It will take me twenty years to get this made to law."

"We have the time." She shrugged.

"Your father is in the Fleet; he will not harm you ever again. I've taken precautions that he will not be released."

"Yes, but Max—what precautions?"

"Guaranteed his loans as long as he is kept in prison." Max grimaced. "It is hardly ideal, but his creditors won't relinquish their claims until everything is paid in full. Nothing will be paid off for fifty years."

"You did this all in a week?"

"No. I've been to your family's home. I began working on it months ago, but I did not want to move forward without your blessing."

"You did not ask for my blessing."

"No. When he did this to you, I decided to act. I should have preferred to kill him. If I had caught him at this, I would have strangled him with my own hands."

A shudder of unease passed through her. She heard his fury and thought he might have been capable of murdering her father. Just as he had slit the poor fox's throat and tossed Lady Malmsbury around the room, bashing her into furniture . . . and the clock. Roxana remembered with sudden clarity why she never wanted to be married.

"Roxana, I promise you that I will never raise a hand to you."

She plucked at his shirt. She believed in her head, but her heart bore wounds that were not so easily ignored.

"Come, love, I have had thirty years of controlling my behavior—I will not allow myself to behave like a beast."

"But what you did with Lady Malmsbury . . ."

"She had my razor. I was afraid she meant to cut you. I would do anything to protect you, or any of my own, but I would never, never strike you." He pushed a hand through his hair. "I cannot promise you I will never be angry, but I would cut out my own heart before I would hurt you."

"I cannot promise that I will not be afraid."

"Ah, my brave Miss Winston. I cannot think that you will be afraid for long. Not just anyone would have set out on their own and established a flourishing business against her family and friends' wishes, especially since you could have accepted my offer of marriage. If I grow too full of choler to contain it, I will kill a clock or some such."

She reached up and pressed a kiss to his chin. "Very well, make me your wife."

"Then I would give you one last gift," he said, and reached into his pocket. He drew out a diamond-and-emerald ring and pulled up her hand to slide the ring on her finger.

"But I have nothing to give you this Christmas."

"You have already given me your heart; what more could I need?"

"Plum pudding," said Roxana, identifying the smell wafting from the basket he had brought.

He glanced reluctantly toward the bed, then pushed her toward her chair. "Finish eating."

"You know, Max, I would speak plainly."

He draped her napkin in her lap. "Yes."

"I am not so injured as to preclude that." She gestured toward the bed. "If you could perhaps allow me the top."

"Dinner is already cold, it can wait," he said, lifting her out of her chair and bringing her up for a kiss.

"I'll warm it on the stove, later." But they never made it back to their meal, for they were too busy sharing their gift of love for each other.

Epilogue

Christmas Eve had dawned cold and dreary, although Max and Roxana were warm with her new stove heating their little love bower. The tree filled the air with pine scent and the waxy smell of burnt candles.

Roxana sat in her padded dressing gown, scraping out the last of the plum pudding bowl with her finger and licking it. Hardly the manners of a future duchess, but Max knew she would never do it in front of anyone but him. He was just happy to see her appetite back, and he suspected there was more than a hint of teasing in her slow sliding of her finger out of her mouth.

Max tied on his last clean cravat and bent over to kiss her. "I have to return to the town house. I have no clean clothes."

"I'm closing the shop early today. I cannot think I will have any customers this afternoon."

He smiled, thinking they would have all afternoon and all day tomorrow to themselves. "This is my happiest Christmas ever," he whispered into her hair. The only thing that could have made him happier was to have his whole family back, but that wouldn't happen.

"Non, non! You cannot go in, sir," protested Madame Roussard. "You cannot see his grace now."

"Goodness, is it that late already?" asked Roxana.

Max pulled out his watch. "It is a little past eight."

"Who do you think it is?" Roxana stretched.

"Scully?" Max shrugged. "They probably found my note."

"I need to get dressed."

"You won't have to tomorrow, love. I promise." Max moved to the door as he heard steps on the stairs.

A head cleared the floor and then a familiar body came into view. It was an apparition. Shock stabbed Max in his chest. He grabbed the partition wall. Then the apparition hit his head on the attic roof.

"You cannot abdicate, old fellow," said the apparition, rubbing his crown. "You'll put a spoke in everything."

Ghosts didn't speak and they did not bump their heads. Max looked back and forth between the two men, barely absorbing things. Scully stood with his arms folded and that annoying look of pity on his face.

"Alexander?"

Roxana stood at his back and put her hand on his shoulder. "I ought to kill you," said Max. Instead he crossed the space and clapped his brother to him. "Who the hell did I bury?"

"More like a what," said Alexander, patting him on the back. "But that is a whole other story."

More Regency Romance From Zebra

Celebrate Romance With One of Today's Hottest Authors

Amanda Scott

Available Wherever Books Are Sold!

Visit our website at **www.kensingtonbooks.com**.